Faerie Fate

by

Silver James

This is a work of fiction. Names, characters, places, and incidents either are the product of the author's imagination or are used fictitiously, and any resemblance to actual persons living or dead, business establishments, events, or locales, is entirely coincidental.

Faerie Fate

Cover Art by *Rae Monet*

The Wild Rose Press
PO Box 708
Adams Basin, NY 14410-0706
Visit us at www.thewildrosepress.com

Publishing History
First Faery Rose Edition, 2010
Print ISBN 1-60154-685-8

Published in the United States of America

The little clock she'd received as a present on her twenty-fifth birthday whirred and chimed the time. One small, tinkling chime. Two. Finally, twelve in all. Midnight between March twentieth and March twenty-first. The vernal equinox. The day when light and dark, good and evil, love and hate all balanced on the finely tuned axis of mother earth.

Voices, strange with lilting accents, whispered somewhere in the darkness of her dream.

****

"She sleeps," said a soft voice, feminine, one Becca didn't recognize.

"Aye," said the second voice. This one was deep, male, arrogant.

"Will she remember?"

"Nay, she'll not."

"How then will she know what to do?"

"She'll know." He sounded confident.

"What of him?"

"Aye, he'll definitely know now. He should have known the last time, but she was too afraid, and he was too full of himself."

"What is so different this time?" She was skeptical.

"She was young then, not matched well to him. Now, she's no young soul. She's had all those lives without him, the lonely nights, and the ache in her heart for all time. This time, she has courage born in the fires of suffering. She'll know not to run from him, but to him."

"You're sure with the knowing of it this time?"

"Aye."

"And, if it doesn't work?"

"Ciaran dies. Again."

A sharp intake of breath came from the woman. *"That cannot happen. Too much went wrong the first time."*

Praise for Silver James...

"Captivating, Timeless and Passionate! FAERIE FATE crosses the boundaries of time and faerie law to reunite two souls in the sacred binding of love. Silver James is a writer to watch!"
~*Jennifer Lyon, author of **Blood Magic**, Book 1 in the Wing-Slayer Hunter Series (Ballentine)*

"In FAERIE FATE Silver James delivers non-stop action and a strong, funny heroine in this time-travel historical. Rebecca finds love lasting through the ages, immortals toying with human lives, and the strength to defy even the Old Ones to get back to her only mate, the one she is bound to for eternity..."
~*Carol Shenold, author of the Tali Cates series, Eternal Press*

"One stand-out story which belongs in a 'best of the year' anthology, is Silver James' [writing as Penny James] CAFÉ MIDNIGHT—a fable where a police officer is helped out in his detecting of a crime by Miss Marple, Hercule Poirot, Sam Spade, Holmes and Watson, and Charlie Chan. Asta, Nick and Nora Charles all have walk-ons. It's affectionate, uncontrived and very well-written..."
~*Andi Shechter, About.com Guide to Mysteries*

Dedication

One of the things a writer dreams about (this one, anyway) is dedicating her book to those who helped along the way. I have so many to thank:

My loving husband and daughter (I promise to buy y'all enough "unmentionables" to make up for lack of laundry services when I'm writing); my oldest, bestest friend, Toy, who first read this book and loved it; my best friend, Justin, for cheers and tech help, despite disliking the genre; my family and friends, Stacie, Kelly, Kier (no relation to the hero of *Faerie Fate*), Cheri and Jeff, and my critique partner, Amanda, who all kept the faith even when mine flagged.

I can't leave out my editor, Frances Sevilla. I also want to thank my own personal Irish leprechaun, Paul, for his help with the language and the setting and for his friendship.

Most of all, I want to thank my dad for giving me a love of books and encouraging me to dream and use my imagination. I know he's smiling as he watches me from Tir Nan Óg.

Prologue

She woke up groggy from a fitful sleep. Bracing for the throbbing ache sure to follow, she stretched her legs, desperate to ease cramped muscles without inducing the agonizing pain that caused those cramps. Rebecca was all too familiar with pain. She groaned aloud as a shooting star shot up the inside of her thigh and into her back, branding skin and muscle with white-hot heat as it traveled.

Taking a deep breath, she glanced at her watch. It was only six o'clock and still dark outside. She was so tired of not sleeping well. When was the last time she'd slept through the night undisturbed by nightmares or pain? Had it been twenty-five years?

Rebecca tossed her head from side to side on her pillow. She clamped her lips shut, trapping the groan welling up to join the tears spilling down her cheeks. Crying didn't help. She'd never found solace in them yet she couldn't stop. Today was March twenty-first, her fiftieth birthday. Half a century, and half of that had already passed her by. Her body felt a hundred. Her mind begged to feel twenty-five again, to be young enough, fit enough, to experience the passion and pangs of first love. Twenty-five years ago to the day, she'd been turned into an old woman overnight.

When the spasms started, she practiced her deep breathing technique to get through them. The familiar routine would see her into the next period of calm. God, she was only fifty. Women in their sixties and seventies had a better quality of life than she did. She was tired—tired of the pain, tired of the loneliness, tired of not being able to live life as she wanted. There was an alternative, one she'd considered several times, but she was too stubborn to succumb to its dark lure. Death was forever.

Rebecca punched her pillow to fluff it. Twisting and turning to find a comfortable position, she sought ever-illusive sleep once again. She wanted to sleep until noon. She wanted to sleep forever, but right now, her body insisted on attention. After a struggle, she made it to the bathroom.

When she'd finished, she leaned against the lavatory, panting as she stared at the face in the mirror. Somewhere in there had to be the twenty-five-year-old who had been so full of life. Her dull gray hair no longer glistened with gold and silver highlights. Skin once softly kissed by the sun now looked like crumpled parchment. The lines etched across her forehead and around her mouth spoke of the pain she'd endured. Scars crisscrossed her chest and arms, as they did her whole body. She'd been an athlete and fought back, willing her body to regain the muscle tone it once enjoyed. As strong as her will was, the pain was stronger. Year after year, it beat her down. She'd had no family left by then. No husband or lover to comfort her and one by one her friends dropped by the wayside, unwilling or unable to watch her decline.

For the past ten years, she'd been utterly alone but for the procession of home health aides who came once a day to help out for an hour or three or five. Rebecca despised herself. She'd planned to do so much with her life before her body betrayed her. Turning from the mirror, she stumbled back to bed, each step excruciating. Gratefully, she sank onto the bed and pulled her legs under the covers. She started her deep breathing, waiting for the pain that would come. When it hit, she was surprised. This time, the bone-jarring ache was relatively mild. She glanced at her watch again, then shook her wrist. The watch still showed six o'clock. "Guess I need a new battery," she mumbled, closing her eyes, praying sleep would come.

Out in the living room, though, time ticked off by seconds. The little clock she'd received as a present on her twenty-fifth birthday whirred and chimed the time. One small, tinkling chime. Two. Finally, twelve in all. Midnight between March twentieth and March twenty-first. The vernal equinox. The day when light and dark, good and evil, love and hate all balanced on the finely tuned axis of mother earth.

Voices, strange with lilting accents, whispered somewhere in the darkness of her dream.

****

"She sleeps," said a soft voice, feminine, one Becca didn't recognize.

"Aye," said the second voice. This one was deep, male, arrogant.

"Will she remember?"

"Nay, she'll not."

"How then will she know what to do?"

"She'll know." He sounded confident.

"What of him?"

"Aye, he'll definitely know now. He should have known the last time, but she was too afraid, and he was too full of himself."

"What is so different this time?" She was skeptical.

"She was young then, not matched well to him. Now, she's no young soul. She's had all those lives without him, the lonely nights, and the ache in her heart for all time. This time, she has courage born in the fires of suffering. She'll know not to run from him, but to him."

"You're sure with the knowing of it this time?"

"Aye."

"And, if it doesn't work?"

"Ciaran dies. Again."

A sharp intake of breath came from the woman. "That cannot happen. Too much went wrong the first time."

****

Fear numbed her whole body, her heart pumping madly as she struggled to breathe. When she opened her eyes, a whirling kaleidoscope of light and dark and fantastic colors swirled and danced around her. Her stomach churned.

"No!" she screamed. The car turned over and over, as jagged glass sliced her skin, and crumpled metal gouged her body. "No," she whispered, knowing if she survived the horrific crash, her life would be changed again, this time for eternity.

****

He bolted up, sweat seeping from every pore in his body. Fear. The emotion tasted cold and coppery in his mouth. He pushed his hair back from his face and took a long, shuddering breath. He needed to remember this dream that left his heart hammering and his lungs gasping for air. Ciaran drew a deep breath to steady his nerves. When he looked up, Niall, the captain of his guard, stood in the doorway staring at him.

The older man's brow knitted with worry, but he tried not to let it show. "The dream again?" Niall already knew the answer. These past few nights passed fitfully for his *Taoiseac*. He would consult his wife the next time he saw her. She was gifted with the sight. Mayhap, she could divine what haunted his young chief.

Ciaran got up and paced, his restless energy propelling him around the room like a stalking wolf looking for prey. "I remember naught of it, Niall, but for the crushing pain and fear." He turned stricken eyes to his old mentor. "Not mine, though. Hers." His hollow voice whispered with echoes from the grave.

Niall rocked back on his heels. This man he'd watched grow from a gangly lad into a warrior prince, the Black Wolf of Connaught, never spoke of the fairer sex, never even noticed the dreamy sighs and covetous glances he left in his wake. There wasn't a cailín in the castle or village, nor probably anywhere in the entire land of Eire, who wouldn't give him a rousing tussle in the hay. Tall, Ciaran stood more than a head above even the tallest soldier in the ranks. His long hair, black as a raven's wing, glinted with the same magical indigo lights in the sun. As cold and mysterious as the sea, Ciaran's blue eyes changed from storm-tossed to sun-glistened in a heartbeat. Broad-shouldered, long-legged, the man was a warrior, stronger than any in his army.

"Hers?" Niall kept his voice strictly neutral.

"Yee heard me. Hers!" Ciaran shouted. "Though I have no knowin' of who she is. She's hurt, Niall, in great pain and lost somewhere in the dark, in a place so baleful that the sun refuses to shine. I don't know how to get to her!" This last admission erupted from his anguished soul.

A cold shiver ran down Niall's back. He had to seek out his wife now. She would have the knowing of it, and if she didn't, she could ask the old Druid who lived in the woods behind her cottage. Niall knew Siobhan took food and drink to the old man, as well as blankets and cast-off clothing. He'd followed her once, making sure she was safe while he watched the two of them from his hiding place in the trees. Appearing older than time, the white-haired old man gazed up at Siobhan with the doting eyes of a father.

Niall had never seen Ciaran so agitated. Even on the eve of their biggest battles, this man was the calm eye of the storm. Now, he stalked to one end of his chamber and back again. Over and over, he paced. He was a caged wolf—an angry, dangerous wolf, black as the night itself. "Who is she?" he snarled at his second in command. "Why does she haunt me?"

"Peace, Ciaran," Niall soothed. "I dunno who the cailín may be. If you will allow, let me go to Siobhan. Mayhaps, she can divine the meaning of your dreams."

"Go, Niall." Ciaran groaned and rubbed his temples. "Go now and bring her to me."

Niall turned on his heel and fled down the hall to the stairs. Never had he heard Ciaran's voice filled with such despair. He clamored through the great hall, issuing orders on the run. Men roused from deep slumber, spurred by the harsh tones of his shouts. One scrambled to his feet, belting on his sword and scurrying up the stairs where he took a post outside Ciaran's door. Another darted out the massive oaken doors ahead of him, already shouting for the fastest horse to be saddled.

Niall waited in the courtyard for his horse and turned his face up to the full moon. He sniffed the air. The stars and moon put the time at just after midnight. *Alban Eiler*, the vernal equinox. A shooting star blazed across the sky. He sighed, afraid naught but evil could come from this night. The portents worried him. He was thankful to be going to his Siobhan. She'd have the knowing of what to do.

Chapter One

Rebecca awoke to unfamiliar pain. Battered from head to toe, her muscles ached, but the shooting stars of branding heat were sated for the time being. She reached deep inside searching for the memories that allowed her to float on top of the pain. Experience, the harshest of teachers, taught her to drift along rather than struggle. No matter how tenaciously she fought, nothing held the pain at bay. She remembered summers spent in the high mountains of Colorado on her grandfather's ranch, riding madly across a meadow, her bare legs caressing the sleek sides of her horse as she rode bareback.

"Ah, colleen," her grandfather teased her, shaking his head in mock despair. "You're nothing but a wild Comanche." Yet his eyes glowed with pride as he watched. She'd never met the horse she couldn't ride, or one she couldn't sweet-talk out of a bad temper. Rebecca had loved those long ago summers.

She shivered. She'd never felt so cold, except for that one time so many years ago, and she didn't want to think about the accident. Her brain refused to move past the memory, forcing Becca to remember waking to a long moment of silence. Antifreeze dripped from the shattered radiator onto the hot motor. The drops hissed and sizzled in the frigid temperature. She'd been lucky it wasn't gas dripping. The real temperature that night had been twenty-two degrees—a cold March night with a canopy of stars shining across the black awning of winter sky. The wind chill brought the temperature down to about twelve—survivable if one had a heavy coat or blanket and could keep moving. Rebecca couldn't move at all. Pinned beneath three tons of crumpled steel, she couldn't even wiggle a toe.

Now a wave of pain built down in her calf. Once again, she sought a safe memory, breathing deep to get above the pain until it crested, and she could ride it down the other side. After twenty-five years of agony, no painkiller worked without addiction, and Rebecca refused to fall into that trap. She'd kill herself before she'd let morphine or other, more powerful drugs control her. Pain already ruled her life—she would allow no other masters. The spasm passed, and she relaxed.

Why couldn't she get warm? Had the pilot light on the old heater blown out again? Becca groaned. Getting to the basement and back up again was a nightmare, but she couldn't put off making the trek. She threw off the covers and swung her legs over the side of the bed—only there was no bed. She lay on cold, hard ground, naked and covered only by the thin woolen blanket she'd flicked off thinking it the covers on her bed.

Feebly, Becca found the scrap of wool and wrapped up in it. In the fetal position, she attempted to generate some body heat. Another wave of pain hit, this time squarely between her eyes. Becca screamed until blissful darkness gathered her up and sent her into oblivion.

****

Niall heard the screaming and turned bleak eyes to the woman he called his wife. They'd never formally married, becoming handfasted at a long ago *Lughnasadh* festival and neither ever turned their back to walk away from the union. Though most of Ireland was nominally Christian, many pockets of the old Celtic traditions survived. He'd have married her in the church if she'd desired, but the handfasting was enough for his Siobhan.

"'Tis the banshee," he whispered. He gripped the hilt of his sword as if that mortal weapon could protect them from the infernal haunt.

"Nay," Siobhan spat. "'Tis a human cry, Niall, one wounded beyond feeling. You must find her and help her."

Niall stared at her. "What do you see, cailín? Is this the one who haunts the MacDermot's dreams?"

Siobhan stilled, looking inward for the answers.

Niall wrapped his big arms around her, and pulled her against the heat of his body. The night was bloody cold. Dread wrapped his heart in an icy fist. He had no doubts this banshee was tied to Ciaran. Reluctantly, he turned Siobhan loose and mounted his horse. Alarmed by the eerie screams filling the night, he needed to investigate them, and would have even without Siobhan's urging. He leaned low over the neck of his sweating horse and urged the animal to run faster.

****

Rebecca heard voices speaking gibberish. Something poked her in the side and she moaned. The gibberish abruptly ceased. The sound of heavy feet shuffling through dry grass stopped a little distance away. A moment later, the men spoke again, but their words were indistinct.

"Help me." Did any sound escape her dry throat? She licked parched lips. "Please help me."

The man who had prodded her with his foot moved closer to take a look at her. He glanced over his shoulder. "Have you a clue as to who she is?"

"Nay," the second one said as he came closer. "There's no knowin' who she could be. 'Tis a bad business, and onc we should walk away from."

"She might clean up enough to warm me bed," the first sneered.

He jerked the scrap of wool covering her body. Another spasm built in her middle. Rebecca was helpless. The shooting star flashed up her spine and splintered into a million pieces in her brain. She screamed and screamed. The sound echoed eerily in the cold air.

Startled, the first man dropped the blanket. Together, the two men ran, barely covering a hundred feet before a company of horsemen cut off their escape. They exchanged panicked looks.

Alarmed by the eerie screams filling the night, Niall leaned low over the neck of his sweating horse and urged the animal to run faster. He rounded a sharp turn on the narrow track and pulled up short, astonished to find Ciaran and a company of horse surrounding two peasants.

"Nay, *Taoiseac,*" the roughest of the two denied, "we dinnit touch her."

Niall slid from his horse and strode to the huddled figure half-hidden in the shadow of an ancient oak. He knelt down and peered at the lump. The creature was probably female, but with her battered face and snarled hair, Niall wouldn't wager a guess on her age. He stared at the battered hands clutching the thin mantle covering her wretched body. A shadow flickered behind him and he looked up. Ciaran stared down from his stallion.

"I'll take her to Siobhan," Niall offered. He bent over and scooped the unresisting body into his arms. Before he could take a breath, cold steel bit into his neck. In one fluid motion, Ciaran had dismounted, pulled his dagger, and threatened his second-in-command. Niall stared, confused by the actions of the man he would follow through the gates of hell. Ciaran's face resembled a stone mask.

The female in Niall's arms stirred, and as he held her he could actually feel the spasm of pain in her as it built, traveling from her midsection and

10

radiating outward. The pitiful thing opened her mouth, but she was so exhausted no sound escaped. The knife slid away from his throat.

Ciaran knelt on the ground, holding his hands to his head, rocking in time to the spasms of pain shuddering through the woman. "I can't take her pain any longer, Niall." He groaned. Slowly, he picked up his dagger, moving his hand and arm in an upward arc, his intent plain. Ciaran meant to kill the woman.

Her eyes flickered open and they shone silver in the pale moonlight. "Please," her lips whispered. "Help me." She stared up into dark, stormy eyes. "Where am I? Who are you?" She sighed. Her long, dark lashes fluttered down to shutter her eyes.

Niall exchanged a look with Ciaran. "What language was that, *Taoiseac*?"

Ciaran stared at the woman lying between them. "I dunno, Niall. I understood naught of her words, but I know in my heart she asked for my help. Honor demands I give it."

"Please, Ciaran, let me take her to Siobhan," the older man pleaded.

Ciaran bristled. "Nay, Niall, no other man will touch her." Snarling, he whipped off his mantle and wrapped it around the shivering girl. He scooped her into his arms and strode to his horse. Holding her in one arm, Ciaran stepped up into the saddle and cradled her across his hard, muscular thighs. "Ride, Niall, and bring your woman." Ciaran wheeled his stallion, shouting to his men to bring the peasants to the castle. He galloped off, leaving the others in the dust cloud his horse's hooves kicked up.

****

"What happened? You said she would not remember," the female accused.

"She won't. He came too soon. The transition was not yet finished," he explained.

11

"They are tied, yet he would have killed her."

"Nay, I would have stayed his hand if he had not."

"Who are you?"

The two voices stilled at the intrusion of the third.

"Who are you?" Becca demanded again.

Silence.

****

"Shush, cailín," Siobhan crooned, brushing the tangled hair back from the woman's face. She winced as she examined the results of the savage beating. "You've been hard used, little one, but you are safe now here at Caisel Ailfenn. Ciaran, *An Taoiseac* of Clann MacDermot, has granted you protection."

The girl moaned again, the words she muttered strange to Siobhan's ears. Young, yet no child this one and as near as she could tell, the girl was still a maiden. Odd that a man would use her so terribly yet would not drink from that cup. Siobhan cleaned her with a soft, wet rag, clucking over the cuts and welts lacing every inch of girl's body. Her nails were torn and bloody, her knuckles covered with cuts and bruises. This one had fought hard.

Every jostling movement the MacDermot made bringing her up to his chamber caused spasms of pain to ripple through the girl's body. To spare her more distress, Siobhan left her naked beneath the down coverlet. The stranger's soft sigh filled the room before she finally succumbed to the gentle hand of deep sleep.

Siobhan rinsed the rag, her mouth grim as she noted the dark red tinge to the water in the basin. She knew the two men waited in the hallway, both anxious for news. Tiptoeing across the room, she cracked open the door. "Yee can come in, but if yee disturb the wee one's sleep, I'll box yer ears," she hissed.

Niall grimaced at her impertinence, but Ciaran ignored her, shoving through the door before the other man moved. Ciaran strode across the room and halted beside his bed, staring at the strange woman. As he reached for the coverlet, she tried to stop him. Niall grabbed her around the waist to keep her from interfering and held her tightly against his side. Ciaran ripped the coverlet back. His face registered shock and she watched him swallow slowly.

"Someone wanted to kill her." He growled the words, his revulsion at the brutality of the attack plain on his face.

Siobhan watched him, the play of emotions a stark reminder of his role as clann chief, but he was also a man. His body's reaction to the girl's predicament surprised her only slightly.

"She fought him." Her blunt statement startled both men.

"Say again, woman?" Niall demanded.

"She fought him," she repeated louder. "Look at her hands. She clawed and hit, and very probably bit as well. Find the man with her marks all over him, and you'll find your culprit."

Niall started to speak but had to clear his throat to get the words out. "Was she forced?"

Siobhan shook her head, not surprised the men would want to know. "Not that I can tell. She had neither blood nor seed spilling from there." She pushed past them and pulled the covers up to the woman's chin, clucking under her breath the whole time. The McDermot was handsome enough to turn the heads of every woman between the ages of six and the grave. As his full lips quirked in a grin fit for Abhean, the faerie piper himself, she wondered why Ciaran had never taken anyone to his bed.

"All right, mother hen," Ciaran chuckled. "I'll not be beddin' her 'til she's healed."

Not at all intimidated by the man who held the

power of life or death over them all, Siobhan faced him down, a bit amused he'd lost his embarrassment so quickly. With her hands firmly planted on her hips, she scolded him. "You'll not be beddin' her a'tall, *Taoiseac*, not 'til she's wishin' yee to."

Niall gulped and stepped between her and Ciaran. He loved her and she knew he would die to protect her. His hand on her arm squeezed, a warning to keep her sassy tongue to herself. He relaxed his grip when Ciaran guffawed.

"Oh, aye," Ciaran chuckled, his grin smug and self-confident. "She'll be wishin' it right enough." He leered at her as he grabbed his groin and adjusted his *boidín* to a more comfortable position.

She snorted, her disdain evident in the inelegant sound. "Away with yee both," she snapped. "Let the cailín sleep. 'Tis the only thing will help her now." She shooed the men out of the room and shut the door behind.

Out in the hallway, Niall and Ciaran exchanged glances. That the cailín had marked her attackers cleared the two men cowering under guard in the great hall. Ragged and dirty, they probably would have ill-used her before finishing her off, but they carried no scratches or bruises upon their faces or arms to prove they'd started this strange affair.

While Niall dealt with the two peasants, Ciaran retreated to his den beneath the stairs. He poked the smoldering fire to life and settled heavily into one of the comfortable chairs in front of the fireplace. He prodded at the puzzle of the girl much like he'd done to stir up the fire. Heat pooled low in his groin. Her nakedness aroused more than compassion or pity. Despite her tortured and abused body, the sight of her lying naked in his bed made him rock hard. No cailín ever affected him this way. That her battered body had the power to do so completely terrified him. A man of honor and virtue, he'd sworn to protect his

14

people. Lust, and visions of the things he wanted to do to her and with her, churned his gut. Had he gone mad?

Niall returned, carrying mugs of rich brown ale. He settled in the other chair, and they sipped their drinks, silently watching the fire, each lost in his own thoughts. A troubled expression settled on Niall's face. Ciaran cocked an eyebrow in question. When Niall didn't speak, he broke the silence. "What?"

The older man stared into the fire, as if he hoped to find the answer in the flames. A long moment later, he spoke. "How? You must have left soon after me. How did you know where to find her?"

Now it was his turn to stare into the fire as he sought the words to explain. "I was pulled."

"Pulled?"

He nodded. "Aye. My heart knew where to find her. My head knew she was in danger. I roused the troop." He shrugged. "Who is she, Niall?"

Neither man had the answer to that one. The fire slowly burned down to glowing embers. He barely noticed when Niall eventually left. He bedded down on the floor in front of the fire. Wrapped up in his mantle, he tried to clear his mind for sleep—not an easy task with the cailín asleep in his bed upstairs.

****

Ciaran stood watching from the doorway. Three days had passed since he'd brought her home. When he'd come to check on the girl earlier that morning, he'd been angry to find his best wolfhound up on the bed with her, sleeping peacefully. The bloody thing actually growled at him. Bemused and hating to disturb the girl, he closed the door and left the dog where it was. His hounds were a rough-and-tumble lot, used to hunting and life bivouacking with his soldiers. Now he discovered his beastie had a soft spot and would probably leave fleas in his bed to boot. He watched the big dog snuggle closer to the girl, and his gut tightened with jealousy. He wisely refrained from marching into the room to shove the dog away and take his place. He wanted, nay needed, to make a good impression on this girl.

"What a good boy you are," the cailín crooned.

He couldn't believe the big dolt actually licked her face. She must be a witch. Bhruic, aptly named for his badger-like temperament, favored no one and barely tolerated Ciaran, yet the bloody cur lapped her face like...like... Ciaran was at a complete loss for words. He suddenly realized the girl was staring at him. A soft growl rumbled deep in the dog's chest. "'Tis not her should be afraid of me," he growled back at the dog.

"If I knew no better, I'd say yee were a wee bit jealous of him," Siobhan all but purred at him.

Ciaran stared at the girl's face. What would she look like once the bruises healed? Her dark lashes were long and thick, but the purple bruises around them overshadowed her silvery-blue eyes. Her right cheek was swollen and an angry red lump marred her left jaw. Her hair remained a snarled mess. His fingers curled into his palms, aching to comb through the blonde tangle. He wanted nothing more than to gather her into his arms and kiss the bruises until they were gone.

"How are yee feelin'?" Surely, he sounded more in control than he felt.

"Like she's been dragged behind a team of wild horses." Siobhan sniffed as she pushed past him, a steaming basin in her hands. "Be gone with yee." She tossed the words over her shoulder. "An' take your great brute of a beastie with yee. Dogs in bed with people," she groused. "Just 'tisn't right."

He'd lost this skirmish, so Ciaran retreated backwards only to be met at the door by Niall. He grabbed the older man's arm and in a conspirator's voice asked, "You actually live with that woman as your wife?" His eyes danced with mischievous lights.

Niall grinned lewdly at the question and ducked his head to answer, "Yes." Niall winked as he leered appreciatively at his wife's backside when she bent over the bed.

She ignored them.

"She does have some attributes to make up for her tongue," he admitted. His wagging eyebrows danced a jig with his smug smile.

"You should teach her to put that tongue to better use," he suggested with far too much male conceit.

"Oh, I have, Ciaran, I have." Niall's chest puffed up.

The men grinned at each other, sharing thoughts only men seem to share. At Siobhan's derisive snort, they retreated downstairs and made their way to the kitchen. Ciaran was hungry though he admitted more than the lack of food made his belly clench.

Upstairs, Siobhan gently cleaned the girl's wounds. Crushed herbs and flowers in the water helped take the sting out. "Have yee a name, cailín?"

Colleen? Rebecca almost chuckled. She hadn't been a colleen for most of her life. She was old, half a century. "Rebecca."

"Well, Becca, if you feel up to it, shove that bloody brute away and sit up. I'll try to comb the tangles from yer hair."

Rebecca flashed the woman a puzzled glance. Her head had been shaved in the emergency room after the accident and since then, she'd spent so much time in bed, she kept her hair cropped short so it didn't tangle. She raised a curious hand and discovered she had hair falling below her shoulders. She combed her fingers through part of it, but they caught and tangled in a knot of leaves and twigs.

Rebecca closed her eyes as the woman combed through the knots in her hair. When she'd awakened, she'd laid very still, afraid to move, afraid to open her eyes, almost afraid to breathe. She'd thought she was back in her bed until she patted the covers and discovered a warm body stretched out next to her. She bit back a scream as warm breath and a low growl tickled her ear. With her heart thudding in her chest, she'd opened one eye to peek. A huge wolfhound, his gray head as large as her own, laid beside her, his tongue lolling out of the side of his mouth. His warm brown eyes watched her intently. When she rubbed his chest, he fell over on her, his back leg scratching in ecstasy. That's when she looked up and saw the man standing in the doorway.

Almost an hour later, her head sore and aching from the combing, the woman bade her lie down again.

"I'll be back in a short, sweet, with a potion for yer pain."

Rebecca lay back against the pillow, thoroughly confused. She didn't own a dog, yet the giant wolfhound still stretched across the foot of her bed. Only, as she looked around, she realized this wasn't her bed. Or her room. Was she dreaming again? Had she relapsed and had the doctors disobeyed her orders about drugs? This dream vaguely reminded her of the one time she'd eased the pain with morphine. The drug was named after Morpheus, Greek god of dreams, for a reason. Hers had been a psychedelic trip, and she feared a repeat performance. This time she was stuck in some medieval castle. At least, she thought it was medieval. What did she know? And who was the young man in the doorway jealously watching the dog, looking as if he had every right to be lying next to her instead? He was gorgeous, she admitted, surprised her middle-aged brain had conjured such a hunk. Black hair, stormy blue eyes, broad shoulders that went from here to there... He had to be a dream.

Well, she'd wanted to sleep forever. Maybe God finally decided to grant her wish. "Ah, to sleep...perchance to dream," she murmured, drifting off.

Chapter Two

Ciaran cracked the door open. He held his breath to keep it from completely escaping his body. She lay on her side, her face turned from him. The sun spilling in through the high window danced over her silken hair, turning it to spun gold and silver. He wanted to bury his hands in its glorious folds. Only supreme will kept him rooted by the door. Bhruic was gone, but two other hounds had taken his place, as well as a tiny bit of fur Ciaran didn't want to think about. One of the kits that chased the mice and rats from his storerooms had found its way to the cailín's side. He was amazed. That small bit of fluff felt perfectly safe sleeping within inches of two of his more savage hounds. Perhaps the cailín truly was a witch. He knew for certain she'd bewitched him. He silently shut the door and retreated to his den. There he could safely drink some whiskey, muse about the strange cailín now sleeping in his bed, and wonder why she affected him so deeply.

Aralt, his father, had been one to enjoy all the pleasures being clann chief granted. He'd spilled his seed often and indiscriminately, yet only begot one child. Ciaran. The MacDermot had never even handfasted with Ciaran's mother, nor with any other. At least the old wolf had enough honor—he didn't inflict his rampant womanizing on a wife. After Ciaran was born, the MacDermot ordered mother and babe to the castle. He gazed upon his only offspring and pronounced the child his heir before sending them to a crofter's hut outside the castle gate. Aralt promptly forgot about them both while he continued his wanton ways.

Niall appeared at the door when Ciaran was six. He'd taken the lad under his wing, teaching him letters and numbers, and swordplay. Niall, though barely more than twenty, was the father Aralt should have been.

Ciaran knocked around the barracks with the soldiers. Most of the cailíns were free and easy with their favors. As heir apparent, he could take his pick. None had enticed him, and he'd not dipped his quill in any ink but one.

He'd been sixteen and celebrating *Samhain*. A young woman, comely and fair, not too much older than himself, came up to him. She took his hand and tugged him behind a tinker's tent, leading him back to a little hut in the woods beyond. Once through the door, she turned loose of him long enough to spread a pallet near the fire. Pushing the bemused boy down on it, she'd straddled his groin and began to unlace his shirt.

Ciaran's reaction took him totally by surprise. His *boidín* grew hard and thick, and of their own accord, his hips began to thrust up at her. She smiled then and bent over to let him glimpse her ample breasts.

"I told him there was naught wrong with you, lad, naught that I couldn't fix with some teaching," she purred, taking his hands and placing them at her bodice.

For the rest of the night, he touched and suckled, was touched and suckled in return, and thrust his cock into every place it could find in the woman's body. She taught him how to kiss, how to pleasure a woman and how to prolong his own pleasure. She showed him how to prevent spilling his seed inside a woman unless he desired to. When they'd finished, he laid there panting and sated. She did the same, curled against him.

The next morning, he left her asleep on the pallet, a smile on her face. He'd closed the door firmly on both the hut and the incident. He had never touched a woman again, had never again felt the stirring deep in his gut, had never grown hard and aching with the need to spill his seed deep within that wondrous place hiding between a woman's thighs. Until now. Now he remembered each sensation his body had enjoyed, each sublime texture that made up a woman's secret places, and he wanted nothing more than to explore, tasting and touching everywhere before burying his cock between her legs.

Ciaran couldn't stand it. The morning dragged by, and he had to see her, had to find out who she was, where she'd come from. He would make her his, one way or another, but if she had kin, he would ask for a betrothal the honorable way. He would even waive any dowry or bride price.

Becca woke. She tensed, waiting for the first spasm to take her breath away. When the pain didn't come, she stretched carefully. Her muscles were tight, but loosened once she'd stretched full out. Soft purring at her shoulder had her lips curving into a smile. A small calico cat snuggled next to her, nose to nose with a different massive wolfhound. A second hound guarded her back. These were good drugs. The pain was at bay. She had animals around her. She'd never admitted how agonizing giving up animals had been for her. Becca was still naked under the covers. She needed to put on something before the nurse came back. Convinced she was back in the hospital, she'd obviously created this fantasy world to see her through the pain rather than face that stark reality.

She shoved at the wolfhound lying between her and the side of the bed. With a growl more grumble than gruff, the huge beast slid to the floor, giving her room to get up. Becca steeled her nerves, then swung her feet off the bed. She'd been tall once, before the accident, a full five foot nine in her bare feet, but her feet still dangled almost a foot above the floor. Becca didn't like this part of the dream. Dropping even that little distance to the hard stone floor would send eruptions of pain up her spine. Still, her body was getting insistent, and she had to find the bathroom. Carefully, she slid off the bed.

Nothing happened when her feet touched the floor. She was stiff, and her muscles were sore but... No pain. No cramps. Nothing. Oh, yeah. Definitely great drugs. Where had this prescription been the past twenty-five years?

Becca snatched a softly woven throw from the back of a wooden chair and wrapped it around her like a shawl. Gingerly, she put one foot forward— still no pain. She cautiously took a second step and a third. Pleased with her body's response, she glanced around the room. Her need for the bathroom hit critical and facing what was out in the hallway, beyond the one door in the room, was not very high on her *To Do* list. Too bad she didn't have a private room. She'd always been shy about her bodily functions. Becca turned around to face the door.

She sucked in her breath. That gorgeous guy lounged against the doorjamb, leering at her. "How long have you been there?" she sputtered.

Grinning lopsidedly, he affirmed her worst fear when he answered, "Long enough, cailín."

The man positively purred at her, and Becca couldn't keep her eyes from straying. Lord, but he was tall, and with all that black hair, that broad chest...not to mention... She jerked her gaze back to his face.

Ciaran really hadn't meant to watch her get out of bed, but when she threw back the covers and was naked... Then she swung those magnificent legs over the side of the bed, and he couldn't force his eyes to look away or his body to behave. He was pleased she'd boldly looked him over. *Tit for tat,* he thought.

The delicate pink tip of her tongue swept across her bottom lip, and he almost groaned aloud. He knew the gesture was unconscious on her part, which made it even more enticing. When her top teeth tugged at her lip, it was all he could do to stand there. Every muscle in his body wanted to sweep her into his arms so he could kiss her soundly. She blushed, and the fact she was embarrassed by her perusal of him amused a man who'd never been amused by a cailín before.

Defensively, she pulled the throw closer around her. "Do you mind?" she snarled pointedly.

"I don't mind at all." His masculine conceit fueled his smug grin.

Becca looked around for something to throw at his arrogant expression. Guessing her intentions, he laughed before ducking out the door and tugging it closed behind him.

She still had a problem. Finding the bathroom was now a matter of *go, or else*. Nervous about having the cute dude hanging around outside the door, she hesitantly opened it and stuck her head out.

Two brawny men with massive swords strapped to their waists spun with exquisite symmetry to block her exit. The look of surprise on their faces mirrored her own expression. She blushed furiously. She needed the bathroom, and she needed it now. "Bathroom?" she squeaked, her face scarlet. Only the word "bathroom" had not come out of her mouth. The word she'd uttered sounded more like "garderobe."

The men tried not to ogle her, and Becca found that almost as amusing as the cute dude giving her the once-over, but then again, she *was* basically naked, and men were men. One man stepped back

24

and gestured down the hallway. The second stepped in front of her and led the way while the first fell in behind. Had she landed in some asylum for the criminally insane? Was that why she had guards? Then again, maybe this was all part of a drug-induced fantasy. When the door to the bathroom swung open, Becca gagged. Slightly larger than a big walk-in closet, the room featured a bench with holes cut in it bumped up against the far wall and a straw-covered floor. The smells emanating from the bench crinkled her nose. Though clean, the room reminded her a bit too much of a bad version of a porta potty at the county fair. Still, it was better than a bedpan. With relief in sight, she looked around for toilet paper and found nothing but a pile of clean-smelling clover straw. She eyed it distastefully but did what she had to do.

Her face still heated from her blush, she scurried back to her room. The men escorted her, ushered her inside, and firmly shut the door behind her. Becca was glad to see the nurse straightening the bed linens, even though both hounds and the kitten had abandoned her. Maybe the drugs were wearing off.

"Ah, and yer looking much better today, cailín," the woman crooned to her. "Are yee hungry?"

Becca realized she was. Ravenous, in fact. She hadn't wanted food in ages. She nodded.

"Good. Yee need to be putting some meat back on yer bones, cailín."

Becca found her voice. "Why do you keep calling me *colleen*? I'm older than you are."

The woman laughed at her. "Older than me? Are yee touched, girl?"

"I'm fifty-years-old," Becca insisted.

"Then I'm nigh a hundred." The nurse chuckled dryly.

A tight knot formed in Becca's stomach. She

clenched her fists, waiting for the pain to take her. She grew still.

The woman eyed her worriedly. "What is it, cailín?" She hurried over and put her arms around her, and the muscles Becca felt grow so tight relaxed.

When the pain didn't come, Becca relaxed a tiny bit more. No pain was good, but what her nurse insisted to be true about their ages was a horse of a different color. Suddenly curious, she checked the walls and furniture, but no mirrors reflected her face. *'Course not, silly. Silvered glass is still a century or two away.*

She congratulated her psyche on the construction of this delicious fantasy. She noticed a large metal bowl and a pitcher on a table tucked against the wall. *Must be what they use for a sink.* A round metal plate, like a shield, hung on the wall above the table. Its highly burnished surface reflected the room like a mirror. Step by hesitant step, like a moth drawn to a flame, she crossed the floor, stared into the shiny metal, and fainted dead away.

Ciaran stepped into the room as the girl looked into the polished shield hanging on the wall. Her faint caught him by surprise. With superhuman speed, he dashed across the floor and caught her before her head smacked against the stones of the floor. He cradled her to his chest for a moment, relishing her nearness and warmth.

The clucking behind him reminded him to get up and get the wee cailín back into bed. He sat on the edge of the bed, holding her on his lap. Reluctant to put her down, he delighted in the fact his arms were wrapped around her nakedness and her bottom fit so perfectly against his groin.

Thanks to Siobhan's healing magic, the girl's bruises and cuts were fading. He searched her face.

High cheekbones curved around to a strong but feminine jaw. Her neck was long and graceful, her nose pert and her lips full, luscious, and entirely kissable. He bent his head, wanting to taste the sweetness he knew he'd find there.

****

"You said she wouldn't remember." That voice was accusatory.

"She shouldn't." That voice was filled with denial.

"Yet she does. 'Tis a complication we shouldn't have to deal with."

"It is an art, not a science."

"What have you done to me?"

****

"Why nothing, cailín, at least not yet, though I was planning on kissing yee."

The deep voice washed over her as warm and sexy as a caress. Becca opened her eyes. The Chippendale dancer she'd talked to earlier now held her cradled in his lap. She stared at his full lips only inches from her own. Something hard poked her bottom and she squirmed. The man's eyes widened in surprise as a look of pure desire washed across his face. Becca sucked in her breath hoping not to break into a fit of giggles. All she could think of was the old Mae West line..."Is that a gun in your pocket, or are you just glad to see me?" In this topsy-turvy time warp of a hallucination, she suspected this male model of a medieval warrior wouldn't know what a gun was. However, he would more than likely know what was in his pocket and would know precisely what to do with it when he brought it out into the light of day. The thought turned her stomach into a cheerleader, flip-flopping wildly as the muscles between her legs clenched.

She felt defensive for some reason she couldn't quite fathom. "I'm old enough to be your mother,"

27

she snapped waspishly, not entirely liking the possessive way he watched her lips.

He arched one eyebrow. He looked roguish and even more kissable.

She resisted the urge.

"Are yee daft, cailín?" He shook his head. "I've thirty summers to my name, and you can't have more than twenty, twenty-five at the most." He glanced down the length of her body and his eyes glinted with male arrogance, possessiveness...and something Becca couldn't quite divine.

Only the thin woven throw separated her naked body from his rock hard one. Becca scrambled to seal the ends across her chest and thighs with her fists, all the while glaring at the gorgeous man.

He roared with laughter at her futile gesture. "Siobhan," he choked out, wheezing as he caught his breath. "Me thinks the cailín is shy and has a need to be covered."

"Aye, *Taoiseac*, she needs a shift and a gown or two to boot."

Almost as if he'd silently commanded it, there was a soft knock at the door. A maid poked her head in, bobbing it in respect. "I've brought the gowns yee requested, *Taoiseac*," she murmured.

Siobhan hurried to the door and relieved the girl of the bundle. Shaking out each one, she laid the gowns across the foot of the bed.

Becca's eyes widened in surprise. These were no common dresses like those worn by Siobhan, but truly gowns of the finest linens and brocades in soft, glorious colors, more beautiful than any prom dress she'd ever coveted. Entranced by the clothing, she missed the flash of possessive pleasure in the man's gaze when he recognized the surprised delight on her face.

Her happiness shouldn't have meant a thing to him, yet he found that it did matter; it mattered quite a lot. That something as simple as picking out a gown enchanted the girl left a warm spot in his middle.

With her hands on her hips, Siobhan unleashed her snappy tongue on him. "Off with yee now, *Taoiseac* Ciaran. Let the cailín dress in peace. She needs no overgrown lout starin' at her like he wants her for supper."

"Ah, yee've a tongue on you, Siobhan, but in this instance, yee're right. I wouldn't mind eating her for supper."

Becca blinked. He meant exactly what he said in every carnal sense of that phrase. Her heart raced and that funny tingling down between her legs started again. *Oh, lord*, she thought. *I am way too old for this fantasy.*

Siobhan scolded the man out of the room and turned back to her charge. The girl would be a beauty when the bruises finally healed, and it was evident Ciaran was completely smitten. She just hoped his feelings were reciprocated. If not, Becca would be in for a hard time of it. Siobhan smiled. She'd seen him adjusting the front of his trews as he'd risen from the bed. Aye, the cailín definitely would be getting a hard time, sooner or later.

Returning to the business at hand, Siobhan smiled at Becca. "Pick yer favorite color, and I'll help yee dress, cailín. Then, I'll fix yer hair."

The retort about her age forming on Becca's lips suddenly died. She'd seen her reflection in the shield, believed it couldn't be her own, yet knew it was. For the first time, Becca seriously doubted her sanity. She'd fallen asleep in the twenty-first century wanting to be twenty-five again or sleep forever. She remembered the book she'd been reading the night before—a romance about a twentieth-century scientist traveling through time and falling in love with a sixteenth century

29

Highlander. This all had to be a dream. Though it seemed real, it couldn't be. Could it? Her pain was gone for the first time in twenty-five years, and the body and face she wore were the ones she'd enjoyed in her youth.

She chose to participate in her dream and picked a sky blue linen dress embroidered with delicate silvery green shamrocks. *Shamrocks? So, not the Highlands of Scotland, but Ireland instead.* Fitting, since her family originally came from County Galway. She sighed, marveling at the way her subconscious wove this tale.

"Be paying the MacDermot no mind, cailín. He's a good man, for all his bully bravado," Siobhan told Becca.

Chapter Three

Siobhan dropped the soft lawn shift over Becca's head and then the linen dress. After the woman laced up the back, it took a few tugs and pushes to get everything in the front seated correctly. Becca glanced down. As a teenager and in college, she'd been tall and athletically built—broad shoulders, high, firm breasts, a small waist tapering to wider hips and long, muscular legs that, as one college football player had mused, went all the way from here to there. There wasn't a sport she hadn't excelled in. Track, softball, swimming. She competed in them all, but her true love was riding. Riding like that "wild Comanche." All those summers on her grandfather's ranch prepared her to compete on the Grand Prix jumping circuit. Her parents insisted college came before her equestrian goals, so she finished her degree in equine management. She'd always known that one day she would compete in the Olympics for Team USA. She was twenty-four when she'd been named as an alternate to the team. And then the accident. Months in rehab, told she'd never walk again, told she was lucky to be alive. Twenty-five years later, Becca wondered when the luck had run out.

****

Siobhan stopped brushing Becca's hair. The cailín had gone as still as a stone, scarcely breathing. Instinctively, she knew the girl had gone far away. She wondered what painful memory caused the tortuous wrinkling of Becca's brow. With slow, rhythmic strokes, she brushed Becca's hair again, hoping the gentle motion brought comfort. She'd known other women abused like the girl, women who withdrew into their minds, merely existing from day to day.

Siobhan laid aside the brush. The girl needed time to heal. That was all. Her strong, capable hands picked up the first gown and folded it neatly and precisely. Opening a large wooden armoire, she rearranged the MacDermot's clothing to make room for the few gowns.

****

Becca blinked. Lost in her thoughts, she now couldn't remember what she'd been thinking about. She found some comfort in the normalcy of Siobhan's tasks. Until she saw the shirts and pants stacked in the cabinet. Men's clothes. Lots of them. She sucked in a breath, her eyes wide.

"Aye, *Taoiseac* Ciaran gives his chamber to you, mistress."

"I am no one's mistress," Becca protested, even as she mulled the strange title around in her head. *Teeshock*. She'd never heard the word before.

"Mayhap not now, but you will be."

Siobhan's answer was a bit too cryptic for Becca's peace of mind. Warily, she watched the woman cross the room to a small table constructed of rough-hewn wood. Siobhan retrieved a metal container and returned, standing in front of her, head tilted as she perused Becca's face.

"A little powder." A tight smile accompanied the explanation. "To dim the worst of the damage."

Confusion was now a perpetual state for Becca. What damage was Siobhan referring to? And powder? Did women always seek to "beautify" themselves? She exhaled, her breath almost a sigh. The scars her body bore would never be dimmed by mere powder or any other cosmetic enhancement. A glimmer danced across the surface of the shield hanging on the wall. The body she'd stared down at in bed that morning and then again as she'd dressed wasn't her own. Covered with bruises and healing cuts, this body bore no signs of the injuries and countless surgeries she'd endured. What had happened to her? Was this some protracted dream? Had she died and entered some sarcastic god's idea of an afterlife? Or had something her professor of physics said was impossible actually occurred? Was she really lost in time? Too many questions that had no answers. She closed her eyes while submitting to her nurse's gentle fingers.

"'Tis time for dinner," Siobhan said. Her lilting voice matched the cheery smile on her face. "Will you come down to eat in the hall or would you rather remain here to eat?"

Becca really wanted to stay right where she was. Every once in awhile, the whole damn situation became so overwhelming hyperventilation was a real possibility. Before she could answer, someone knocked.

"Is she decent?" a gruff voice growled through the door.

"Aye, too decent for the likes of you," Siobhan retorted tartly.

The heavy door swung open and an older man almost as tall and powerful as Ciaran blocked the doorway. Mercurial expressions flickered across his ruggedly handsome face, surprise, admiration, a touch of lust, a hint of confusion. Then he smiled. Becca saw her reflection in his eyes. That exquisite creature could not be her. She swooned again.

The man caught her in strong arms and lifted her up, trying to hold her without being too familiar with her body. "He insists she dine with him, Siobhan," he hissed at the other woman. "I have no choice but to escort her down."

"'Tis too much excitement too soon, Niall," she

hissed right back. "And, if he catches her in your arms, you'll be drawn and quartered for sure."

Becca pushed feebly against the solid wall of the man's chest. "Uhm? I'm not feeble-minded. You want to talk about me? Then talk *to* me." She thumped the man's chest again. "I'll be fine," she insisted. "Just put me down."

Hesitantly, he set her on her feet, a strong hand on her elbow to steady her. Becca swayed for a minute and then regained her equilibrium. "What you must think of me," she demurred. "I'm not really the fainting type."

Niall smiled, the look in his eyes softening. "I never thought you were, cailín. You wouldn't be alive otherwise."

Siobhan slapped his biceps, the smacking sound of her palm on his bare skin as loud as a gunshot, and glared up at him.

He glared back, refusing to be chastised. "Well, she wouldn't, Siobhan, so leave off."

Niall escorted Becca and Siobhan to the great hall, the two guards who'd been stationed at the chamber door trailing them. Deafening noise rose from the large room below. Becca hesitated at the top of the steps. Niall took her elbow again to steady her and urge her along, despite the hissed warning from Siobhan.

As Becca's bare feet delicately trod the first few steps, twenty voices abruptly stopped talking. All eyes looked up. Hands stilled halfway between plates and mouths. She faltered mid-step, suddenly shy and uncertain, sure she couldn't face all those strange people in this strange place. She felt twelve instead of fifty. Then *he* appeared at the bottom of the stairs. Ciaran. *An Taoiseac* of Clann MacDermot. He took her breath away. He gazed up at her, his hand lifting as if he was reaching for her.

She stared into his eyes. They were the color of

the Colorado sky just as a thunderstorm moved across the mountains. He gazed at her, his eyes sweeping her from top to bottom. She shook her head slightly sending a silken tendril of hair dancing enticingly next to her ear. His eyes tracked the movement like a hunting hound. As she watched, his emotions played across his face. Admiration. Bemusement. Lust. Oh, yes. There was definitely lust, obvious by the way the front of his trews stretched, drawing her eyes there. Dragging her gaze upward, she saw the breath hitch in his chest as he watched her. Michelangelo could have chiseled his face from granite. Her heart stuttered and she couldn't catch her breath. He was the most amazing man she'd ever laid eyes on. His arms were long and roped with muscle. His shoulders broad, his chest thick, and his legs? Oh, his legs could make her swoon again. What would it feel like to have those thick thighs touching hers, skin to skin? She could actually feel warm liquid drip down her thigh.

She laughed, a sharp bitter sound. She was having an honest-to-god wet dream. Old enough to have hot flashes, she should have been way beyond such fantasies. "No! This is stupid," she snarled. "Wake up!" She was so focused on berating herself for her out-of-control emotions, she failed to notice the darkening of those eyes shining up at her or the thundercloud of anger marching across the perfect face below her.

She closed her eyes and shook her head vigorously to wake up. As she opened her eyes, the tantalizing dream who'd been waiting for her at the bottom of the stairs disappeared. She faltered. The knot of pain always hiding in her gut unraveled. She doubled over and fell to her knees, bruising them on the cold stone step. The pain radiated out from her core, stretching into her fingers and toes, even to the very ends of her hair. Excruciating, it was worse than anything she'd ever experienced before. She thought she screamed, but she didn't know if any sound actually escaped. Inky blackness swirled before her eyes and her stomach churned. *Oh, God,* she moaned. *Not again. I can't survive this again.* She screwed her eyes closed, desperate to shut out the whirling cyclone of light and dark.

Ciaran stormed into his den and raged at his foolishness. Infuriated, he growled under his breath. He'd stood there like a foolish lad, wearing his heart on his sleeve for everyone to see. Like some faerie queen, she'd descended toward him, wearing the gown he'd personally chosen because its color matched her eyes. Her shoulders, wide for a woman and showing unusual strength, sloped up to the slim column of her neck. His *boidín* hardened as he imagined nuzzling the soft skin in the hollow of her throat.

Standing there at the bottom of the stairs, he'd reached for her, spellbound by her beauty. Her silvery-blue gaze locked on his, and he'd offered his heart when he reached for her. If she had but looked, she could have seen it there in his palm, pulsing and beating only for her. Instead, she'd barked out a derisive laugh and mocked him. Ciaran was certain every man in the great hall heard her deny him. Infuriated, he howled in frustration.

****

"You must make her forgot." The female's voice was panicked.

"I have tried but she is too strong. Mayhap the pain of that life is so overriding she cannot get beyond it to live in this one." He sounded perplexed.

"She must or all is for naught. He cannot die without issue."

"Who are you?" Becca screamed the question into the whirling vortex.

"She hears us. How can that be?" She was

alarmed.

"I know not, but what can she learn? Naught to help her." He was confident.

"No, nor naught to help us." She wasn't.

"We must be patient. Have faith," he counseled.

"Bah. Patience is for those with short lives and faith is for those who cannot see beyond the next sunrise."

****

Becca lay still, steeling herself for the next crushing wave of pain. She was so cold. She couldn't remember how long she'd lain here. She couldn't feel her feet or her hands, except when the pain roared through her body. She whimpered and choked back tears, desperate to remember what had happened. She shivered. She'd been driving, the road was slick. No, that wasn't it. Two men. Ugly men with fists and hard boots had pounded her body. No. She shuddered. Cold. Hard ground. More men. Speaking a strange language. She shook her head and pain formed a starburst behind her eyes. Wait. She'd been coming down a long staircase. Someone was waiting for her. *He* was waiting for her. Tall and rugged, with eyes filled only of her. Had she fallen? Hit her head? She was wearing a prom dress. Had she tripped on the unfamiliar hem and tumbled head over heels down the steps? Why couldn't she remember?

She refused to open her eyes, knowing the whirling dervish waited for her if she did. Her stomach roiled and she gagged, afraid she was going to vomit. A strobe light pulsed beyond her eyelids and the roaring in her ears drowned out all other sound. She tasted the bile rising in her throat. She groaned. The pain built again, like myriad shooting stars burning through her entire body.

"Hold her head up," Siobhan ordered. "She'll choke else."

Niall sat on the bed, the girl propped against his chest. He obediently held Becca so her head lolled back against his shoulder. Siobhan grabbed the basin she'd used to bathe the girl earlier and held it just in case.

Niall wrapped his arms tighter as the spasms hit. He heard Ciaran roar down below, and he turned stricken eyes to his mate. "What devil resides in her that torments them both?" His voice and breathing were both ragged.

Siobhan could only shrug in reply. She had no answers.

They both turned to face the door, recognizing the heavy footsteps coming their way. Ciaran threw open the massive oaken door with such force, it shuddered as it hit the wall behind it. His hair was disheveled, as if he'd tried to pull it out by the roots. His eyes were wild and as dark as a storm-ravaged sea.

"I cannot stand her pain," he spat out between gritted teeth. "Kill her and free me from her ensorcellment."

Siobhan gasped, moving to protect the girl.

Niall groaned, loath to follow that order, yet hesitant not to. He loved Ciaran as a son. His pain was every bit as great as the girl's, and he could stand neither's suffering much longer. "How can this be?" he asked his wife, praying she knew of a way to free them all.

"I've not got the knowin' of it," Siobhan admitted sadly. "That they are tied together is obvious, yet Ciaran has never sworn the binding. I have never witnessed such, Niall. Mayhaps Odhran will know," she prayed.

Ciaran sank to his knees, his head falling forward until his chin rested against his chest. "By all the gods, Niall, kill her before she kills me." His whispered plea sounded like a death rattle.

Siobhan dropped the bowl she'd been holding and hurried to a small table near the fire. Boxes and jars littered the top of it. She took a cup, added a bit from one vial, and a pinch of another. Finally, she poured wine into the cup and stirred the mixture, murmuring softly. She carried the full cup back to the bed.

"Lay her head back, Niall, so she can drink."

He looked up at her in shock. "You think to poison her? Why not let me plunge my knife cleanly into her heart and be done with it?"

"'Tis but a sleeping draught, husband. 'Twill put her beyond the pain." She nodded toward Ciaran and added, "He will follow." She tipped the liquid into Becca's mouth and stroked her throat so the girl would swallow. Within a few moments, Niall felt her body relax. Her breathing deepened, filling her starved lungs with oxygen. He shifted so he could lay her back on the bed. Siobhan pulled the covers over her as her husband hurried to Ciaran's side.

"She's a witch, Niall. We must kill her," Ciaran panted.

"Nay, lad, we can't," he protested. "I believe that what befalls her will befall you. The O'Neills grow ever more hungry for our land, and I fear what will happen if you are not here to lead us." When Ciaran nodded weakly, Niall stood and helped the bigger man to his feet, grunting with the effort. "I'll take him to another chamber," he told Siobhan over his shoulder.

"Nay. Put him in bed beside her where I can watch over them. Then ride yee to Odhran's hut and bring him here to me." When he started to protest, she held up her hand in warning. "This is beyond my knowin', Niall, and I, too, fear for both of them. This is the truest binding I have ever seen, one for all eternity. We must protect them until the gods sort this out. Ride, husband, ride hard, and bring me

Odhran."

Niall helped Ciaran around to the far side of the bed and eased him down. Ciaran groaned as he laid back, and Niall lifted his feet up onto the bed. He stood uncertainly for a moment, indecisive for one of the few times in his life.

"Go," Siobhan hissed.

Niall turned on his heel and fled, banging the door closed behind him.

A knot of worried men awaited him at the foot of the stairs. To a man, they'd seen the vision in sky blue float down the stairs toward their *Taoiseac*. They'd seen the great joy radiating from the MacDermot as he awaited this woman who was obviously his chosen one. To a man, they saw the rage suddenly vanquish the joy and the MacDermot turn and leave. Shocked, they watched the woman fall, Niall too slow to catch her. They heard her screams, and they heard the answering howls erupting from Ciaran's den. Even the more educated among them were scared.

Niall could take scarce time to allay their fears, so he motioned two of his lieutenants to follow him to the stables. They had to jog to keep up with his long-legged dash as he briefly filled them in on Ciaran's condition, that of the woman, and his own mission.

He rode hard and fast, slowing only when the trail narrowed dangerously. The ride took far too long for him to reach Siobhan's cottage. He barely slowed as he guided his horse onto the narrow trail on the other side of his mate's herb garden. Half a league into the forest, Niall found the small clearing and the old Druid's hut.

"Odhran," he shouted, pulling his horse to a sliding stop before the door. "Come quickly. *An Taoiseac* has need of you."

The door to the hut creaked opened and the

tired, wrinkled face of the Druid stared out. "But I have no need of him," the old man snapped.

Niall was shocked silent. His fist closed convulsively around the handle of his sword and pulled it half way out of its scabbard. Through clinched teeth, he snarled, "Your very life has need of him, Odhran. If he dies, I will personally run my sword through you."

Odhran watched him for a long moment, as if trying to read his thoughts. The man's eyes flickered then he dipped his chin in an almost imperceptible nod. "Aye," he agreed. "Ciaran is in need of aid though I may be a poor choice. Still, I will do what I can." He ducked back into his hut and emerged a few moments later with a worn leather satchel looped across his shoulder. "Let us go."

Niall clasped the old man's hand and swung him up behind him. Odhran felt frail beneath his robes and he wondered just how ancient the old Druid actually was.

****

Ciaran dozed lightly. The pain had finally left his head. Siobhan puttered around over by the fire. He tracked her movements by the swish of her skirt as she mixed potions and such. A soft puff of air tickled his ear. The woman next to him sighed in her sleep. The pain had finally left her as well.

He gathered her into his arms and settled her next to him, her head on his shoulder, her soft breasts pressing into his side. The woman stirred, moving one leg over his. Absently, he rubbed his chin on the top of her head, relishing the soft silkiness of her hair as its strands caught in his beard stubble. A sense of peace and contentment stole over him. This was the way life was meant to be, he mused. He grew hard and smiled, reveling in the fact that he had. Though he would never have admitted it even to Niall, he'd often wondered why other men bedded women with abandon, but he'd never had the urge beyond the one time. And, if that long ago cailín hadn't taken the bull by the horns, so to speak, he'd probably be a virgin to this day.

"'Tis no shame in that, *Taoiseac*," Siobhan said softly from where she sat on a bench near the fire. She flashed him a knowing smile when he opened his eyes only to glare at her. "Not all men need to be a bull with a herd of cows. Long ago, Ciaran, before the gods even gave us the sacred fire, before the cauldron, spear, sword, and stone, they gave every man a woman. Each man was to care for and protect his own and if he did so, life would be good." She cocked an eyebrow and gave him a saucy grin. "If yee gather my meaning?"

Ciaran grinned back knowing exactly what she meant. He nodded, wanting her to continue.

"Because this kind of love was so deep and abiding, the gods knew that one lifetime would not be enough. They promised as long as each man kept his covenant with his true mate, even though the dark sleep of death might part them in this life, the two would be reunited in the next." Siobhan sighed. "Mortals being what they are, they forgot what a wondrous gift true mating was. They got greedy and hungered for others. They had no patience to await their one true love. This angered the gods. They gathered all the mortals together then separated the men from the women. Every god gathered a handful of each and tossed them to the four winds. This went on until all the mortals had been scattered. If a man is lucky enough to find his true mate, win her, and keep her, then the gods will keep their covenant with that man. He will get to keep her for eternity, finding her again in each life, to have and to hold."

Ciaran studied her for a long time. "What are you saying, Siobhan?" Almost afraid to hear what she'd say next, he held his breath.

"Not a thing, Ciaran. 'Tis just an old tale, but I suspect you might be the rare man who will recognize the truth in the telling of it."

She'd called him by his first name, rather than his title. He started to smile until he saw her forehead wrinkle as she stared at the girl in his arms. That's when he noticed the beads of sweat dotting Becca's forehead. Siobhan glided toward the bed carrying two cups.

"Drink, Ciaran, then help me dose Becca. I fear sleep is the only respite I can give the two of you for now."

He took the cup and sniffed it suspiciously. Putting the rim to his mouth, he tossed down the contents in one swallow. He handed the cup back to Siobhan. In one smooth movement, he sat up, bringing Becca with him. He cradled her limp body to his chest with one hand tenderly cupping her cheek and turned her face toward the other woman.

She slowly poured her potion down the girl's throat, making sure she swallowed. Then Siobhan turned her back to prevent him from seeing the smile curling her lips. Her reflection in the shield hanging on the wall gave her away.

Relieved, he laid back down, still cradling Becca. He settled her against his side. Her eyelids barely flickered during the process, then she sighed and snuggled closer. Ciaran closed his eyes, savoring the feel of her body molded to his.

He'd had a huge, empty hole in his life, but had never been able to discern what was missing. Now he knew. He'd longed for this feeling his whole life, but could never define what he sought. This woman puzzled him. He knew only her first name, knew nothing of her sept or clann, nor nothing of her, yet she had come to mean the world to him.

He was afraid—afraid for the first time in his life. He was afraid of needing her so much. He was afraid of losing himself in her. He was afraid of losing her. That was his last thought as Siobhan's draught sent him to sleep.

****

Niall could not make the return trip to the castle nearly as quickly as he'd ridden out. In his haste to get Odhran, he hadn't even considered taking a second horse for the old Druid to ride back. As it turned out, his forgetfulness was probably for the best. The way the old man clutched at his belt, Niall suspected he probably could not have sat a horse by himself. As time passed, Niall opened up and confided in the Druid, telling him of Ciaran's dreams and the screaming banshee who turned out to be Becca. He spoke of how they'd found her and Ciaran's possessive protectiveness from the very moment he'd laid eyes on her. He told Odhran about Becca's pain and its affect on Ciaran. And he revealed his own worries for the health and safety of his clann chief. Times were too unsettled, too dangerous to lose Ciaran. The clann needed him. The king needed him.

When they arrived at the castle, Niall helped Odhran to the ground, and then dismounted himself. He led the Druid inside and up to Ciaran's chamber. Siobhan met them at the door. With fingers to her lips, she ushered them in. Becca's head rested on Ciaran's shoulder and his strong arms enfolded her, as if to keep her close and safe. Both breathed deeply.

Odhran stared at the sleeping couple and felt his heart stutter. What Siobhan had sensed, he knew absolutely. This truly could be a mating granted by the gods, if the couple could only work through the obstacles placed before them.

Ciaran instinctively mistrusted his feelings for this woman. That she could bring out such strong emotions and feelings—protectiveness, lust, rage, fear, even pain—disturbed the man. Odhran understood that. Ciaran was a warrior, a leader within the scattered clanns. In battle, he was quick, decisive. In ruling, he was fair. He was a man always in control—or had been until this waif appeared in his life. Now he was adrift on a sea of unfamiliar feelings.

Odhran turned his gaze to the woman. A little glimmer of insight niggled at his brain, like a worm dangling on a hook waiting for the fish to bite. The woman in Ciaran's arms looked young and with her beautiful features and hair of gold spun with silver, there was a large portion of appealing waif to entice a man. Yet at the same time, Odhran sensed there were two in the place of one. Deep inside the waif, there was another. That other was dark, yet not evil.

He wished the woman would wake. He wanted to look into her eyes. That other being seemed as old as time and full of pain. Odhran wanted to look into the mirrors of her soul to see. Surely the gods wouldn't toy so cruelly with a good man like Ciaran.

The Druids believed the human soul made a long journey through many lives in the course of its existence. Odhran was curious about this woman's soul, guessing it had survived many lifetimes. As he watched, the woman slipped her right hand into Ciaran's shirt and rested her palm above his heart. The couples' legs were entwined like wild ivy and her hair cast a golden net across his chest. Even in sleep, the woman sought the binding. Then the pain hit.

Niall rushed to the old Druid's side. The man clutched his chest and fell to his knees. He panted, biting back moans. Niall looked helplessly at his wife, but her eyes were on the couple in the bed. Neither moved. Her sleeping draught had put them far beyond the pain's reach. Siobhan knelt beside the old man and took his face in her hands, forcing him to look at her.

"Is the pain hers?" she asked. He nodded. She continued to hold his face and stare into his eyes. Within moments, the Druid's breathing returned to normal and he relaxed. Siobhan released him, and Niall helped both of them up.

"Well?" the big soldier demanded.

Siobhan turned sad eyes toward her husband. "They have much to conquer in this life, but if they persevere, they will have great rewards."

Niall walked the two of them over to the bench by the fireplace and settled them onto it. He oftimes got lost in his wife's cryptic pronouncements and this was definitely one of those times.

Siobhan absently patted the old Druid's hand. The smile she offered him did nothing to hide her fatigue. "She is no witch, Niall, despite what you think. Nor is this some illness or disease that will infect us all."

Niall opened his mouth to protest, worried that the Druid had also succumbed to her pain.

"Your wife speaks true, Niall," Odhran confirmed quickly. After a pause to catch his breath, he added. "The girl is changing into a woman."

"Nay," the big man spat. "I've never seen a cailín suffer that change as this one does."

Odhran shook his head, thinking for a moment. "Mayhap, my big friend, 'tis the other way around. The woman is changing into a girl."

Niall stood there, a look of total confusion splashed across his face.

Siobhan cut her eyes to the Druid. The old man patted her hand now. "You feel it, too, daughter. There are two within her. Until one or the other wins out, there is little hope. And, if the wrong one does..."

"What gibberish is this?" Niall demanded. "You said she was not a witch, but then how can there be two?"

Siobhan stood up and laid a restraining hand on his forearm. "She's no witch, Niall. I will vouch for that with my life." She turned to face the Druid. "The pain comes from the joining?"

The old man nodded, suddenly worn out. "Aye. The one who is must become the one who was."

"What of the MacDermot?" Niall demanded, still confused by the Druid's ramblings.

"What of him?" Odhran blinked owlishly.

"Her pain is fearsome and it becomes his. Can she survive it? Can he?"

"She may not." Odhran sighed. "Mayhap, he as well." At Niall's sharp intake of breath, Odhran hastened to add, "Nay, his life will not be forfeit. His heart? That is yet to be seen."

Later, after Odhran had been fed and given a place to sleep, Niall sought out Siobhan. He'd checked on Ciaran and Becca, confirming both still slept peacefully, wrapped in each other's arms. Niall stood in the doorway, watching the man he'd helped raise from boy to clann chief. A look of peace gentled Ciaran's face, the expression was one Niall hadn't seen since Ciaran's childhood. Shutting the door, he'd bid the guards good night.

Siobhan had taken a room not far from Ciaran's so she could tend to Becca as needed. She was already in bed when he entered. She looked fetching with the coverlet pulled up to her chin, and he suspected she had nothing on underneath. He started dropping his clothes at the door. Siobhan, her lips curled in a cheeky grin, urged him to hurry.

"'Tis been too long, dear heart," he growled. He kicked off his boots and his trews quickly followed. He dove under the covers Siobhan held up and gathered her into his arms. He found her full breasts, one with a rough hand, the other with his mouth. He loved her long into the night. He loved her until they were both exhausted and sleep claimed them.

Just before dawn, Niall woke Siobhan and loved her all over again. When they were both satisfied, he pulled her close.

"I am a man thick with no wit, my love," he admitted. "I dinnit get much that was said last night by the Druid. Can yee straighten out my thinking?"

Siobhan kissed his chest then laid her head on the spot. "Odhran thinks Becca's soul has gotten lost," she explained. He made a sign to ward off evil but she stayed his hand. "He thinks her soul came back to find Ciaran's. When she was here the first time, they missed each other, and so her soul went on to other lives. But there was no living for her without him, so she's come back. The two parts of her must become one, and that coming together is the source of her pain."

"Ciaran should just grab the bull by horns," he snorted.

"Oh?"

"Aye." He looked smug and superior, positive he had the answer. "He needs to tup her until she has no idea who she is." He grinned wickedly at her. "Just like I'm going to do to you."

Siobhan kissed him deeply, thinking, *Nay, he needs to tup her until she* knows *exactly who she is.*

Chapter Four

When he awoke, Ciaran fought the urge to rip the gown from Becca's body and spend the morning losing himself in her. From the moment he'd first seen her naked in his bed, despite her battered and bruised body, he'd wanted her. He wanted to cup her firm breasts in his hands while he kissed her long and deep. He wanted to explore every inch of her body with his tongue, and bury himself so deep inside her core, he wouldn't know where he ended and she began.

Becca stirred restlessly in her sleep and her right hand trailed down his belly to rest lightly on his manhood. He sucked in his breath. By the gods, he wanted that, too, wanted her mouth and hands touching every part of his body.

Ciaran was about to throw caution to the wind when he heard the guard on the outer wall issue a challenge. Moments later, several horses clattered into the courtyard. Trying not to wake her, he reluctantly disentangled himself. Still dressed from the night before, he took only a moment to readjust his erection to a more comfortable position in his trews and run his fingers through the tangles of his hair. He snagged his mantle from the foot of the bed and wrapped it around his shoulders as he headed straight to the great hall.

Niall was already there greeting the three riders who'd come in. The colors in their mantles proclaimed they came from the O'Conor, King of Connaught. Two of the messengers asked only for a quick drink and fresh mounts. They were away even as the third began to recite his message.

Conchobhar O'Conor, King of Connaught, had issued an *ard fheis*. Each clann chieftain in the O'Conor *tuatha* was to answer with the minimum of a detachment of men and provisions for both men and horses to last for at least three months. The messengers had been riding night and day to issue the edict to all those owing fealty to the O'Conor *tuatha*. The MacDermots had long held military responsibilities within the *tuatha* and were probably among the first to be notified.

"What comes?" Ciaran asked when the courier paused for a breath.

"Clann O'Brien raids from the south, *Taoiseac* MacDermot," he stated coldly. "The O'Conor thinks to drive them from Connaught before midsummer. He is calling the clanns together. Will you attend?"

Niall watched his liege carefully. He was the only one who'd noticed Ciaran's glance up the stairs during the recitation of the *ard fheis*. This might be a solution to Ciaran's current dilemma. Odhran and Siobhan had talked of a joining of the two selves within Becca. If Ciaran were away, perhaps things would come easier for the cailín. He also hoped it would be easier on Ciaran with half the country between them. He had little doubt Ciaran would do his duty. Ciaran's words proved him right.

"Aye, we'll be coming and about time, too. I bring a company of horse and a company of hobelars. Have you time to rest?"

The messenger shook his head. "Nay, *Taoiseac* MacDermot, though I thank you for your offer of host. I ride for Ros Comain, but I ask a boon. Spare me a fresh mount?"

"Granted," Ciaran replied, handing the man a cup. "Drink now and have a bite while we bring yee a horse."

Ever efficient, Niall strode toward the door,

shouting orders even as a maid hurried forward with a plate of roasted meat and half a loaf of fresh bread. The man wolfed it down where he stood.

Upstairs, Siobhan heard all the commotion and suspected what had transpired. She finished dressing and went to check on Becca. She tapped softly on the door. When there was no response, she eased it open. The cailín still slept, but Siobhan was pleased with the girl's appearance this morning. Her face had some real color in it instead of the pallor and bruising of days past. The only shadows under her eyes were cast by her long lashes.

****

"He has not bound her," the female sighed.

"Nor has the covenant been consummated," said the male.

"He cannot go 'til it is done. He cannot tempt fate this time."

"What about me?"

With the third voice, the others grew silent.

"I know you hear me. Why won't you answer?"

Still silence.

"Please? Just tell me what's going on. Is this a dream?"

One finally broke the silence with a sharply indrawn breath.

"Do not," the female chided.

"I must lest all go for naught," the male argued. "Child of the Mortals, 'tis no dream we weave. You have journeyed long through Imrama Anam. *You have been returned to* An Domhan *to fulfill your destiny."*

"My...destiny? Oh, these are very good drugs." Becca choked on a giggle.

"Child, the veil closes. Our time here is short. You must listen. You must be who you have become, else the you who was will be no more." The man was insistent.

"Oh, that's as clear as mud. What are you talking about?"

"Seek within your heart, Child," the woman murmured. "Seek with your heart to find what is missing."

"Your fate is tied to his, Child, and his to ours. Do not fail us."

****

Becca woke up feeling light-headed and with a mouth tasting like cotton. Her stomach growled loudly reminding her of how terribly hungry and thirsty she was, as if she'd gone days without food.

"Other than a bit o' broth and my potions, there's no telling how long it's been, cailín," Siobhan chirped at her.

She stared at the older woman. "How do you do that?"

"Do what?"

"Read my mind."

Siobhan smiled. "No mind reading, cailín. I heard your wee tummy complaining all the way over here." She watched for a brief moment. "What troubles you, Becca?"

She wasn't sure she wanted to discuss it just yet, but she had too many questions without answers. This woman was kind to her and seemed to take many things in stride. Besides, she lived in this century, and Becca didn't. She really needed some answers. "Siobhan, what is *Imrama Anam?*"

The older woman took a step backward. "Why do you ask, cailín?"

She shrugged. "I heard it mentioned somewhere, and I don't know what it means," she dissembled.

"Methinks you would do well to seek counsel with Odhran," Siobhan said softly, watching through narrowed eyes. "You can trust me, Becca," she finally added.

Becca opened her mouth to speak, but stopped.

If this wasn't a dream, and she *was* back in medieval times, they'd probably burn her for a witch if she spoke of her life in the twenty-first century, not to mention those mysterious voices echoing in her head.

Siobhan remained quiet, giving her ample opportunity to speak, then smoothed over the silence when it stretched too long. "Would you like a bath, cailín? At the very least, you need a change of clothes. That dress wasn't meant for sleeping."

Becca blushed. "I would love a bath," she said, wondering that such would be possible. She was woefully ignorant of this life. "But I really need to, um..." Her hands fluttered in a vague gesture.

Siobhan grinned. "Can you find your way?"

She nodded, her face now flaming. Siobhan opened the door and she fled down the hall, gainfully trying to ignore the guard hard on her heels. She made it to the garderobe and took care of business. The guard waited for her, but she steadfastly refused to look at him as she skittered back to her room. Stepping through the door, she was suddenly reminded it wasn't just *her* room.

That devastatingly handsome man who was so much a part of this fantasy banged about the room pulling out clothes. He grabbed a few other items and stuffed everything into a well-worn leather satchel.

She hesitated just inside the door, afraid to disturb him. The man's frenzied activity slowed.

He stilled and turned. His gaze devoured her. She vaguely wished she'd had that bath and had on fresh clothes, but the burning desire in his eyes brushed the thought away. She could be wearing rags and it wouldn't matter a bit to him.

"Ah, cailín," he sighed, looking her up and down. "Would that I could stay and explore what is to be between us." His voice held so much promise.

She remained very still, her heart in her throat.

He took a deep breath and was all business again. "The O'Conor, my king, has sent out the *ard fheis*. Clann O'Brien invades Connaught. We leave for Tuam and the south as soon as we can provision."

She had no idea what he was talking about. She'd never heard of Connaught or Tuam, or any king named O'Conor.

Something on her face must have revealed her bewilderment. He strode across the room and took her suddenly cold hand in his big paw. "The O'Brien clann is raiding again," he told her. "All *tuatha* loyal to Conchobhar O'Conor rally with an army to defeat them."

A shiver skittered down her spine. Ciaran was leaving. Echoes whispered in her mind. *He cannot go 'til it is done. He cannot tempt fate this time.*

"What troubles you, cailín?" He released her hand and raised his arms as if to hug her.

Becca stepped into the warmth of his embrace. Grateful for this gesture, his open arms encircled her. She was tall, the top of her head almost as high as his chin. He rubbed it across the silkiness of her hair.

"I do not understand what is happening, Ciaran," she whispered. "I do not know who I am, or who you are, but I fear for us both if you go away."

His lips brushed across her forehead as his heart leapt for joy. Witch she might be, but she had wrapped around his heart just as her arms now wrapped around his body. He could not let her go. "Three months, cailín, and the invaders will be defeated. I'll be back before *Albun Heruin*."

Again, when her face betrayed her confusion, he added, "The summer solstice."

Becca opened her mouth, but couldn't think of anything to say. Instead, she simply turned her face to his, tears glistening in her eyes.

He bent his head and tasted her lips, his mouth gentle and hesitant, as if this was the first time he'd ever kissed a woman. His lips were strong but soft, and his tongue flicked across her teeth, inviting her to open her mouth to him. He pressed his whole, hard length against her soft yielding one, then he shuddered, his arms tightening around her. She felt him harden, and she wanted to grind her hips against him. Instead, she kissed him back, her tongue seeking his. Her arms tightened around his back.

"Nay, cailín," his mouth murmured into hers. "I must go, though my heart aches to stay with you. Honor demands I answer the summons." He tried to put distance between their bodies, but his was as reluctant to part as hers.

She closed her eyes, unwilling to see the yearning in his. Her body felt heavy, achy, and in need of his touch, yet her heart and her mind shied away from what she wanted.

"The binding," the female voice demanded in her head.

"The covenant," the male insisted.

"Oh, shut up," she shouted.

Ciaran released her so quickly she almost fell. She'd spoken out loud, and he assumed she was talking to him. She caught the flash of hurt in his eyes as he turned away from her and resumed his packing. "Crap," she murmured under her breath. "Why do I keep doing this?" She waited a moment to see if her ghosts, as she now thought of them, would answer her. When they didn't, she stepped closer to him.

She reached out to touch his broad back, her fingers trembling as their tips brushed his shirt and found the man beneath the linen. It was like touching a wall but hard and smooth with muscle rather than stone. "Ciaran?" she whispered. He flinched away from her voice and her touch. "I'm sorry," she added. He ignored her. "I'll leave you to pack." She turned to leave. As she reached the door, she felt the stirring of those voices in her head.

"Why can't you just leave me alone?" she demanded.

"As you wish, mistress," Ciaran's cold voice answered.

Becca whirled to face him, realizing she'd spoken out loud again. She'd lived alone for so long it was second nature for her to talk out loud to herself. Some days, her voice had been the only live voice she heard. As crazy as it might seem, the conversations she'd held with herself had been comforting.

Ciaran glared at her, anger etched in every line of his face. She wanted nothing more than to run to him and kiss his hurt and anger away, but a part of her rebelled, chafing under her overwhelming, and inexplicable, need for him. Becca screwed her eyes shut and took a deep breath, letting it out with a slow huff. "I didn't mean you, Ciaran." She kept her voice carefully neutral.

He spread his arms to encompass the entire room. "I see no one else," he snarled.

Becca dipped her face to her hands and rubbed her temples. She was getting a raging headache, probably from those two fiends arguing in her head. Another deep breath helped steady her nerves. "There is no time, Ciaran, to convince you, and I'm not sure I could if we had all the time in the world."

You could, a voice whispered, *with the covenant.*

She shook her head, but wisely refrained from retorting to that voice in her head.

"I don't want you to leave, though I know you must. I...I don't want your anger between us." She walked toward him warily, watching his fury build like a thunderstorm on a hot summer afternoon, all sound and fury as it boiled higher into the sky.

Emotions flickered across his face as quick as lightning. Standing in front of him, she had to tip her head only slightly to look him in the eye. A muscle jumped along his clenched jaw but he remained silent. "There is something between us, something I don't understand, and it frightens me. I fight *it*, foolish as that may be, but I do not fight you."

She touched his cheek and felt him shudder all the way to his toes. His arms hung straight at his sides, while his fists clenched and unclenched. She wondered if he wanted to embrace her or throttle her. "Forgive me, Ciaran. I would not see you hurt. You have been nothing but honorable toward me, and I have repaid you badly. Please do not turn away from me because I am dimwitted at times." Her hand traced his strong jaw, then trailed down his chest to lie against his heart. She could feel its strong, steady beat beneath her palm. "Stay safe, Ciaran, and return to me so we may resolve what is between us." She waited a heartbeat, then two. He was still angry and refused to reply. Disheartened, she turned to leave again.

As her hand withdrew, he snatched it and brought it to his mouth. His lips placed a searing brand in the exact center of her palm. With a growl, he loosed her hand and stormed out of the room after grabbing his leather satchel.

Her knees shook so hard she sank to the floor as the door slammed behind him. Tears streamed unheeded down her face. Becca's heart had been ripped out. No, she amended. Her very soul had just stomped out that door.

Ciaran found Niall in the stable trying to bring order to chaos. The older man took a good look at his liege. He couldn't remember a time when he'd seen the man this angry but could only guess at what had made him so. As he opened his mouth to ask, Ciaran spoke up.

"Why, Niall?" he snarled. "What have I done to the gods that they would do this?"

Niall rocked back on his heels, surprised at the vehemence in Ciaran's voice. "But, Ciaran, you've been spoiling to fight."

"Nay, Niall," the other growled. "I welcome the clean battle of war, for that is a fight I understand. 'Tis the other I don't comprehend. Why is it the only woman to ever stir my blood is an addlepated waif who beguiles me on the one hand and rebukes me on the other?" Ciaran let out a huge sigh.

Niall choked back a snicker. "She's a woman," he finally managed to say, almost choking on his suppressed laughter. Ciaran just looked pained. Niall allowed himself a brief moment of familiarity by putting his arm around the other man's shoulders. That love should come so late to his *Taoiseac* was entertaining, despite the misgivings he felt about the tie between the two. Remembering the circumstances in which they'd found Becca, he reminded Ciaran. "We don't know what befell the cailín before you rescued her. She still heals. Leave her to Siobhan and the Druid. We will go fight glorious battles against the O'Brien. When we return victorious, you can settle what is between you." He thumped Ciaran heartily and led him off to finish preparations. "When we return, yee need to tup her before either of yee can think about it," he counseled with a knowing chuckle.

Siobhan found her huddled on the floor. Becca felt completely drained and her brain threatened to cease functioning. Overwhelmed, she could only look up at Siobhan helplessly. Giving her a hand up, the older woman led Becca down to the kitchens. Cooks and maids bustled about, getting provisions ready for the march. Siobhan found an empty bench near one of the hearths and parked Becca on it. In a few moments, Becca had a bowl of stew and a slice of cheese melting on a hunk of hot bread. Grateful, she tasted the stew and decided it was the most delicious thing she'd ever put in her mouth. When she expressed that opinion, Siobhan just laughed.

"It's been so long since you've eaten, week old gruel would be a feast," the woman teased.

As she ate, Becca watched, fascinated by all the activity. Life in a medieval castle wasn't anything like she'd imagined. Maybe this wasn't a dream. When she'd mopped up the last bit of liquid in her bowl with the last crust of bread and wolfed it down, she looked around for Siobhan. Her nurse was nowhere to be found. A maid hurried by, saw the empty bowl in Becca's hands. She dropped a curtsy and snatched the bowl before sailing away. Feeling in the way, Becca slipped out of the kitchen. She found her way back to the great hall. Men rushed around, and she was afraid she'd get run over. Deciding her room was safer, she wearily climbed the stairs.

She found Siobhan directing the filling of a tub with hot water. A dozen buckets lined the hearth, gently steaming. As Becca entered, Siobhan shooed out the men who had carried up the tub and the buckets.

"Come, cailín, out of those clothes and into the bath," she directed.

She didn't need a second invitation. Siobhan had her out of her dress in moments and Becca peeled off the shift underneath. She trailed her hand through the water, relishing its warmth. Stepping into the tub with care, she sat down and sank up to her chin. This was pure heaven. Warmth seeped into her muscles and she relaxed. The fragrant steam rising from the water smelled of roses and something spicy she couldn't put a name to. Once she was settled, Siobhan scurried out the door, intent on some mission of her own.

Half asleep, Becca didn't hear the door open, nor did she hear Ciaran's sharp intake of breath when he saw her. *By the gods, but she is beautiful,* he swore. Her breasts were full but firm. Her narrow waist flared to hips perfect for cradling a man. Ciaran grew so stiff his trews actually strained the laces. Golden curls nestled at the top of her thighs. Then he got a good look at her legs—long, muscular, with dainty ankles. He yearned to have those legs wrapped around his middle as he plunged into her time and time again. A strangled cry tore its way from his throat.

Becca knew without looking who'd made that sound. She held her breath waiting for him to speak, hoping he would, afraid he wouldn't.

"Ah, cailín," he cried. "If yee'd but let me love yee..." His anguished voice trailed off.

Becca wanted nothing more than to jump up and run to him, throw her arms around him, and kiss him until the hurt went away. She'd never felt this way about any man before, and it bewildered her. Still, she longed to comfort him.

"Please," she whispered, "don't let me blow it this time." Louder, she simply said his name, trying to put all of her feelings into the one word.

"If I touch you now, cailín, I'll never leave." He groaned. "My honor—" His voice thickened with emotion, and he couldn't finish.

"Then go, Ciaran. Go quickly so you can return to me that much sooner."

Before Becca could voice her next thought, Ciaran scooped her out of the tub and kissed her. His heart pounded an urgent rhythm against her breast as his mouth devoured hers.

She responded, cupping his cheeks in her hands. He carried her to the bed still ravaging her lips with his. She squirmed against him, her hands working inside his shirt, seeking bare skin.

Ciaran laid her on the coverlet then broke away. He stood swaying with the effort it took to release her. "Ah, cailín." Those two words whispered across her naked skin, a caress as warm and seductive as a lover's touch. His eyes memorized her body.

Becca closed her eyes, waiting for what she was sure would come. She opened them when she heard the door close quietly. Her body didn't feel like her own. She was hot, achy, and her middle was tied in knots. Her breasts ached for the feel of his hands, and her lips felt cold without the touch of his.

"Wow," she sighed. "Nobody should be able to kiss like that."

Chilled and stark naked, she wrapped up in what she thought was a dark plaid blanket tossed carelessly across the foot of the bed. Woven of rusty red and gray wool, with touches of yellow and lavender, it smelled of Ciaran—wild, woodsy, clean—like the outdoors, but with an underlying musky scent, too, one that was all man. That scent twisted her insides all over again.

The blanket was warm, as if Ciaran had just thrown it aside. Becca found an intricate brooch pinned to one corner. This was Ciaran's mantle— more than a cloak, less than a blanket—a very practical combination of the two. She buried her nose in it and inhaled, wanting to keep Ciaran's scent with her always.

Shouts from outside and down below in the great hall propelled her to her feet. The men were leaving. *Ciaran* was leaving.

Becca wrapped the mantle around her like a toga. She ran from the room but stopped on the top step of the stairs, unaware her guard had stopped behind her. Men milled about the great hall, Niall and a few others shouting orders. Ciaran stood in the midst of it all, a wild warrior tall and strong.

Becca couldn't breathe. He wasn't just handsome. He was beautiful in the way the Rocky Mountains were with their rugged majesty, the way a desert sunset was all crimson fire, blazing across a blue sky, so brilliant one had to squint. Her eyes filled with rainbows as she blinked away tears.

Ciaran looked up and stopped breathing. Like some ethereal *fae*, Becca stood at the top of the stairs wrapped in his mantle. Her hair framed her face and bare shoulders in a golden nimbus. The subtle reds and grays of his plaid suited her. His chest swelled as he remembered to breathe. The sight of her standing on the stairs wearing nothing but his colors was one he would gladly take to his grave. He touched his heart with his fingertips then made a fist. Extending his clenched hand toward her, he opened his fist, hoping she'd understand.

Becca recognized what Ciaran's gesture meant. She stretched out her hand and envisioned it gently wrapping around his. She drew back her fist, laid it above her heart and then spread out her hand. Ciaran had offered her his heart. In return, she'd taken over the safekeeping of it in her own.

Ciaran smiled at her, lust, need, and something deeper, more profound shining in his eyes. Becca kissed the tips of the first and second fingers on her left hand and blew him the kiss. He caught it and pressed his hand to his lips. Abruptly, he turned away from her, his voice rising above the babble around him.

"We ride!"

Chapter Five

Realizing she'd be able to see the courtyard from the window in Ciaran's chamber, Becca sprinted back down the hallway. Stretching up on tiptoe, she could just barely look out the high window. Frustrated, she grabbed the bench by the hearth and tugged it over. By standing on it, she could lean out the window to see the gate and most of the courtyard. Two detachments of mounted men awaited their commander. One group carried shields and either long swords or lances. The other detachment had bows and quivers full of arrows. These were the famous Irish hobelars—mounted archers who could dash from one crucial front to another in a battle.

Becca recognized Niall as he gracefully vaulted onto his warhorse. Her heart lurched, and her throat closed off as Ciaran came into sight. Already mounted, he was utterly magnificent, like some pagan war god.

Their eyes met across the distance. As foreign as the idea seemed, she truly cared for this man. He was a stranger, yet that mattered little. She was afraid for him. Would he be safe? Her emotions were in turmoil. She feared he wouldn't come back even as she was afraid he would. Once Ciaran returned, all that was between them would break open like some raging flood smashing through a dam.

She finally understood this man held her fate in his hand, just as she did his. She laid her hand against her heart to show him she was keeping his safe. He smiled and she watched the stormy ocean blue of his eyes soften to the color of the summer sky.

She returned his smile even as she raised her chin in a show of bravery she didn't necessarily feel. She would survive this as she'd survived everything else in her life. She held his gaze until he wheeled his stallion and called his troops together.

Horses snorted and stamped, kicking up a fine coating of dust. Metal jangled and leather creaked as the troop lined up for departure. A few wives darted forward for a last kiss. Children and dogs milled around creating little eddies in the tide of people.

Ciaran watched the controlled turmoil with a practiced eye. In his heart, he was a soldier. Until this moment, he'd lived for the call to arms. Now? Now, his heart ached at the thought of leaving Becca.

Earlier in the great hall, his men had been too busy to notice her dressed only in his mantle standing at the top of the stairs. He'd forced himself to turn away and chuckled, now thinking, *Aye, and I would have had to kill any man who noticed.*

As he was about to give the order to ride out, movement in the window of his chamber caught his eye. She was there, framed by the dark stone of the castle walls. The wind caught the golden web of her silken hair and playfully tugged it toward him, as if she were casting a net to catch and hold him. His stomach clenched. Only his willpower and devotion to honor kept him in the saddle. Every muscle, every sinew, every part of him longed to rush to her side, to hold her and kiss her and bury himself inside her, making her his for all time.

Gods, but she was beautiful. She drove him to distraction with her vacillation, but once he returned from this campaign, he'd have her one way or another. The thought of her lying beneath him rode him hard, a burr under his saddle festering into a sore spot. Then she touched her hand to her heart. Ciaran steeled himself to turn from her, to tear himself away from the promise in her eyes.

He rode through the gate at the head of his troops, not once turning to confirm she was there. Ciaran knew. He could feel the warmth of her gaze burning into his back. He planned on making short work of the thieving O'Brien so he could return to his golden witch. *Nay,* his heart whispered, *not witch but fae.*

****

The troops had long since passed from sight and the people gathered in the courtyard to see them off dispersed but still Becca stayed at the window, hoping to catch some stray glimpse, some whispered echo of Ciaran. Shadows lengthened, the sun sliding past midday. Clamoring down from the bench, she wandered around the room listlessly.

Becca needed to get dressed. She finally opened the wooden cupboard and noticed some of Ciaran's clothes were still there. Without thinking, she pulled out one of his shirts and put it on. It swallowed her, but she didn't care. It carried his scent and her skin craved the feel of fabric that had once touched his. Rummaging around, she found a soft leather strap and wrapped it around her waist like a belt. She rolled up the sleeves and searched for footwear. His boots were obviously too big.

She grinned lasciviously. She couldn't wait to find out if the old wives' tale was true—the one about the size of a man's shoe and hi... She forced her salacious thoughts away from that riddle and back to the situation at hand.

His shirt fell almost to her knees but Becca also needed something to cover her legs. There was a pair of trews in the armoire, but they would swallow her. Not to mention, she'd probably set the castle on its collective ear if she showed up dressed as a man. She eyed the gowns for a brief moment. Just not her style. At least not until Ciaran returned. As a last resort, she bunched, knotted, and hitched the mantle until it made a passable skirt. She looked like a fashion disaster but didn't care. Screwing up her courage to face the outside world, she was saved by a soft tap at the door.

"May I come in?" Siobhan's voice called.

Becca rushed to the door and pulled it open. The older woman's eyes were red-rimmed. Becca's heart went out to her. Siobhan was married to the master-at-arms and likely felt even more bereft than she did. Once Siobhan got a good look at her attire, a wicked smile creased her face, chasing away any lingering sadness.

"Ah, cailín," Siobhan chortled fondly. "Yee can't go wanderin' around dressed like that." Despair welled up in her chest and she saw a shadow of her own feelings flit across Siobhan's, too. "Do you miss him that much, then?"

Becca nodded. The flood of tears she'd been holding back for so long suddenly broke the dam of her self-control. She sank to the floor, tears streaming down her face as sobs wracked her body.

Siobhan joined her. With their arms wrapped around each other, the women bawled until they had no more tears. Becca finally hiccupped and giggled. A bit embarrassed yet relieved by their crying jag, they washed their faces in the basin of tepid water and put on brave expressions.

"Yee still cannot go traipsing around in the *Taoiseac's* clothes." Siobhan's tone and the hands firmly fisted on her hips were insistent. "'Twouldn't be seemly for you to go about dressed like a ragamuffin." She arched a brow. "Nor dressed like a man."

"But the dresses, the gowns... They're too fine for me," Becca protested.

Siobhan looked shocked. "Do yee not understand, cailín? When the MacDermot returns, the two of you will be wed, and you'll be the mistress of the castle." That almost made Becca start bawling again. "Nay, cailín, he's a good man and 'twill be gentle with yee when it comes to the tuppin'," Siobhan hastened to reassure her. "'Tis obvious for all to see that he cares about you, and I'm thinkin' you might feel the same about him."

"It's not that," Becca stammered as she drew in a ragged breath. How was she going to explain to this woman what the real problem was? How could she explain that she was from hundreds of years in the future? "I don't know a blasted thing about running a castle," she finally blurted out. Then she thought a moment. What the hell was tupping? If it was what she thought it was, she wasn't going there.

Her partial confession rocked Siobhan back on her heels. She stared at the girl, shocked. "Y'er well bred, cailín, 'tis obvious to see by looking at yee. How can it be that yer dam dinnit teach yee what a mistress would be needing to know?"

Without thinking, she exclaimed, "Because my mother lived in a two-story ranch house in Aurora, Colorado." As soon as the words burst out, Becca clapped her hands over her mouth.

Siobhan stepped away from her, the woman's hands going to her chest in a protective gesture.

"I'm not from here," she admitted, daring to trust this woman. "I'm not from now."

"ODHRAN!" Siobhan yelled at the top of her lungs. She dashed across the room and tore open the door. Grabbing the burly guard, she ordered, "Bring me Odhran the Druid now!"

A few minutes later, the old Druid was pushed through the door. Disheveled and stunned by the suddenness of his summons, he stared at the two women. Siobhan dismissed the guard, telling him to go get something to eat and not to come back until he was called. His dissent died on his lips as she firmly shut the door in his face. Siobhan whirled to face Becca. "Tell him," she ordered. "Tell him what you just told me!"

Becca's brain whirled. Had she made a huge mistake? "That I know nothing of running a castle? I'm just a peasant girl, Siobhan. How could I know what I've never been taught?"

"Bah," Siobhan spat. "Do not hide the truth, cailín. This is too important. Now tell him."

She remained silent, so Siobhan turned on the Druid. "Then you tell her, Odhran. Tell her what is *Imrama Anam.*"

Becca sucked in her breath, suspecting she was about to learn something very important.

"Why that lesson, Siobhan?" The old man tilted his head, his gaze darting from one woman to the other.

"Because she asked me," the woman hissed.

The Druid took her right hand and led her to the bench still positioned under the window. "Sit, child, and tell me. How do you know of *Imrama Anam*? This is not common knowledge these days."

"I don't know anything," she replied. "That's why I asked Siobhan. I don't know who I am or where I am." After a moment, she added in a quiet voice, "Or *when* I am."

The Druid silently stared into her eyes for a long moment then nodded his head. "She speaks the truth, Siobhan. She knows nothing of the old ways, though there are traces of power within her."

Odhran spoke then, keeping his voice soft, spinning a spell, entrancing Becca. He told her of the old religion and the gods of the Celts, of the *Tuatha dé Danaan*, the mythical people now called faeries who settled Ireland and then withdrew, leaving the land to the mortals. Odhran told her of *Imrama*

Anam, the journey of the soul as it traveled through eternity seeking *Tír Nan Óg*, the Land of the Ever Young. He revealed his own thoughts about her predicament and questioned her about the voices in her head.

"Oh, hell." Becca jumped up to pace the floor. "I'm screwed. I didn't major in quantum physics, and I sure didn't study history. I know enough to understand that if I mess up here, then the whole future is out of kilter. This can't be happening," she groaned. Then her stomach growled.

Odhran and Siobhan stared at her, totally perplexed. "Quantum physics," Becca reiterated. "The study of... Oh, never mind. I'm so hungry I can barely think. Look, the point is that where I'm from...*when* I'm from, there is a theory about time travel. If a person goes back in time and changes things, then things are also changed in the future."

Odhran beamed. "Exactly. That is the whole point." He smiled proudly, the professor praising a student who finally understands.

"No," Becca argued. "You don't get it. It always changes things for the worse."

Siobhan exchanged a long look with Odhran, then left. Odhran patted Becca's hand. "Cailín, the timekeepers will not allow that to happen."

"Timekeepers? Who or what are they?" Becca was losing this argument. Even so, it was important she at least try to win.

"The timekeepers. Certain *Tuatha dé Danaan* shepherd our souls through our lives. It is they who make things right when they go wrong. Your being here is not a random act, Becca. In fact, I think you were plucked from your time for a very specific reason."

Becca's mouth opened and closed several times, making her look and feel like a fish out of water. She grinned at the analogy. She *was* a fish out of water.

Siobhan returned with a platter laden with bowls of stew and crusty bread. She passed them out then settled on a stool by the fire to eat.

Becca was so hungry she all but swigged the soup from her bowl. When she'd finished, she looked at the older woman across the room. "I really am fifty years old," she told Siobhan, flashing a sly grin. "And old enough to be his mother."

"He doesn't need a mother," Siobhan reproved, but with a chuckle lurking just below the surface of her gruff words. She arched an eyebrow and stared at the bed, her meaning plain to see. "Let us hope the young pup can teach his old dog new tricks." Her lips quirked in a lascivious smile.

"Siobhan!" Becca blushed crimson all the way to the roots of her blonde hair.

Odhran swallowed the bread he'd been chewing. "Consider yourself blessed, cailín," he sighed, looking her up and down. "What I wouldn't trade to have back the body of my youth."

Becca's face flushed a deeper shade of red. Odhran's leer was much too reminiscent of the looks Ciaran gave her. At the thought of him, her heart constricted. "Who is he?" she whispered. "Why do the too-ah...the twah...the faeries care what happens to him?" She couldn't quite get her tongue around the Gaelic words, not fully realizing she'd been speaking Gaelic since she'd first fully awakened in Ciaran's bed.

"What do you mean, Becca?" Siobhan asked, her gaze and voice both sharp.

"Those voices, the ones in my dream. They spoke of him. They said he'd know what to do, that things had gone wrong before because I was too young." Becca paused, deciding how much to reveal. "They talked about a covenant. Some sort of binding." She watched Siobhan's face closely.

"'Tis the truth, then," Siobhan sighed. The

woman glanced at Odhran who still stared at Becca.

His gaze remained focused on Becca, trying to read meaning into her hesitant confession as he looked into her soul. "What else did they say, child?" he persisted.

"That Ciaran would die...and that he could not die without issue," she whispered, the words dragged from the very depths of her soul. "They didn't want him to leave until we'd..." Becca hesitated to finish the thought out loud. "Tupped," she finally admitted, choosing the local terminology.

Siobhan and Odhran watched her like two cats waiting at a mouse hole. "Have you?" Siobhan asked pointedly. "Could you be with child?"

Taken aback, Becca was insistent. "No! We haven't and I'm not. In fact, I've never..." Her voice trailed off. She was distinctly uncomfortable with the direction of the conversation.

"You *are* still a maiden," Siobhan confirmed, smiling.

"Old maiden," she groused.

Siobhan burst out laughing. "How did you survive to the ripe old age of fifty with no one plucking your fruit? Either you were a hag or the men of your time were without wits."

Becca was indignant. "I was not a hag. As a matter fact, when I was younger, I looked pretty much like I do now, thank you very much. And it wasn't for lack of trying on the boys' part. I just never found the one I wanted..." Her eyes clouded over with memories from her previous life. She managed a shrug meant to show she didn't care. "Then, it was too late."

Odhran patted her hand, the gesture meant to comfort. "Tell us, child."

"I was in a car accident," she began then realized the others looked confused. "A car. A vehicle with a motor. Uhm, a wagon that moves by itself

71

without horses... Oh, God. I just did it. I just screwed up the space-time continuum. I can't do this," she wailed.

"Hush, cailín," Siobhan comforted her. "Tell us of this accident."

"The car...uhm, the wagon went off the side of a mountain. I was pinned in the wreckage and it took forever to get me out. The doctors... The healers said I wouldn't live, but I did. Then they said I'd never walk again, but I did. It hurt like hell, but I kept getting up every morning and surviving one more day." Her voice dropped to a whisper. "Day after day, for twenty-five years, I kept surviving. I went to sleep on my fiftieth birthday and woke up here." She shivered. "Who am I, Odhran?" Her voice cracked and she had to clear her throat before she could continue. "Am I in someone else's body? Is their soul in my body back in the twenty-first century living my life as I'm living theirs?"

Odhran shook his head. "Nay, cailín. You are who you are supposed to be. Ciaran and Becca were destined to meet. I suspect you've been sent back to right a wrong which occurred in this lifetime."

"Oh, God," Becca complained. "Trying to keep the space-time continuum straight is hard enough. Now you're talking about parallel universes and lives. Stop it, Odhran. You're making my head hurt!"

Odhran stood up. "Sleep, cailín. We will talk again." He shuffled to the door and let himself out.

Becca stared at Siobhan. "When am I, Siobhan? What year is this?"

Awestruck, Siobhan shook her head. "You've come over a thousand years from the future. 'Tis nine hundred sixty-one, Becca. The twenty-seventh day of Mhárta, just before the new moon of Aíbreán."

Becca automatically translated the date without stopping to wonder how she did so. March 27, 961. Okay, so it was the tenth century, the beginning of the medieval period. She could cope with this. She'd have to. She shivered and wrapped her arms around her waist to keep from shaking apart.

The burly guard had not reappeared, so Siobhan called for him and others to come as well. Becca turned her back on the room, retreating to the window to stare out into the inky darkness while servants emptied the cold water left in the tub and then removed the tub itself. The fire in the hearth died to embers. Becca shivered again, this time from the cold. Another servant appeared and stoked the fire. In a few minutes, the fire blazed in the grate, and at last the room was empty but for Siobhan and Becca.

The woman joined her at the window. "Odhran is right, cailín. You need to sleep. This has been a momentous day."

"Will he be all right?" Becca asked without turning around.

"Aye, cailín," Siobhan assured her. "Ciaran is the boldest, most cunning warrior in the land, descended from the legendary Fenian Warriors. 'Tis why King Conchobhar comes to him first. Niall says Ciaran is charmed in battle. No enemy can touch him. No weapon can harm him."

Becca put her arm around Siobhan's shoulders. "Thank you."

"Ah, yee might be thankin' me now, but wait 'til tomorrow," the other woman replied tartly as she moved toward the door.

"What do you mean, Siobhan?" Becca glanced over her shoulder and quirked a brow.

"Tomorrow you learn how to be mistress," Siobhan warned.

"Don't count on it," she promised as the door closed behind the other woman.

****

The troop rode hard all day. Cheery evening

fires burned surrounded by tired men lounging near the heat. Horses snorted and stamped in the dark. Bhruic lay next to Ciaran, his head on the big man's knee. The dog's wide, soulful eyes stared up at his master. "Aye," Ciaran admitted to the wolfhound. "I miss her, too, though I hardly know why."

Niall finished setting the perimeter guards, and he dropped to the ground beside his commander. "All is quiet, *Taoiseac*," he reported. His voice sounded as tired as he looked. He wrapped his mantle tighter against the chill March night.

Ciaran stared at the fire but acknowledged Niall with a brief nod without looking up.

"'Tis only the O'Brien," Niall reminded his clann chief. "Bent on thieving cattle and not much else."

Ciaran lifted one shoulder in a negligent shrug, his attention elsewhere.

Perplexed, Niall pushed for an answer. "If not the O'Brien, then what troubles you, *Taoiseac*?" Ciaran finally raised his eyes and stared at his second-in-command. Niall sucked in a deep breath as he recognized Ciaran's despair and for the first time since Niall had known him, fear as well. He automatically reverted to his role as mentor. "What troubles you, Ciaran?"

"Who is she, Niall? Why has no one raised a hue and cry?"

"Becca?" Niall asked, already knowing the answer.

Ciaran flashed him a disgusted look. "Who else? She's well-bred, though ill-used, and left to die. Why has her clann not set the countryside ablaze looking for her?"

"Mayhaps, she comes from too far away?" Niall gave the notion some thought. "Think you she is an O'Brien?" That idea vexed him. Had the O'Brien come not to raid but to reclaim their kin? That would mean an all out war for he was fair certain Ciaran

74

would not give her up.

"Mayhaps. But there is something, Niall, something I can't name."

"Can't? Or won't?"

Ciaran stared into the fire, marshaling his thoughts. "I first thought her witch, now..." Niall waited without speaking, letting the other man form words from his chaotic thoughts. Ciaran finally sighed softly. "*Tuatha dé Danaan,* Niall. I think she's faerie."

Niall snorted. "We've both touched her, Ciaran. She's real. She's flesh and blood!" He paused while formulating another argument, finally adding, "Had she been a daughter of Danu, think you a mortal could have so abused her?"

Ciaran pondered that. All but immortal and powerful, the *Tuatha dé Danaan* were full of magic. They could scarcely be harmed by mortals. Then an unrelated thought struck him. "Suppose she was outcast?"

Niall opened and closed his mouth several times, but no words of wisdom tripped off the tip of his tongue. Finally, he could only shrug, waiting in silence once again for Ciaran to continue.

"She spoke strange, Niall, when we first found her. And, even now, she does not seem to fit in. Odhran sensed a trace of power in her."

Niall shrugged again. "You and I, Ciaran, we've kept the old ways longer than most. Me, because of Siobhan. You? You, I think, have a bit of the fae about you yourself."

Ciaran started to interrupt but Niall stayed him with a raised hand. "Nay, hear me out, lad. I knew both your sire and his brother, and I tell you true. The clann would have been better off if Fionn had lived to be *An Taoiseac.* You are much like him, Ciaran. You know the tales, for I told them to you when you were but a lad."

He nodded, remembering the stories Niall had told him. Tales of the great battles between the *Tuatha dé Danaan* and the *Milesians* and *Fir Borg*. Stories of how mortal humans had been caught in the middle. He'd thrilled to the legend that one of his forebears was a Fenian Warrior and saved the life of one of the faerie. To repay that first MacDermot, Finvarra, a king of the *Tuatha dé Danaan,* had gifted the clann with a covenant. Once in each generation, the clann would be honored with the birth of a true warrior to guide and protect them.

Niall knew that Fionn had been given the gift, but he'd been killed by treachery. None could prove it was Aralt behind his brother's death. Aralt had been a bane to the clann. Niall recognized the gift in Aralt's son and sought out young Ciaran, teaching the lad what he needed to know to become *An Taoiseac* when Aralt finally passed. There was one part of the legend Niall had never divulged to his charge. The gift from Onagh, Finvarra's consort. The warrior was to be blessed with a true mate, one he could bestow the MacDermot Knot upon. The Knot was a brooch of gold and silver intertwined through eternity and sealed with the faerie's tear. A brilliant stone, shot with fire, the likes of which none had seen before or since.

Legend had it that Onagh herself wove the knot from a lock of her long, golden hair and a thread from her silver gown. As the knot was finished, she shed one tear of joy, and that tear hardened into a precious stone caught forever in the web of the eternity knot. Once the MacDermot warrior gave his heart to his true mate and gifted her with the Knot and the binding words, their lives were bound together, beginning without end, until the end of time.

Fionn died before he'd found his mate. Aralt, not having the gift, traveled from bed to bed never able to scratch the itch that annoyed him. Niall watched Ciaran eschew the favors of the cailíns, knowing almost from the beginning that he'd received the gift. Now the woman left behind in Ciaran's bed was more than likely the fulfillment of the covenant between faerie and mortal. All Niall had to do was keep his clann chief alive long enough to woo and win the woman.

Chapter Six

Becca spent the next several weeks learning to find her way around the castle and grounds and, more importantly, the nuances of the language and customs. Though she still thought in modern terms, the archaic words for them rolled more easily off her tongue. Siobhan spoke of moons rather than months, and fortnights and sennights, meaning two weeks and a week. Becca slowly released the self-portrait she carried around in her head, that of a fifty-year-old woman too crippled in body to enjoy life. For whatever reason, she'd been granted the use of this young, lithe body, and she planned to exploit it to the fullest.

She spent time in Ciaran's den. The room often overwhelmed her with male regalia and scent, but it reminded her of him. Spending time there eased the ache of missing him. The castle's accounts were stored there, and Becca familiarized herself with the ledgers. Siobhan taught her the inner workings of the castle, how each area was its own small kingdom. The kitchens and larder were the demesne of the cook, and none dared argue with the man. Since moving into the castle, Siobhan had taken over the maids and serving staff though she nominally granted authority to a man named Gair, a retired soldier who, though the castle's steward, was at quite a loss catering to the women now occupying the household. A small village clustered around the walls of the castle where a tanner, a weaver, and a blacksmith all enjoyed autonomy. Beyond the village, crofters and shepherds lived their lives among their fields and herds.

Day after day, the stables drew her. Eachan, the gruff Master of Horse, never noticed her presence or perhaps simply chose to ignore her. Even though Siobhan was determined to teach her the place of the mistress of the castle, Becca sensed ambivalence toward her from most of Ciaran's household. He'd not handfasted her in the old way, nor formally betrothed her in the way of the Church before he left. Though his men sensed his intentions toward the strange woman who now occupied Ciaran's chamber, they still remembered the peculiarity of her coming and the illness that dogged her. Then there were the women. That was a whole other situation, and Becca didn't want to look too deeply into their motives. The young ones were jealous. The old ones were skeptical. Becca was caught in the middle.

Bhruic and most of the wolfhounds had accompanied Ciaran and his troops. Two stayed behind, though, and shadowed Becca silently as she passed through the busy days and lonely nights. Often, the calico cat would also join her entourage. She started calling the trio Winken, Blinken, and Nod. People often stopped what they were doing to watch the odd parade go by. Becca, flanked by one of the big brutes, followed closely by the second, with the tiny fluff of a kit dancing along in the rear presented quite a sight. Those who sought the blessings of the Church crossed themselves after she'd passed. Those who didn't smiled, believing one of the fae had come to grace their clann. Most had seen the look on Ciaran's face as he'd stared up at the window of his chamber before turning his horse to ride away. He'd chosen the cailín with his heart even if he hadn't voiced that choosing.

Ciaran had been gone close to a month, and the last remnants of winter dug tenacious claws into the month of April. The day dawned raw and blustery with a north wind whipping around the corners. Rain threatened to fall from thick, gloomy clouds. Restless, Becca threw a mantle about her shoulders and braved the bleak weather, the hounds at her side. As her feet often did, they dragged her toward the stable. As she stood at the stable door hesitant to enter, two boys raced out almost knocking Becca down. Both hounds bared their teeth and growled, but the boys were gone too quickly for the dogs to retaliate. She heard shouting coming from inside and peeked around the door.

Eachan was a huge hulk of a man with red hair and a beard as wild as the mane on one of his stallions. He bellowed at the top of his lungs as stable hands scurried willy-nilly to do his bidding. The hubbub fascinated Becca until Eachan shouted for a sharp knife. Curious, she crept forward until she could see into the stall behind the big master. A beautiful mare was down on a bed of fresh straw. Looking closer, Becca saw marks in the dirt made by the mare as she struggled to get up. The mare's distended belly indicated she was trying to foal but something had gone terribly wrong. The horse had worn herself out and was down now. If something weren't done soon, both mare and foal would perish. The fact that this mare looked just like her grandfather's favorite horse didn't help matters any.

"Bring me that knife," Eachan roared. "We'll cut the foal out."

"You'll do no such thing," Becca commanded, her voice cutting through the hubbub. There was dead silence in the stable as every eye in the place turned to stare at her. Becca swallowed hard, realizing she might have stepped on her poncho this time. "Well, in for dime, in for a dollar," she muttered. "I know the mare is down," she added quickly to Eachan. "But I might be able to save them both. She's too beautiful to lose without a fight."

The master stared at her unblinking. Rumor had it that this was the *Taoiseac's* chosen, and if so, she'd be his mistress when the MacDermot returned. A shrewd man, he knew he had enough witnesses if both colt and dam were lost. Their demise would not be on his head but hers. He nodded, giving his permission. At this point he had nothing to lose, and if the cailín could save them both, he had everything to gain.

Becca knelt beside the mare, crooning to her while running knowing hands across her swollen belly. She could tell by feel that the foal was transverse, and if there were any chance of saving them, she would have to turn it. There wasn't much time left. The mare was almost out of fight.

Becca stood up and faced Eachan. "I'll be right back," she told the gruff man. She hitched up her skirts and ran, tossing over her shoulder, "Don't touch her!" She sprinted to the castle.

Every man in the stable stood there agog at the sight of her shapely legs. "*An Taoiseac* is a lucky man," the master sighed, speaking for them all.

"Siobhan!" Becca yelled at the top of her lungs as she entered the castle. "Siobhan, I need hot water, soap, and rags."

The older woman appeared from the kitchens. "Slow down, cailín," she cautioned. "Tell me what's wrong."

Becca grabbed a quick breath. "Hot water and soap, Siobhan, and rags. Lots of rags. There's a mare in trouble. The horse master wanted to gut her to save the foal. I can save them both, but you've got to help me." She took another breath. "And you've got to do it now. There's no time to waste."

As Siobhan called for the items, Becca sprinted back to the stable. Siobhan followed not too far behind carrying an armful of soft rags.

Calmly, Becca checked the mare. There'd been no change. She tried to push up the sleeves of her gown but they were so tight she couldn't even get them past her forearms. "Where's that sharp knife?" she asked the horse master. With a quizzical look, the big man handed it to her. Becca passed the knife to Siobhan who looked a little surprised. "Cut the sleeves off," Becca ordered the other woman. "I don't have time to explain, Siobhan," she implored. "Just do it."

Siobhan cocked an eyebrow, wondering what the cailín was up to. Wordlessly, she sliced through the seams at the shoulders of Becca's gown.

Impatient, Becca ripped the first one free before Siobhan had finished. Several boys appeared with steaming buckets of hot water. Becca ripped the second sleeve free. Moving around the stall to get to the buckets to wash up, she caught her toe in the hem of her gown and fell flat on her face.

"Bloody hell," she muttered, pushing herself off the ground. "I'd kill for a pair of jeans right now.

Siobhan and Eachan both stared at her, tasting the unfamiliar word. Becca fumed a minute. "Trews," she finally translated. "I'd kill for a pair of trews."

That set everyone within earshot to wagging their eyebrows. Unceremoniously, Becca reached between her legs, gathered up the back hem of her skirt, and pulled it through. Grabbing the front hem, she tied the two together. It wasn't jeans but it would have to do. She couldn't waste any more time trying to con a pair of trews out of Siobhan.

There wasn't a man in the stable with a closed mouth or without a lustful thought in his head at the sight of the cailín with the tied up skirt. Every well-defined muscle in her legs was there for them to savor, and they did so openly.

Oblivious to their leers, Becca knelt by the

mare's head, talking to her and rubbing her neck. Becca leaned away and washed her arms and hands in one of the buckets. Still crooning softly to the mare, Becca moved to kneel behind the horse as she carefully moved the mare's tail. When Eachan figured out what she was doing, he moved to stop her but Becca stayed him with a glare. With infinite gentleness, Becca inserted her arm up to the shoulder and searched the mare's womb to find the colt. The mare tensed and she braced, but the contraction was so mild she barely felt it. That was a very bad sign. After careful manipulation, she got the foal's head down between its forelegs. There wasn't time to turn it.

"Rope," she said softly, withdrawing her arm. "I need a rope with a noose on the end."

The stable master handed her a rope, and Becca washed it as well, causing eyebrows to rise again. With the noose clutched in her hand, Becca plunged her arm back into the mare. She managed to get the noose looped around the colt's head and its forelegs. She had to keep the colt's head positioned between his forelegs so he could fit down the birth canal.

"Draw the rope," she ordered. "Slowly."

Eachan took the rope in his big, calloused hands but pulled with gentle and steady pressure. The mare shuddered, and Becca's face turned white. That contraction completely numbed her arm—a very good sign. Now, if the mare would fight, she might be able to save them both. She crooned to the mare.

"Again," Becca whispered to the horse master.

In a short while, a chestnut colt spilled into Becca's lap. She tore at the amniotic sack and pulled off the rope. Grabbing clean rags, she vigorously rubbed down the colt. He lay still, not breathing. She said several very unladylike words under her breath and shifted her weight. Grabbing the colt's head, she covered his nostrils with her mouth and blew. After several tries, the colt's sides gave a little heave, and he started breathing on his own.

A murmur rustled through the gathered crowd. The horse master stood, hands on hips, completely amazed. As he watched, Becca thrust the colt into Siobhan's arms and told the other woman to keep rubbing him until he was dry. Becca crawled back to the mare's head and cradled it in her lap.

"Listen to me, Maggie May," Becca whispered, naming the mare after her grandfather's horse. "You have a fine, strong son who, like most males, took the hard way into this life. Now it's up to you. You have to get up, Maggie. I know you're tired but the afterbirth is to come, and you need to nurse the little brute."

Becca stood up and tugged on the mare's halter. The horse blew a gentle puff of air through her nostrils but refused to move. Becca sat back down. "Okay, Maggie, here's the deal. I need new boots. Horse hide is supposed to make soft ones." The mare rolled her eyes and snorted. "Not to mention the fact that these barbarians probably eat horsemeat." With that, the mare lunged up and stood shakily on all four feet. Becca scrambled up with her and hugged the horse's neck. "Ah, sweet Maggie," she sighed in the mare's ear. "You are the bravest, most wonderful horse in all the land."

The little colt, shaky on his long, spindly legs, wobbled over to his dam's belly and nudged her. In a few moments, he found what he was seeking and nursed hungrily. Becca, feeling as shaky as the newborn colt, walked over to a bucket of now-tepid water and half-heartedly washed. Stained and ripped, her gown was in shambles. The slippers she'd worn were completely ruined, too. She definitely needed more durable footwear, wishing belatedly for a pair of boots.

Siobhan, always the model of efficiency, was already on her way back to the castle calling for a hot bath to be prepared in Becca's chamber. Becca bent to gather up the bloody rags. As she reached to snag one, a giant boot descended and trapped it.

"Nay, mistress," the huge horse master roared. "Yee've soiled yer hands enough this day. You'll not be picking up like one of the maids."

Becca squared her shoulders and faced the man. "I am quite capable of picking up after myself."

The big man guffawed. "Aye, cailín, you're quite capable of most anything yee put yer mind to, and *An Taoiseac* MacDermot has met his match this time fair certain. Let the stable boys earn their keep. You've more than done so this day. 'Tis the best mare in the herd you've saved along with her fair son as well." After a long pause, he spoke again. "How know you to do this thing?" he asked, his voice filled with wonder. He'd known the foal was turned wrong but it had never occurred to him that something could be done to rectify it.

Trying to explain the vet med classes required for an equine management degree at Colorado State University would be futile. She shrugged and simply replied, "Something my grandfather taught me."

"Do you ride as well, cailín?"

"Oh, yes," she breathed, her eyes shining.

"I'll have a horse picked out for you."

"Oh! Please, may I pick out my own?"

Eachan grinned at her. "Doesn't surprise me that you'd want to, cailín. Just let me know when."

****

Back in her chamber, Becca stripped out of her bloody clothes and gratefully sank up to her chin in the hot, sudsy water. Clucking like a hen, Siobhan gathered up the ruined clothing and deposited them outside the door. After grabbing a jar smelling something like sweet clover, Siobhan pulled up a stool. "Here, cailín," she scolded. "Yee've even got blood in yer hair." She dunked Becca and then started washing the younger woman's hair.

"Oh, this is heaven." Becca closed her eyes, sighing.

When the water cooled off, she reluctantly climbed out. Before Siobhan wrapped her in a thick blanket, the woman checked her body closely. "Aye. 'Tis good, cailín. Yer hurts have all but healed." She bustled about for a moment. "I've laid out another gown for yee," Siobhan said over her shoulder. "You'll be hungry after all that work and dinner will be served up soon. Come on down to the great hall when yer dressed."

Becca grimaced at her, not wanting to put on the gown. "Siobhan, could you get me a pair of trews and a shirt?" Siobhan snorted her answer to that question as she swept from the room. "Well, it was worth a try," Becca told the door. "Can I at least have boots?" she hollered.

****

The next day dawned bright with a promise of warmth and blue skies. Becca found a pair of soft leather boots near the hearth. With a whoop of excitement, she pulled them on. They fit perfectly. She finished dressing and headed down for breakfast.

Anxious to get to the stables to check on Maggie and her new son, Becca gobbled down her meal. She ran to the stables but stopped short. Mare and colt were in the paddock, mother chewing the greening grass contentedly while the baby tried out his wobbly legs with an occasional nudge from his dam. Becca felt the joy build inside her as she watched them.

The huge horse master joined her. "And have yee come to hold me to my promise, cailín?"

"Aye, I have."

"Come around to the back, then. I had some horses brought up from the field. Some is broken, some is not."

Becca trailed him through the stables and in a pen at the back of the stable, a small herd of horses milled about but the horse in a second pen caught her eye. Jet black, his coat reminding her of Ciaran's hair. A man Becca hadn't seen before tried to halter the horse. He wasn't having much luck. The horse reared and danced out of his reach whenever he got close. He tried again and the horse laid back his ears, nipping at the man. Without success, Eachan tried to draw her attention to the docile horses in the next pen. Becca remained fixated on the little drama playing out before her.

Becca stared at the man in the pen. Almost as tall as Ciaran and about the same age, he was sunset to Ciaran's midnight. Auburn hair blazed like fire in the sun, and his amber eyes glinted with flecks of gold. He had the body of a horseman—long, muscular legs, narrow hips, broad shoulders with strong arms and hands.

"Why does he approach from the front?" Becca wondered aloud. "He should come from the side where the horse can see him."

"And why would that be, cailín?" Eachan asked.

Becca gave him a look that implied he was dense. "A horse can't see straight ahead," she explained. "If he can, you don't want him because he's too narrow between the eyes. You have to come up on his side, where he can see you, so you don't spook him. Waving your arms about like he's doing, why that's utter nonsense."

The man stared at her, his eyes narrowed in speculation. She refused to acknowledge what his leer suggested.

Glancing at his audience, the man in the pen noticed the wisp of a cailín standing with the horse master. Tall and well made, her hair was spun gold in the sunshine, and her eyes were as blue as the water in Galway Bay. Her appearance created a familiar tightening in his trews. He'd been gone for over a month, away when the *ard fhias* came. Niall had sent him out to survey the outlying farms and fields, looking for likely candidates to train as soldiers and more importantly, to find the best horses. Riordan had just returned, and chafing at having missed the *ard fhias*, he planned on breaking several horses while he waited for Ciaran and the troops to return. Now, as he looked the cailín up and down, he considered a ride of another sort, glad for the opportunity.

"Nonsense is it?" the man in the pen growled. "And I suppose a mere slip of a cailín like you can break a horse better?" He stomped toward them, angry that the girl dared mock him, and the horse was getting the better of him in front of her.

"I suppose I can," Becca retorted, "because I don't intend to *break* him, but gentle him."

"Then do it," he snarled. Frustrated, he flung the halter at her.

Becca caught the halter in midair and slipped through the rails on the pen before either man could react. She waited until the stranger perched on the top rail to watch, gloating at her. Becca harrumphed under her breath. She caught Eachan's low chuckle and took it for disdain. *Well, I'll just show them,* she vowed. Squaring her shoulders, she marched toward the nervous horse. Halfway to him, she stopped, keeping her hands by her sides.

"Aye, and what a wild boy, you are," she whispered to him. The horse pricked his ears and tossed his head. Becca stepped nearer, making sure she held his attention. "That nasty man doesn't have a clue, now does he," she crooned. "We know that you and I are going to be friends." The horse nickered and stretched his nose toward her. She reached for his shoulder and placed a gentle hand on the hard muscle there. The horse blew softly, nibbling at the sleeve of her gown with velvet lips. "Aye, just like a male, all soft lips and loving, aren't you?" she whispered in his ear. She carefully rubbed the rope halter against his shoulder, then his neck, and then down his cheek. She let him sniff the rope before she slipped it over the end of his nose and up behind his ears. He tossed his head, but didn't try to pull away from her. She patted his neck still murmuring sweet nothings to him.

"Tell me, Eachan," she called over her shoulder, her voice still calm and soothing. "What do you prize most when you're breeding?" Her hands ran over the horse's neck and chest.

The man on the fence choked, and Eachan pounded him on the back. "Easy, Riordan." The older man chortled. "'Tis no ordinary cailín you're dealing with here," he explained to Ciaran's lieutenant. "What do you mean, cailín?" the horse master called to Becca.

"Beauty or spirit?" she asked.

"Why both, cailín," the big man replied. "But if I can't have both, then 'tis spirit I want."

"Does that include bad temperament?" she asked.

"Nay, cailín," Eachan answered. "I'll not abide an ill-tempered horse."

"Just so we're in agreement," Becca told him. "Have you a bridle and saddle?"

Riordan jumped from the fence to fetch the items. With deliberate steps, he carried them out where the girl and the horse stood, not wanting to spook the animal. He stood just behind her, fascinated as much by the view of her *tóin* as he was by her ability with the horse. The gown she wore, though plain, emphasized her strong back, tapering to her nipped-in waist, before draping over the soft curves of her behind. Yes, he definitely wanted to get a better feel of her *tóin*, thinking the curve of it would fit nicely in a man's hands as he rode her.

"Lay them there," the girl told him with a point of her chin.

Riordan deposited the saddle and laid the bridle across it. He was utterly intrigued by her now. He withdrew slowly so as not to startle the horse.

Becca reached down without breaking eye contact with the horse and snagged the bridle. As with the halter, she rubbed it against his shoulder and neck before slipping it over his head. The bridle held no bit. She much preferred a horse that would respond to a hackamore than one forced because of the metal in his mouth. Letting the reins trail in the dirt, she picked up the saddlecloth and let the animal sniff it. Rubbing it along his neck and shoulder, she settled it into place across his withers. She did the same with the saddle. Without tightening the girth, she led him around the pen a few times, letting him get used to the weight and feel of the saddle on his back. When the horse quit laying back his ears and shaking his head, she slowly cinched the girth until it was tight. She led him around before tightening the girth again, knowing most horses blow up so when they let out their breath, the girth would be too loose.

Eachan chuckled, his delight evident. The cailín knew her stuff. He'd never met a female who could saddle her own horse, much less one who knew all horses were wise to the way of the saddle and would take advantage of the unwary.

He glanced at Riordan and chuckled again. The man was positively flummoxed. Eachan had a great deal of affection and respect for the younger man. Had Riordan not been such a fine soldier, Eachan would have claimed him as his successor as horse master.

Becca would have given most anything to have on a pair of trews at that moment. Somehow, she knew if she brought up the subject, there would be hell to pay from the rakish man perched on the fence. She led the horse away so she could mount with the horse between her and the two men. She checked the length of the stirrups and figured out how to shorten them without having to ask Eachan.

Whispering to the horse, Becca said, "Here's the deal, my handsome friend. I don't have a stitch on under this bloody skirt, so you are going to be a quiet boy until I get settled. Okay?"

Bunching up her skirt, she put her foot in the stirrup and swung her other leg over the horse's back. Bracing her feet in both stirrups, she pulled and tugged until her skirt formed a reasonable barrier between her bare bottom and the saddle. She took great satisfaction in the sharp intake of breath from both men as she sank down astride the horse and nudged him forward with her heels.

As soon as she settled into the saddle, the horse tensed and bunched beneath her. At least he'd given her time to get her skirt fixed. This was going to be a hellava ride, and she hoped she was up to it. Being thrown head over heels in a gown with no underwear on was not the way she wanted to start the day. The horse ducked his head, pulling against the reins, and kicked both hind legs into the air. Then he reared only to drop back down on all four hooves to crow hop several times. Becca hung on, enjoying the challenge. The horse wasn't truly trying to buck her off. He was just trying her mettle.

Eachan and Riordan jumped into the pen as soon as the horse started bucking. They thought to flank the horse and rescue Becca. Then Eachan realized the girl was smiling. He laid a hand on Riordan's arm and pulled him back to the fence. "Let them be," he told the younger man. "I suspect the cailín is tougher than she appears."

The horse finally stood stock-still in the middle of the pen, head up, nostrils flaring and eyes wild. Becca patted his neck as she leaned forward and whispered into his ear. The horse quivered a moment then became so still it was as if he'd turned into a statue. Carefully, Becca nudged him with her heels again. The horse walked sedately. After several circles around the pen, Becca nudged him again using heels and knees to urge the horse into a trot. She circled him around and trotted the opposite direction. When he'd trotted nicely for several rotations, she pushed him to a canter. He had an easy, collected gait, much like a rocking chair. He carried his head low, and that was another trait Becca liked in a horse.

Eachan turned to Riordan. "She has a better seat and hands even than Ciaran," he admitted.

"Aye," Riordan agreed. "A rare cailín indeed." He made a slight adjustment to the front of his trews. *A cailín most extraordinary, and one I'm looking forward to gentling myself.*

Becca made another lap at the canter, longing to turn the horse loose for a headlong gallop but she needed open countryside for that. She slowed him to a walk and with an easy tug on the reins, stopped. Becca patted his neck, pleased with him. She stepped down and led the horse over to where the men stood.

"And tell me, cailín, just what did you whisper to him to make him behave?" Riordan asked, his eyes twinkling with more than good humor.

A dimple appeared in her cheek when she gave him a smile. "Why, I told him that if he ever wished to see the ladies again, he'd best ease his temper."

Riordan guffawed, wanting this saucy cailín more than ever. He moved toward her, but was cut off by the big horse master.

"Methinks we need to talk, Riordan." Eachan snagged Riordan's arm and pulled the lieutenant out of earshot. "You don't know who she is, Riordan, and yee'd best be finding out before you commit a killing offense."

Killing offense? Riordan speculated on that for a long moment. Those were rare in Clann MacDermot. Riordan stared at the other man, waiting for him to continue.

"Though not formally betrothed, she belongs to *An Taoiseac*," the horse master informed him. Riordan's lower jaw dropped. "Pick up your teeth, man, and keep your eyes and your hands to yerself. I'll not be telling Ciaran what you've been thinking, or been lookin' at." He chuckled, the sound both amused and lascivious. "I have enough to tell him with the birth of the colt and this."

Eachan left Riordan standing there and returned to Becca's side. "He'll not be bothering you again, cailín."

Becca choked back a laugh, but as Riordan approached them, she realized Eachan had done something more than just put the younger man in his place. He looked so somber, she quickly hid her smile and quenched the laughter dancing in her eyes. He'd been fun to tease, but the difference in their positions suddenly hit home. He was one of Ciaran's soldiers, and she was to become Ciaran's wife. Arthur and Lancelot came to mind, but she tossed the thought away immediately. She was no Guinevere, and though this man was fun to flirt with, only Ciaran had the power to make her go weak in the knees.

"Mistress," Riordan greeted her formally. "Please forgive any offense I may have inadvertently implied. I dinnit know who yee were. Please accept my fealty. As I protect Ciaran and all that is his, so shall I protect yee."

"Thank you, Riordan," Becca replied formally. Then with an impish grin and dancing eyes, she turned to Eachan. "Is there any way you can steal a pair of trews for me so I can ride properly?"

Chapter Seven

The nefarious deed took Becca near a sennight, but she finally managed to snag a pair of trews from the washerwoman. Old and soft, she hoped they wouldn't be missed. The last thing she wanted was to get the woman in trouble. After much cajoling, Eachan finally agreed to let her ride the countryside, but only if she took an escort.

"These are unsettled times, cailín," he told her. "And if aught were to happen to you, I shudder to think what the MacDermot would do."

"All right," she relented. "Will you find me an escort while I go change?"

Eachan nodded. "I suppose I know which horse you'll be wantin'."

Becca grinned cheekily. "Aye, if you can catch him, I'll ride Arien. If not, I'll catch him myself."

"Arien," Eachan snorted. "And what kind of a name is that for a horse?"

"A very proper one, thank you very much," Becca retorted. "Arien was the magical horse born to Poseidon." When Eachan looked perplexed, she continued. "Poseidon was the Greeks' god of the sea."

"Ah," Eachan nodded sagely. "Like Manannan Mac Lir. But you must be very learned to know of the Greeks and their gods."

Becca giggled. "Not really. Greek mythology wasn't really my..." She'd started to say it wasn't her thing, but knew the slang would only confuse Eachan. "I found other studies more interesting," she finished. "Anyway, back to the subject at hand. About that escort?" She planted her hands on her hips refusing to be deterred.

"Aye, cailín," he capitulated. "I'll get you an escort. Taidhg will have to go, as well as another."

"Taidhg? Is that my guard's name?" Becca had tried asking the man's name, but he would never speak to her. *Teague.* She rolled his name around in her head.

Eachan nodded. "Ciaran trusts him completely, which is why he was left behind to watch over you."

Becca mulled that over as well. No wonder the man looked morose most of the time. He was a soldier, and he'd been left behind to protect a silly woman because his clann chief deemed it necessary. Becca determined to make it up to him somehow. Maybe getting out of the castle and into the countryside would help. Taidhg lurked around the front of the stable. He was a very good guard because most days, she forgot he was there. "I'll tell him on my way to change while you come up with another *escort.*" She emphasized the word, letting Eachan know she found it both distasteful and amusing.

"Change? You aren't trying to steal trews, are you?" Eachan squinted one eye and glared.

"I've already stolen them," Becca informed him in a voice as tart as green apples. "But I'll wear them beneath my skirts so no one will know. Will that suffice?"

Eachan guffawed. "Aye, but yer a cailín full of fire and vinegar, fair certain. I can't wait for the MacDermot to return. He's in for a most memorable time, and I want to watch every spirited moment of it. Things are sure to be lively."

Flustered by the direction her thoughts took, she stared at him while trying to think of a retort. When nothing came to mind, she lifted her chin defiantly to cover her embarrassment.

"Aye, Becca, I'll find another to accompany yee,

and I'll naught be tellin' a soul what's beneath yer skirt." Still chuckling, he strolled away. "Since I can't be goin' with yee, Riordan will. His honor will keep him immune to yer charms."

Becca headed back to the castle with Taidhg in tow. "I'm going riding," she informed him. "I think we both need to get away for a bit." He stopped dead still behind her. She turned to face him. "Taidhg, I'm sorry. I know you want to be with the troop, and I wish Ciaran had taken you."

"Nay, mistress," he whispered, shocked that she'd called him by name and a little surprised that she'd be concerned for his feelings. "'Tis your life I've been charged with. I saw the *Taoiseac* when he found you. You are his chosen. Naught may happen to you for 'twould kill him fair certain. Captain MacDonagh will guard the *Taoiseac's* back, while I guard you."

Becca was speechless. She could tell by the way the man carried himself, and from the scars on his face and arms, he was more than just a soldier, he was a warrior. She suddenly felt very cherished. Though her eyes glistened a bit, she smiled bravely at Taidhg. "Well, I still think we need to get out and let our horses run."

Taidhg relaxed and smiled back. "Aye, mistress. 'Twould be good to feel the wind in my face."

Lighthearted now, Becca skipped up the stairs to her chamber. She put on a plainer gown and slipped on the pilfered trews beneath it. Snagging Ciaran's plaid mantle from the footboard of the bed, she draped it around her shoulders and pinned it with the brooch. It was a beautiful thing, gold and silver entwined in a Celtic knot with a fire opal shaped like a teardrop set in the center so that all the strands wove underneath it. Becca briefly pondered how a fire opal had found its way to medieval Ireland. "Faerie tear," she murmured as she stroked the stone a moment before sending the thought away. The sun was shining, and a horse was waiting. Time for action, not history lessons.

Taidhg waited for her at the bottom of the stairs, and together they went to the stables. As promised, Eachan had found Riordan, who was already mounted, and waiting for them. Becca stuck her tongue out at him as she mounted Arien with a slight boost from Eachan. Riordan vainly tried to ignore her.

With the two wolfhounds on their heels, the three exited the keep gate and trotted through the collection of huts and cottages built next to the wall. Becca heard a faint meow and turned to find the little calico following with bounding leaps. Laughing, Becca reined Arien around. "Go home, Nod. We go too far today for you to follow."

Riordan and Taidhg sat stunned as they watched one of the hounds return to scoop up the cat and carry her back inside the gate where he deposited her gently at the door to the stable. He then loped back to them, his tongue lolling happily out of the side of his mouth.

"And you're very pleased with yourself Master Winken," Becca called to the wolfhound. The dog's happy bark sounded like laughter.

Riordan took the lead, and Taidhg brought up the rear. The two dogs ranged from side to side, noses testing the air and the ground for prey. Riordan led them to a long meadow. Without a thought, Becca whooped for joy and nudged Arien into a gallop. She leaned over his neck and savored the feel of his mane whipping against her face as his strong legs pounded the ground beneath them. This is what she'd missed most, the exhilaration that came with flying across the ground. Muffled curses behind her and the pounding of two sets of hooves meant she'd caught the men flat-footed, and they were not happy with her.

Becca spied a trail leading off into the woods. She slowed Arien slightly so he could turn onto it. Riordan called her, but she ignored him. She'd been denied this particular freedom for over twenty-five years in her time, and she was not going to give it up so easily. Even Taidhg called after her, imploring her to slow down and let them catch up to her.

She glanced over her shoulder to see where they were, and when she looked back to the front, a low branch caught her chest high and swept her off Arien. She didn't remember hitting the ground.

****

"She wears the Covenant," the female said.

"Aye," the male agreed, "but she knows naught of it."

"He is vulnerable without it," she persisted.

"Are you going to talk to me this time?" Becca was determined to get some answers.

Silence.

"You two are really pissing me off, you know. Why can't you just tell me what's going on?"

"Don't," the female whispered.

"Who are you?"

"She willna remember," the male whispered back.

"Yes, I will."

Silence.

"At least tell me if you are real. Or are you just a figment of my imagination? Am I going to wake up in the hospital? If I am, just let me die now. I can't go back. I won't go back."

****

"Easy, cailín," Riordan soothed. "You'll not be dyin', and we have to take you back." Becca griped his arms. The strength in her hands amazed him. She was a most uncommon cailín indeed. "You took a tumble from Arien," he explained. "We need to get you to Siobhan."

The two wolfhounds pushed past Riordan and licked her face. Becca waved them away. Slowly, she opened her eyes. "Oh, God," she whispered. "I'm still here." Tears glistened in her eyes. "I was afraid they'd take me back," she choked.

Taidhg's hand griped his sword hilt. "Who, mistress? Who would dare take you?" He looked around warily, afraid someone was watching from the woods.

Becca shook her head. "Not here," she mumbled, closing her eyes against the bright sunlight. "They aren't here, Taidhg. Don't take me to the hospital."

Her words confused Riordan, and he worried she had a head injury. "Catch Arien if you can," he told Taidhg. "If you can't, leave him to find his own way back. We have to get her to Siobhan."

Taidhg nodded in agreement. Arien had returned to stand quietly with the other two horses. The guard snatched the reins on all three and led them over. Riordan mounted his horse while Taidhg picked up Becca and handed her to the other man. Holding Arien's reins, he mounted his own horse, and they started back to the keep. Every instinct urged Riordan to put his horse into a full gallop and get Becca home as quickly as possible. However, he knew that if she'd injured her head in the fall, the gallop could do more harm. They were just a league away. He could stay his anxiety. He would not risk further injury to her.

Becca sank back into the place where the darkness was soft and gray instead of the all-encompassing black of unconsciousness. Maybe those others were still lurking about in there, and she could ask them more questions.

****

"She wants to know who we are," the female reminded him.

"As if she'd recognize us," the male replied disdainfully.

"There are those who would," the female argued. *"And this one would ask."*

"You are the one who gave the Covenant," he accused.

"And you are the one who promised it," she reminded him.

****

When Becca awoke, she was back in her bed. *Ciaran's bed!* She all but cried in relief. Siobhan and Odhran hovered over her, and she suspected that Riordan and Taidhg clustered outside the door. That Eachan waited with them would have surprised her. The dogs and Nod milled about getting in the way. Siobhan had shooed them off the bed several times and tried to keep them out of the room before finally throwing up her hands in defeat.

"You can't be taking such chances," Siobhan chided her. "Yee nigh frightened a year's growth out of all of us."

"Chill out," Becca told her, grinning when she realized Siobhan hadn't a clue as to what the phrase meant. "I'm fine," she added. "That wasn't the first time I've come off a horse, and it probably won't be the last."

"Aye, it will," Eachan roared from the door. "I thought yee had more sense, cailín. Yee'll not be ridin' one of mine like that again."

Becca smiled at the huge man, knowing he was all bluster and bluff. "Is Arien all right?"

"Aye, through no thought of yer'n, though."

"I'm sorry, Eachan." She raised her voice. "And that goes to you two lurking out there in the hall. You might as well come in and have a go at me as well."

Riordan and Taidhg entered hesitantly. Relieved Becca sounded so normal, they breathed sighs of relief. They both wanted to lay into her with sharp tongues for what she'd done, but they were both so thankful she wasn't hurt, neither could unleash their wrath.

"I was stupid, okay?" she told the room. "That's what happens when I'm cooped up. I go a little crazy. My head quits working. I promise it won't happen again. I really am fine." She stretched and winced. "Well, nothing that a hot bath won't cure."

Siobhan stood apart with her hands on her hips scowling at Becca. She cleared her throat and glared a little harder.

"All right, already. I promise not to ride recklessly. I promise not to run off and leave Taidhg and Riordan behind. I promise to be a good girl. I promise not to cause any trouble until Ciaran gets back. Does that satisfy you, Siobhan?"

"And why don't I believe a word of it?" the other woman scoffed. "Trouble follows you like a shadow, Becca."

Becca shrugged and tried to look sheepish.

"Out with yee all," Siobhan ordered the men. "Taidhg, send up the tub and hot water, will yee?"

Becca closed her eyes. The relief on everyone's faces humbled her. By leaving Taidhg behind, Ciaran took her safety very seriously, and now her gut churned with guilt. If something had happened to her, Riordan and Taidhg very likely would have forfeited their lives for her foolishness. She resolved to be more responsible.

As the next few days passed, Becca noticed a great deal of activity both in and out of the castle. Out beyond the village, on a hill above a wide green park, a great pile of wood sprouted, and everyone seemed to be obsessed with cleaning. She needed more information before she made a tactical error so she finally asked Siobhan.

"'Tis *Beltane*," the older woman explained. "The

first of May. All the hearth fires will be extinguished, and at dark on Beltane, the bonfire will be lit. Each family will light a brand from the fire to take home to relight the hearths. Did you not celebrate it in your time?"

Becca shook her head. "May first in my time was called May Day but no one celebrated."

Enchanted by all the activity, Becca avidly watched the preparations. As Siobhan had indicated, when May first arrived, all the fires were extinguished, and people scrubbed all the hearths clean. Everyone in the castle, village, and the outlying crofts dressed in their finest and gathered on the green just before dusk. Food-laden tables stood everywhere, and casks of wine and other drink were opened and shared. Pipers played lively tunes while couples danced.

As dark fell, Odhran lit the bonfire, and the night blazed with flames. Entranced, Becca wished Ciaran was there to share it with her. Before she could brood too long, Riordan appeared and claimed her for a dance. Laughing, she admitted she didn't know a reel from waltz, but he swung her around to the lively music and just managed to keep his boots out from under hers. After a few jigs, she sent him off to find a more willing cailín.

Siobhan clustered with other women whose husbands were soldiers. Though Becca could tell from their faces they were worried and missed their husbands, they still managed to enjoy the festival. A few of them danced together, and they all ate, drank, and laughed.

Becca felt out of place again. As the MacDermot's intended, she was not part of the village, but since she wasn't his wife yet, she wasn't part of the castle either. Lonely, she found a space a little away from the crowd. She spread Ciaran's mantle and sank down on it. Winken, Blinken, and

Nod immediately appeared and nestled around her. She tried very hard not to think about Ciaran but as she watched Riordan draw a comely young cailín off into the dark, she couldn't help herself.

"You don't have to miss out on the festivities, Taidhg, just because I choose a quiet place," she said softly, knowing the man was nearby. His clothing rustled as he moved behind her.

"'Tis all right, cailín," he replied, his voice as quiet as hers. "I have no wife, and my head is too old to suffer the effects of drink on the morrow."

At midnight, a small trail of fire flickered, joining a small pile of brush with the main body of the bonfire. By ones and twos, and then whole families, the villagers lined up to jump across the smaller fire. Becca had no clue why they did so.

"'Tis for luck," Taidhg explained, sensing she didn't understand. "And to protect us from evil."

"Then we'd best go have a leap."

He held out his hand to help her up. As she approached the end of the line, Riordan suddenly appeared at her side. "Since the MacDermot 'tisn't here, will you allow me to be his proxy?"

Becca grinned, her dimple showing as her eyes danced with mischief. "Haven't you already jumped across with that little brunette? How much luck and protection do you need?"

Riordan ducked his head in mock chagrin, but Becca saw the impudence shining in his eyes. "'Tis not for me, cailín, but Ciaran. I fear he will need all the luck he can garner when he returns to deal with you."

Laughing, Becca grabbed his hand, and the two of them ran and leaped across the flames. Ever faithful, Taidhg followed close on their heels.

Odhran was the last person to leap the fire. All the heads of household then came to the bonfire and lit a torch. With their raised brands chasing the shadows away, everyone drifted back to their homes. Riordan lit the torch for the castle, and he now led that procession back.

"'Tis *An Taoiseac* who would do the honors," Taidhg told Becca as they followed close on Riordan's heels. "So now Riordan stands in for him."

Becca mulled that over for a bit. She'd assumed Riordan was just another officer in Ciaran's service. Now she wondered. There was so much knowledge everyone else took for granted, and about which, she had no clue. Desperate to fit in, she acted like she understood, even when she was reluctant to ask what she didn't know.

For the next fortnight, Becca stayed very low-key around the castle. She let Siobhan teach her needlework. It bored her to tears. Though there was some satisfaction in watching a picture eventually take shape. It just took too long to suit her. During the long years of her rehabilitation and decline, several nurses had tried to teach her to embroider, needlepoint, and knit. Becca had always been active, and the inactivity her injuries forced upon her body chafed her. She purposely stayed away from the stables, though she watched Maggie May and her foal from the courtyard. Becca did find some satisfaction out in the herb garden learning the names and uses of the herbs.

One of her grandfather's ranch hands was a Cheyenne and his mother lived on the ranch with them. She was a fascinating old woman who wove amazing tales of her people and was a deep well of knowledge of both folklore and native medicine. Micco, her son, often used herbal remedies on the horses. Many of the same herbs with the same uses grew in neat rows behind the kitchen.

She'd found peace and contentment in her predicament. Missing him terribly, part of her still dreaded Ciaran's return. A whole new can of worms would be opened when he did. She was thankful his absence allowed her to adapt to her new life. Becca still harbored the fear she'd suddenly wake up back in the twenty-first century, and she couldn't bear that thought. When Ciaran returned, she'd deal with the problems he presented. At fifty, she'd long ago decided any semblance of passion was long past her capability but the things that man could do with just a kiss absolutely curled her toes, and it frightened her to death.

Chapter Eight

She couldn't breathe. Stabbing pain in her left side just above her hip. *No!* Panicked, Becca forced her way up through stifling darkness. Finally able to open her eyes, she focused on the wolfhound lying across her feet. He was real. This room was real. Becca touched her side, expecting to bring away a bloody hand. Nothing. This pain was not hers.

Ciaran! He'd been hurt and grievously so. Her heart pounding, Becca knew only that she had to get to him. She threw off the covers and ran to the door. Flinging it open, she caught Taidhg curled up in front of the door, asleep.

"Ciaran," she panted. "I must go to him."

The man stared up at her stupidly, still half asleep. "But, mistress, he's far away. Fighting." He pushed up to a sitting position.

Exasperated, Becca glared at him. "I know that, Taidhg. It doesn't matter. He's been hurt, and I have to get to him. Do not argue with me. Get me a guide, provisions, and horses." When he still didn't move, she yelled. "NOW!"

The commotion in the hallway woke Siobhan. She stumbled out of her room, blinking the sleep out of her eyes. "What is it, cailín? 'Tis not even dawn yet."

"It's Ciaran, Siobhan. He's been hurt. I must go."

"Nay, cailín, 'tis too dangerous. The O'Briens are raiding, not to mention some of the other clanns. And there are those who are less than loyal to the O'Conor. They also have axes to grind with the MacDermot. If they caught you, cailín..." Siobhan's

107

voice trailed off. She did not want to think about the bloody war that would ensue if anyone harmed the young woman.

"I'll just have to make sure that doesn't happen," Becca snapped. She grabbed the other woman's arm. "Siobhan, he'll die if I don't get there in time." Her voice broke, and she blinked back tears.

"We'll need at least a company." Taidhg hoped to dissuade her.

"No. That would leave Ailfenn undefended. Two men. We ride hard and fast. Go, Taidhg." Becca remained adamant. She took Siobhan's arm and pulled her into the chamber. "I need clothes, Siobhan. Trews and shirts. Heavy boots. And a first aid kit." Realizing she'd used a twenty-first century term again, she explained what she needed.

Within the hour, she was ready. Taidhg and Riordan awaited her in the courtyard. Becca had raided Ciaran's den and found a sword light enough for her to handle and a dirk. Belting them on, she sent up a quick thanks for the fencing lessons she'd received when the captain of the Modern Pentathlon team had tried to lure her away from the equestrian team. She swung the blade experimentally. It was certainly different from the foil she'd trained with and was far more deadly but Becca might have need of deadly force before all was said and done.

She swept through the massive doors of the keep just as the sun rose. The first rays of dawn bathed her in a golden nimbus, and her appearance caught everyone by surprise.

"She could pass for a warrior," Taidhg whispered to Riordan.

The other man simply nodded, too stunned to speak. *She could be a Fenian Warrior come to life,* his mind insisted. Who was this woman who had so ensorcelled his kin? *And me,* he added with honesty.

Becca was tall for a woman and muscular with

broad shoulders. She'd tied her hair back with a leather thong and wore her trews and boots like she'd been born to them. Riordan knew of no woman who would be so comfortable, so confident in male garb but Becca looked like a Celtic warrior queen of old.

The horse master himself held Arien's bridle. Becca needed no help to mount now that a skirt no longer encumbered her legs. Eachan patted her thigh with far more familiarity than anyone else in the keep would have dared.

"Take care of him, and he'll take care of you, cailín," he whispered to her.

Becca nodded, not trusting her voice. Instead, she put her heels to her horse and cantered out the gate, Riordan, Taidhg, and the two wolfhounds hard on her heels. Once beyond the gate, Becca motioned for Riordan to take the lead. She had no clue which way to head.

The three rode hard but wisely, keeping their horses as fresh as possible. Every sinew and synapse within Becca screamed that she run Arien until he could run no more. Her need to get to Ciaran was that great.

****

As that first day slid into evening, her grit astonished both Riordan and Taidhg. She never complained, never slowed them down, never expected cosseting like most ladies would have demanded as their due. They'd made excellent time and were much farther than Riordan had anticipated. When the night grew too dark to ride safely, Riordan called a halt. He'd found a small copse of trees not far from a stream.

Becca unsaddled Arien and rubbed him down with handfuls of sweet-smelling grass. When she finished, she led him to the stream to drink his fill. Taidhg strung a picket line while Riordan watered their mounts.

Becca sat on the bank of the stream, and Riordan hunkered down on his heels next to her. "'Tis a cold camp tonight, mistress," he apologized.

"Aye," Becca agreed. "I, too, hope the three of us can pass through unnoticed."

Riordan nodded, astounded by her acumen. She was indeed well matched to the MacDermot.

They settled the horses and huddled together in the copse, their mantles wrapped around them. Taidhg broke open a pack and dug out some journey cake and dried venison. Becca shared a measure of hers with the wolfhounds now snuggled on each side of her.

"Will you tell me, Riordan?" Becca finally broke the silence. "Will you tell me of the clann?"

Riordan grinned at her, cocky good humor twinkling in his eyes. "Curious are you of the clann you'll be joining soon enough? Well, those of us tied to the MacDermot are more a sept than a clann," he explained. Becca felt utterly confused.

Taidhg, more familiar with her background, broke in. "A sept denotes direct lineage from common parents, mistress. Riordan and the MacDermot belong to the sept of MacDermot."

"Why do you call him *the* MacDermot?" she asked. Taidhg and Riordan exchanged uneasy glances. "Oh, hell," she sputtered. "I know you've heard the rumors about me. I'm not daft. I just can't remember much of what happened in my life before Ciaran and Niall found me."

"Captain MacDonagh was nigh beside himself that night," Taidhg explained to Riordan. "Not to mention the *Taoiseac*," he added with a wry grin.

"As you wish, cailín," Riordan acquiesced, falling into the more familiar address. "A lesson in clann history then. As Taidhg said, a sept is a familial group descending in direct lineage from common parents. I am a MacDermot, a direct cousin to Ciaran. Ciaran is *the* MacDermot. He's the head of the sept and the clann. The clann, which includes the MacDermots and the septs owing fealty to them, descended from one common ancestor. Captain MacDonagh is a distant cousin, as is Taidhg. Several clanns form a *tuatha,* which is like a kingdom. We owe allegiance to the O'Conor of Sil Muredaich. Conchobhar O'Conor is King of Connaught. Have you no idea of your family, cailín?"

Becca shook her head. Her grandfather's last name had been Connor, which was much too close to O'Conor for comfort. The voices in her head had insinuated she'd lived in this time, but they'd given no indication of who she had been. She sure didn't want to make any rash statements about her ancestry. Her surname was Miller. Common enough in the twentieth century, but too chancy in the nineth.

"Mayhaps 'twill come to you, mistress," Taidhg said. His smile was meant to encourage her.

Becca's whole body slumped as exhaustion set it. She'd been running on adrenaline since dawn. Before she could catch it, a huge yawn stretched her face.

"I agree," Riordan laughed. "'Tis been a long day with more just like it to follow. We'd all best bed down."

"I'll take the first watch, Riordan," Taidhg offered.

Riordan nodded his assent, rolled up in his mantle and was softly snoring within moments. Taidhg moved away from the group and found a place in which to conceal himself.

Becca nudged Winken with a toe. "Go with him and guard him well," she told the dog. With a deep sigh, the huge animal stood up, shook, stretched, and padded over to where Taidhg had hidden himself. Becca then poked Blinken who was lying beside her. "And you'll go with Riordan when he relieves Taidhg." The dog yawned but Becca knew he'd obey.

She bundled up in her own mantle. With her nose buried in the woolen wrap, she sniffed deeply. It still smelled of Ciaran, and her stomach knotted in an unfamiliar but enticing way. She knew what it felt like to awaken in his arms. Enough time had passed, though the memory was more like a hazy dream than reality. She closed her eyes. What would his arms, broad chest, and muscled abdomen feel like pressed against her when they embraced skin to skin?

Ciaran was always fiercely aroused whenever he was near her. Though she'd never actually seen a naked man, Becca was well aware of the mechanics involved with the act itself. She'd supervised the mating of her share of stallions and mares. Unbidden, the image of Ciaran covering her body like a stallion over a mare seared across her psyche, and she squirmed as inner muscles contracted. Flushing, she remembered how his erection pressed against her. Though she had nothing to judge from except some half-hearted teenaged memories, comparing him to a stallion might be just a little too accurate for comfort.

Becca sighed. If she didn't quit thinking about his body, and what it might do to hers, she'd never get to sleep. Tomorrow would be just as exhausting as today, and the urgency to get to Ciaran still rode her hard. Resolutely, she forced all thought of him out of her head.

****

"He gave the Covenant without the binding." The female was complaining again. "Its power is diminished, and look what has happened."

"There was magic enough to deflect the blow. He

will be able to ensure the line." The male sounded cocksure of himself.

"He should have made the binding." She was insistent.

"How could he? Fionn died before his Covenant was fulfilled. That fool Aralt wouldn't know a true mate if she bit him on the toín."

"Enough! No more excuses. Ciaran must learn the binding oath before he becomes the biggest fool of all." She was adamant.

"He has until Lughnasadh to complete the binding." Did he sound a bit unsure?

"What happens if this binding thing doesn't occur by then?"

Silence.

"Fool. She still hears." The female was upset.

"Nay, dear heart," the male denied. "No fool am I. 'Tis fools these mortals be."

"And what of you who tied the MacDermot's fate to our own?"

"'Twas in the heat of the moment," he answered defensively.

"Pray she gets there in time. The line can't die."

"What happens if I don't?"

More silence. Becca sighed. Eventually, these people had to give her answers.

****

Becca woke up shivering. Both dogs pressed against her as Riordan brushed her hair back from her face. "What is it, cailín? What ails you?"

"'Tis not me," Becca replied groggily, trying to get her bearings. "'Tis Ciaran. He has a fever." She pushed herself upright. "What time is it? Can we safely ride? I fear each moment I'm apart from him."

Riordan nodded. "Aye, 'tis not even first light yet, but if we travel slowly, we can ride."

Taidhg was already up and saddling the horses. Becca retreated to a bushy tree some distance away and took care of her morning absolutions. She mounted up and followed Riordan's lead, Taidhg once again bringing up the rear.

The day passed uneventfully, and as dark descended, they pressed on through the night until it was again too dangerous to ride. Once more they made cold camp, this time Riordan taking first watch. Becca was so tired she fell asleep with a piece of journey cake still in her hand. Blinken dutifully followed Riordan while Winken nestled at Becca's back. Taidhg wrapped up in his mantle a few feet away and fell into a light sleep.

They followed this same routine for almost a sennight before they caught up to the first stragglers of the O'Conor's army. As they passed each group, Riordan asked about the location of the MacDermot men and news of Ciaran. At last, the captain of a troop of horse being held in reserve knew where their troops could be found.

Becca fought back tears. They'd threatened to fall the entire journey but she was so close to their destination, losing control was an eminent possibility. Each passing day weighed heavily on her. She could feel what was happening to Ciaran's body, the fevers and pain that ravaged him. Would she be too late? He was gravely wounded and ill. Her heart and soul were positive she was the only one who could save him.

The sun was gone and shadows lengthened in the murky dusk when the first MacDermot guard challenged them. "Riordan MacDermot," Riordan answered. "With Taidhg MacDonagh and *an Taoiseac's* lady."

Becca and Riordan had already passed the sentry, but Taidhg caught the measured look the man sent after the girl. Taidhg had heard the talk in the barracks and at the table. These were battle-hardened men, and they were none too sure of the

MacDermot's choice for a mate. Her startling arrival, strange appearance, and behavior was odd enough. Add the MacDermot's reaction to her, and the whole affair left them puzzled. With battle imminent, she was a distraction the troop did not need.

The three of them rode into the encampment. Niall MacDonagh swept Riordan into a rough hug as soon as the younger man stepped down from his horse. Niall nodded up at his kinsman, Taidhg, and stared at Becca, finally recognizing her.

"What does she here?" he demanded of Riordan, his voice harsh with accusation.

"*She* does what she pleases," Becca retorted. She swung off her horse with assured grace as Niall stared at her mannish attire. He opened his mouth to chide her, but she preempted him. "The countryside is unsettled. Three men were less likely to draw attention than a woman and her escort. Where is he?" she demanded.

Flabbergasted, Niall simply stepped back and pointed. A crude tent had been erected, and the shadowy shape of a body was visible among a pile of furs and blankets. Becca let out a little cry and rushed to Ciaran's side.

Sweat left a sickly sheen on his handsome face, now creased and wracked by pain. He thrashed about, caught in a fevered nightmare. Becca laid a cool hand on his hot forehead. "Rest easy, Ciaran. I'm here now."

He grabbed her hand and almost crushed it with his brute strength. She stroked his cheek with her other hand. "Becca?" his voice grated out between dry, cracked lips.

"Shh," she soothed. "Everything will be fine now. I'm here to take care of you."

"Nay, *muirnín*," his parched voice croaked. "'Tis no place for you. Who was fool enough to bring you?

Not Taidhg. He swore his life for you."

Riordan slipped up beside Becca and knelt down. "Twould be me, cousin," he said in hushed tones. "This one you have chosen has a mind of her own. Near a sennight ago, she awoke and demanded we bring her to you."

Niall sucked in a deep breath. Ciaran had been wounded in a sneak attack just before dawn a sennight ago. He stared at Becca, his expression thoughtful. "So the binding goes both ways," he muttered.

Ciaran grasped Riordan's arm in greeting. "'Tis glad I am that you are here, cousin. Niall will have need of you. The O'Brien think to attack soon." He turned feverish eyes to Becca. "You are getting back on that horse and going home," he ordered with some semblance of his old authority.

Becca snorted, the inelegant sound saying it all. "The hell I am," she added for emphasis. Over her shoulder, she called to the other man hovering at the tent flap. "Taidhg, get the bag Siobhan packed for me from my saddle."

She reached for the blanket covering him, but Ciaran grabbed it. She pushed his hands away and stripped it off. Tears filled her eyes when she saw the raw, gaping wound in his side, just above the hipbone. The gash was an angry red, swollen and full of pus. Becca hoped she'd arrived in time to stop the infection. When Taidhg appeared with the bag, she gave him whispered instructions.

Within a few minutes, a bucket of steaming water appeared at her elbow. She tossed in a cake of soap and washed up. With hands as gentle as she could make them, she probed the wound, ever conscious of each breath Ciaran sucked in. She winced each time his muscles clinched and knotted or when his hands fisted to keep from pushing hers away from him. Though deep, the wound hadn't bled much. Becca was grateful. No major arteries or veins were involved. The infection and the attendant fever worried her. The wound must be cleaned and drained before she could cauterize it. None of it would be pleasant for Ciaran. She glanced up to find Niall guarding the entrance to the tent.

"Whiskey?" she asked the captain of the guard. "Or something equally strong." She wanted the strong liquor for two reasons: first to get Ciaran roaring drunk so he wouldn't feel as much of the pain, and second to help disinfect the wound. Food mold was still centuries away from being distilled into penicillin.

"You have to go home, cailín," Ciaran whispered to her. "I couldn't bear it if aught happened to you."

"Nothing is going to happen to me, Ciaran. And if I don't kill this infection, you are going to die. Where would I be then?" she retorted.

Ciaran smiled and relaxed a little. That she'd considered life without him, and she didn't want him gone was a major stroke to his ego and gave him great comfort. He didn't want to admit how often in the past two months he'd almost mounted his horse and ridden home to claim her fully. He worried she truly was fey and would disappear before he could return.

While she waited for the whiskey, Becca bathed his face and chest with a wet cloth. His men had piled blankets and furs on him hoping to sweat out the fever. Becca knew this fever had to be cooled rather than sweated. It was so high the fever itself could kill him. As her hand trailed the cool water across his chest, his hand found its way to her leg and rested on her thigh for a moment. It didn't stay still very long as caressed her.

"At ease," Becca ordered with a small giggle. "Is that all you ever think about?"

Ciaran cupped himself and grinned at her. "'Tis

too late, cailín, to make *an boidín* stand down."

Becca glanced at his erection. Her breath whistled sharply as she sucked it in. So that's what had poked her in the behind. She tried not to stare, but she couldn't drag her gaze away.

"Aye, look your fill now, sweet Becca, for as soon as I am up, I'll be burying him deep between your legs."

"You are up," she retorted, ignoring the little shiver of anticipation skittering up her spine. "And you are in absolutely no shape to be putting that thing anywhere but back to sleep." She glanced over her shoulder after hearing a discreet cough. "Ah, Niall," she greeted the other man with relief. "'Tis about time. Pour that stuff down his throat 'til he can't think anymore." She haphazardly threw a blanket over his midsection and stood up. Ciaran groaned and reached for her. She danced away from his hand. "I'll be back when you are good and drunk," she informed him. While the tone of her voice brooked no argument, her eyes glinted with mischievous lights.

"I'm always good, even when I'm drunk," he shot back.

Niall dropped beside Ciaran and propped him up. "Drink, Ciaran. I wouldn't want her coming after me with that sharp tongue of hers."

Ciaran smiled, remembering a different conversation with Niall concerning the same subject. "I can't think of anything more pleasant," he mumbled around the mouth of the wineskin Niall held to his lips.

Becca found Riordan and Taidhg sitting at the fire. Riordan handed her his plate but she shook her head. "Thanks, but I'm not hungry."

"'Tis as bad as it looks, cailín," Riordan stated, his worry leaking out in his voice.

Becca shook her head. "It's bad enough but I

think he'll live. I have much work to do tonight, Riordan, and it will be hard on him. Niall is getting him drunk now so he won't feel as much of the pain. Can someone build a small fire closer to the tent? I'll need a continuous supply of hot water, and when it comes time to cauterize the wound, I'll need to heat the knife."

Riordan and Taidhg both grimaced at her words, but Taidhg stood to do her bidding.

"You seem inordinately fascinated by hot water and soap," Riordan mused.

"Heat and soap cleanse," she told him. "Both kill that which would fester in a wound." Her face was etched with fatigue as she pushed her hair out of her eyes. "That which festers in a wound would kill a man."

Riordan nodded. Eachan had told him of her part in the birthing of the foal. He was not surprised she was wise in the healing arts. Once again, he wondered where she'd come from. In the dark midnights on their way to find the troop, he and Taidhg often talked, speculating about her. Taidhg told him of her battered body and the strange language she'd spoken when they'd found her; of Ciaran's immediate and possessive reaction to her. She acted like no other woman Riordan knew, and there were still times strange words and phrases came out of her mouth.

As Aralt's nephew, under Brehon law, Riordan could have made claim to become clann chief when Aralt died. Though his father's acknowledged heir, Ciaran was still Aralt's bastard. Like Niall, though, Riordan recognized something in Ciaran so he hadn't pressed his claim, choosing instead to swear his fealty to his cousin.

Riordan stared into the fire watching the crackling flames dance as he wondered. Was she a witch as some in the castle believed? If so, he'd seen nothing but good magic come from her hand. When he'd gazed upon Ciaran's face earlier, Riordan would have sworn the man wasn't long for this world. Then he'd seen his cousin's reaction to the girl. A man near death could not evidence that much lust. Riordan grinned as he remembered the first time he'd laid eyes on the girl. She'd had the same effect on him.

A sudden burst of song erupted from the tent, the words slurred and bawdy. Riordan and Becca exchanged smug looks. Ciaran was rip-roaringly drunk.

"He'll need to be," she murmured as much to herself as to Riordan. "What I must do tonight might kill a lesser man."

She stood up and headed back to the tent, her steps measured and resolute. Riordan stayed where he was, wishing for a bit of whiskey himself. It would not be the last time he made that wish in the long night that followed.

Back in the tent, Becca stared at Niall and Taidhg. Her gaze never wavered as her mouth formed a tense line. "This will not be easy," she told them. "What I have to do will hurt him and though he is drunk, it will not be enough to block all the pain. You will have to hold him down. Know that I seek only to save his life and trust me to do what is necessary though you may not understand." She gazed at each man for a long moment, taking their measure. "Will you help me?" She held her breath waiting for their answers.

"Aye, mistress," Taidhg replied without hesitation.

It took Niall longer to reply. He scrutinized Becca with a hard eye. "What comes to him comes to you, cailín," he finally replied with a soft growl.

Becca wondered if there was an implied threat in Niall's words. If Ciaran died, would Niall kill her?

She blinked. With perfect clarity, she realized that if Ciaran died, she wouldn't want to live. Becca took a deep breath before nodding at the big soldier to show she understood. "We begin."

It was near dawn when Becca finished, so exhausted she had trouble lifting her arms. Niall's cryptic statement made perfect sense now. She'd felt each slice of the knife as she cut away dead and diseased flesh. Her muscles could recite each stitch she'd taken in the muscles of his abdomen. She'd worked with tears streaming down her cheeks as Ciaran moaned and thrashed. She'd almost passed out herself when she'd finally cauterized the wound. Now, she wanted nothing more than to fling herself down beside him, rest her head on his muscled shoulder and sleep for a week.

Wearily, she washed his blood from her hands, then packed the wound with an herb poultice. She bandaged him and pulled the blankets up around him.

Though still feverish, he was not as hot as he had been. The killing fever had broken at last, and Ciaran finally slept peacefully.

Through the whole ordeal, Niall watched her closely. Only he suspected the toll it had taken on her. "Sleep, cailín," he ordered, his voice gentle. "I'll be here to watch over the two of you."

Becca gratefully curled up beside Ciaran. Niall found her mantle and tossed it over her. Surprised to find the MacDermot Knot pinned to it, he stared at Ciaran for a long moment before gazing at the girl. The Knot had never left Ciaran's possession since he'd first received it. Upon assuming the position of *An Taoiseac*, the Knot came to Ciaran even though Niall couldn't recall Aralt ever wearing the thing. Conversely, he couldn't remember Ciaran ever without it.

'Twas most curious for sure. Niall could recite

many of the old tales, but he obviously didn't know near enough.

As soon as they got home, he would consult Siobhan and Odhran, the Druid. Surely one of them would have the answer.

Chapter Nine

Becca didn't want to open her eyes even though the camp stirred outside the tent. Men and horses snorted and stamped. Ciaran had wrapped his arms around her at some point, and all three wolfhounds, Bhruic, Winken, and Blinken, were curled up at her back. She was still so tired she could barely move and guessed she'd only slept two hours or less. At least Ciaran's fever had broken, and he was sleeping easier.

She moved and Ciaran's arms tightened around her. He growled softly in his sleep. "You're as bad as the dogs," she complained. "I'm just checking the bandage." She fought loose from his embrace and sat up. She pulled away the covers and wasn't surprised to find Ciaran aroused. "I swear," she swore under her breath, "all he thinks about is tupping." The bandage was soaked through with nasty yellow pus, and she yanked it away. The wound looked less angry now though it still drained. She replaced the herb poultice and bandage with fresh and was just about to lay back down when all three dogs snapped to ferocious attention. Panicked cries echoed from the outlying sentries, and suddenly the area around the tent erupted with violent activity. Men ran this way and that, drawing swords and looking for the enemy.

Alarmed, Becca found her sword belt and cinched it around her waist. The dirk she'd used on Ciaran's wound was back in its scabbard, hiding beneath the blanket she'd wadded up to use as a pillow. She snagged it, jammed it through her belt, and then reached for her boots. Ciaran stirred, his hand reaching for his sword.

"No," Becca told him firmly. "You're in no shape to fight."

"I can't just lie here, cailín," he growled weakly.

"Not only can you, but you will," she growled back. She did move his scabbard closer so his big fist could close around the hilt. "As a last resort," she cautioned, turning to leave.

His hand snagged her ankle. "Where are you going?" Groaning, he pushed up on an elbow. "You have to stay here where I can protect you."

Becca shook her foot loose and danced out of his reach. "You'll be lucky to protect yourself." She smiled to take the sting from her words, knowing it was vitally important to him and his honor that he keep her safe. "I am not without ability with a sword, Ciaran. I will protect myself. Stay with him," she ordered the hounds as she slipped through the tent flap.

"Nay, with her," Ciaran told the dogs. The three dogs obediently followed her out into the melee.

Becca found Riordan and Taidhg standing shoulder to shoulder in front of the tent, their swords drawn. Eddies of men clashed all around the campsite. The hobelars were at a distinct disadvantage. They were bowman, used to being mounted and mobile. In the hand-to-hand fighting taking place, their bows were useless. The troop of horse carried both sword and lance, and those soldiers were more adept at fighting on foot. As they watched the fight, Niall seemed to be everywhere.

Then suddenly, he was nowhere to be seen. The men exchanged worried looks. Becca turned to Riordan.

"Go," she ordered. "Taidhg and I will guard *him*," indicating the tent with her chin. She pulled her sword and brandished it in the air.

Riordan hesitated just a moment for he'd spotted Niall surrounded and about to be overcome. Then he was gone, diving into the fray.

Taidhg gave her an apprehensive look.

Becca smiled at him. "You have my back, Taidhg, as I have yours. Together we shall keep the MacDermot safe this day."

Her voice was filled with such utter conviction Taidhg did not doubt her words. Before he could reply, two men were upon them.

The wolfhounds dashed everywhere, nipping and tearing where they could sink their teeth into flesh, but darting away too quickly to take a blow from the swords or dirks aimed their way. Becca and Taidhg fought shoulder to shoulder. Taidhg finished off his man and turned his sword on Becca's. In short order, that man was dead, too. Slowly, the MacDermot troops got the upper hand. The pile of bodies in front of the tent continued to grow. Riordan and Niall split up, each working their way through their soldiers to rally them.

At one point, Niall turned to check on the tent. He groaned when he realized Becca and Taidhg were back-to-back, fighting off four attackers. There were too many O'Brien fighters between them for him to get there in time. Then, as he watched, Becca slashed the throat of one, and her sword continued in one smooth motion to block the thrust of the second. Her left hand followed the path of her right, and she buried her dirk up to its hilt beneath the arm of the other attacker. Like a dancer, she whirled, freeing the dirk and spinning to take on the second man attacking Taidhg.

"Makes you want to weep for joy, doesn't it?" Riordan laughed as he appeared at Niall's shoulder. "What babies the two of them will make!" With that, the younger man was off seeking other prey.

"Aye and aye," Niall agreed before turning to

find his own quarry.

As the sun neared its zenith, horsemen galloped into the camp, and the last of the O'Briens broke and ran. Most of the horsemen raced off to chase the retreating foe, but a small knot stopped in the center of the camp. The obvious leader of the group called to Niall.

"Captain MacDonagh," the rider acknowledged. "How fares the Wolf of the MacDermot?"

"He lives to fight another day, King Conchobhar." Niall bobbed his head in a respectful nod.

The king glanced around the campsite, noting how many O'Briens lay dead compared to the small number of dead and wounded MacDermot soldiers. His gaze stopped on Becca.

Her hair fell in loose waves about her shoulders, and there was no hiding her gender. The look on his face sent a shiver up her spine. Gauging the look on the king's face, she was in peril of losing more than her life. Rather than run, she squared her shoulders and marched out to join Niall.

Riordan and Taidhg closed on either side of her. They would fight even the king himself to keep her for Ciaran and the MacDermots.

Conchobhar watched her speculatively, noting the bloodstained sword and dirk she carried in each hand and the stains on her clothes—men's garb no less. He glanced at the pile of O'Brien bodies in front of the tent. She was every inch a woman, as the trews clinging to her lovely curves proved, and a beauty.

She met his gaze defiantly, chin lifted stubbornly as her eyes bored into his. This was a woman of deep passion, and he wanted to taste what she had to offer. He was, however, surprised a female fought with the MacDermot's troop. Ciaran was nothing, if not a traditionalist. Conchobhar's gaze raked over her, lingering on her curves, his desire plain for her to read. Any other woman would be pleased to have elicited the notice of the king. She merely raised her chin another notch and glared at him.

The king saw her knuckles tighten as she gripped both sword and dirk tighter. Then he noticed that Niall, Riordan, and Taidhg had all drawn their weapons and that the rest of the MacDermot troops watched warily, their weapons unsheathed.

Whoever this woman was, Clann MacDermot would not let her go without a fight. "And who might you be?" he purred, still intrigued by her audacity.

Before she could speak, Niall stepped in front of her. "Becca MacDonagh, sire, daughter of my brother Dubhgan and chosen by the MacDermot to be his bride."

That gave the king pause. She was blood kin to Niall and all but wed to Ciaran. Aye, if he tried to take her, there would be bloodshed and an allegiance with blood ties as old as time would shatter. He looked past the group to the man who appeared at the front of the tent. No matter how much Conchobhar wanted her, he didn't desire her that much.

"My blessing, then," the king intoned. "Need you help to clean up this mess?" He glanced around at the dead and dying.

"Nay, King Conchobhar," Niall replied. "We'll take care of our own and bury theirs."

"As you will." With a gesture, Conchobhar led the rest of his men in pursuit of the fleeing O'Briens.

Becca had held her breath from the moment Niall stepped in front of her. He'd blatantly lied to the king, and if his duplicity was discovered...well, she didn't want to consider the consequences. Suddenly overwhelmed, she felt an absolute compulsion to sit and sank to the ground.

"NO!" That panicked cry was torn from a throat still ragged from pain.

As one, Niall, Riordan, and Taidhg turned to find Ciaran swaying in front of the tent. He wore naught but his mantle draped around his waist. Ciaran clutched his side and blood oozed between his fingers. The point of his sword buried in the earth was the only thing that kept him upright. Becca turned to look at him, and her heart melted at the sight of him. Absently, she took Riordan's proffered hand, and he helped her back to her feet. Tired, but determined, she marched over to Ciaran.

"I told you to stay put," she snapped.

He straightened with a great deal of effort and ran his hands all over her body, needing the reassurance that none of the blood on her clothes belonged to her

"Satisfied?" she retorted, arching one eyebrow. "To bed with him, Taidhg," she ordered.

Taidhg took one arm, and Riordan grabbed the other. Ciaran knew that in his present state the two men outmatched him, but he vowed to get even with them when he had healed. The two half carried, half dragged him back to the pallet in the tent. Gently, they laid him down, and Becca knelt by his side. She swatted his hands away and pulled off the bandage to look at his injury.

"You've reopened the wound, Ciaran," she scolded. Reaching for her pack, she prepared another herb poultice. First, she daubed the blood away and checked to make sure that none of the sutures had pulled loose. Satisfied he hadn't done further damage, she applied the poultice and bandaged the wound again. "If you don't stay still, you'll never heal," she admonished. "And if you never heal..." The corner of her mouth quirked in a half-smile as her voice trailed off, leaving the implication open to interpretation.

He groaned, knowing full well what she meant.

Once she'd taken care of Ciaran, Becca checked the other three men. Niall had a slight cut on one arm, and Riordan a slightly deeper wound on a thigh. Like Becca, Taidhg came through the battle unscathed. Becca doctored Riordan and Niall, then moved to duck under the tent flap.

"Nay," Ciaran protested, his voice hoarse.

"I have to see to the others, Ciaran." Becca's voice was no-nonsense. "Your men fought bravely this day, and I'll not leave them to their wounds unaided." She turned on her heel and was gone before he could speak again.

Like a shadow, Taidhg drifted out after her. Reassured Taidhg would keep her safe, he turned back to Niall and Riordan. "So tell me," he demanded.

"I, too, need to check the men," Niall said. "Riordan, you tell him."

Riordan sank down on the blankets where Becca had slept scant hours before, thankful to take the weight off his thigh which burned and ached now.

"'Tis a right uncommon cailín you've found for yourself, cousin." He started at the beginning, from the time she'd bested him with Arien, including the story Eachan told him of the birth of the foal. He mentioned her accident in the woods and her gentle melancholy at the *Beltane* fire. "Methinks she missed you, cousin." Riordan smirked. Then he spoke of the night she'd awakened with pain in her side, insistent that Ciaran would die without her, and their fast journey to find the troop. "She fought like a demon today, Ciaran," Riordan added. "Half the pile outside your door belongs to her." Riordan flashed the injured man a cocky grin. "Not only is she a fighter, but have yee noticed how her *tóin* looks in a pair of trews? If you don't marry her, I will." Riordan barked a hearty laugh as Ciaran growled at him.

"No one shall touch her but me," Ciaran grumbled. "And if I'm not touching her soon, there'll be the devil to pay."

Riordan laughed harder, looking down at the blanket covering Ciaran's midsection. There was a definite lump there. "Aye, I'd say she's got you fair certain, cousin." He snickered, but he couldn't help but admire the big man lying beside him. Less than twelve hours ago, Ciaran had been closer to death than any of them wanted to admit. Now, his body made demands that a whole and healthy man would be proud of. Pushing to his feet, Riordan flashed his cousin a wicked grin. "I'll see if I can't send her back this way."

Outside the tent, the MacDermot men had been busy. They'd piled the O'Brien dead in the woods, and several soldiers dug a shallow grave. Once they vacated the area, some of the O'Brien would undoubtedly sneak back to claim their kinsmen. Only two of the MacDermot soldiers had died, and even now, several men readied their bodies for the long journey home. Both of these men had died bravely in battle. They would be buried on MacDermot ground.

Becca and a handful of others tended those more seriously injured. Like a faithful dog, Taidhg followed her around with a bucket of soapy water and an armful of rags. When Riordan got close, he noticed how drawn and tired Becca looked. Her pale face emphasized the dark circles smudging her eyes. She was all but asleep on her feet.

"Enough, cailín," he said, pulling her to her feet and taking the rags from her. "Yee need to look after yourself," he reminded. With a grin, he added, "Not to mention my cousin pines for your company."

She swayed on her feet and Riordan steadied her. "Becca, yee've slept a scant two hours between healing Ciaran, the battle, and healing the rest. Yee've done enough, cailín." He added softly, "He needs yee as yee need him. Go. I'll see to the rest." He gave her a little push toward the tent, and as she took an unsteady step, he realized she was about to fall flat on her face. With a swallowed curse, he scooped her up in his arms. "Aye, he'll have our hides for sure now, Taidhg."

Riordan carried her back to the tent, stooping low to bring her inside. He shook his head at Ciaran. "She's exhausted, Ciaran, that's all. Both of you need to sleep."

He laid her beside Ciaran who immediately wrapped his arms around her and pulled her head down on his shoulder. "I have need of you, Becca," Ciaran whispered in her hair.

"Wash your hands, Riordan," she ordered, her voice slurred. "Before you tend the wounded." With a contented sigh, Becca let go of consciousness and sank swiftly into a deep sleep.

****

"He lives," the female sounded awestruck.

"I told you to be patient." The male smirked.

"There is still the oath of binding," she reminded him, sounding prim.

"Humph, all in good time."

She waited until he was finally gone, and she bent over the sleeping couple, watching them closely. The man stirred as if sensing her presence. She smiled, whispering in his ear. His arms tightened protectively around the woman. She nodded. It was good.

****

Ciaran awoke slowly. Becca lay wrapped in his arms, and he kissed her hair. He needed to do something. He needed to say something to her, but like a will-o'-the-wisp, it danced just beyond his memory. Shrugging the need away, he kissed her awake as he'd longed to do since he'd first lain with her in his bed two months ago. Her mouth was just as sweet as he'd remembered.

Becca opened her eyes and stared into the stormy blue ones watching her intently. "We must be feeling better," she teased. What had the king called him? *The Wolf of the MacDermot.* That was certainly apropos. He looked like he was going to eat her alive.

Before she could say more, Ciaran's mouth covered hers, his tongue teasing her lips. Her hands tangled in his hair as her lips and tongue fought back. Her breasts strained against the soft linen of her shirt, desperate to break free so they could touch his bare chest. One of his big hands found a breast, and she pushed against his palm. He smiled as he teased her already hardening nipple into a rigid peak. Rolling her backward, his mouth broke away from hers. He grinned at her little moan of protest then his mouth covered a nipple through the linen of her shirt.

Becca gasped as his mouth teased and suckled her breast. *So this is what I've been missing,* a small part of her brain complained. Her hands remained wrapped in his soft hair, and she squirmed against his hipbone when another part of her body demanded equal attention. As his mouth worked on her breast, his now free hand traveled languidly down her ribs, across her hip and down between her legs. Becca moaned again and pushed against his hand.

Ciaran wished she wore a gown, for she'd have been free and open to him at that moment. While the trews she wore left little of her curves to the imagination, the leather created a formidable barrier between them. Despite the trews, his thumb still found the tiny nub guarding her womanly entrance, and he teased it. Becca clamped her legs around his hand. Ciaran groaned. Ah, to have those lovely legs wrapped around him as he pushed into her hot depths. He didn't think it possible, but he grew harder and thicker with the thought.

He rolled on top of her and groaned again, only this time from pain not passion. Becca immediately pushed him off and away. She sat up and checked the bandage on his hip. Despite the pain he was in, Ciaran grinned at her. Her lips were swollen, her skin flushed. A wet stain surrounded her still taut nipple, and its rosy bud was visible. He was the one who evoked that passion within her. He was the one who would one day soon make her his.

"You'll pull out the stitches," she chided as she pushed her hair out of her eyes.

"Stitches?" he asked. "An' what have yee done, cailín? Have yee sewn me up like a fine, linen shirt?"

"Something like that," Becca replied distractedly as her fingers tenderly checked his wound. "Ciaran, you almost died," she scolded, at last satisfied he had done no damage. "You still could. I won't take a chance with your life."

He grabbed her hand and placed it around his thick shaft. "What of my *boidín*?" he asked with a wicked grin. "His life is in danger as well."

For a long moment, Becca savored the feel of his erection—satin smoothness over steel, a hard ridge running up the underside and a flap of soft skin covering the tip. The muscles between her legs constricted, and she felt a gush of wet heat. She bent her head to taste him, her tongue caressing his swollen tip then swirling around the top of his shaft. His hips thrust helplessly at her, and she opened her lips to take him into her mouth.

Ciaran's hands fisted in her hair, and he dragged her head up. "Nay, cailín," he whispered, his voice husky with barely controlled lust. "Not until I can finish by burying myself deep within you." He pulled her up and kissed her hard, his tongue sweeping in and out of her mouth in a preview of what the rest of him would do to her once he healed.

"You could at least wait until you get the cailín home and in a proper bed before you go about tupping her," Riordan groused, poking his head through the tent flap. A sardonic grin spread across his face, and his eyes twinkled with droll humor.

Embarrassed, Becca rolled away and got to her feet. "Yeah, I, uh, I need to... I'll be back," she stammered. She ducked through the tent flap and sprinted for the woods like a banshee was hot on her trail. The three wolfhounds and Taidhg followed at a slightly more sedate pace.

Riordan chuckled, amused by Ciaran's state of arousal. Sobering a little, he reminded his cousin, "Siobhan says she's still a maiden, Ciaran. Do the cailín a favor and at least give her the vows and a proper bed the first time."

Vows. Something clicked in Ciaran's memory. An oath. There was an oath he was supposed to remember, one having to do with Becca. His mind worried the thought like a dog with an old bone, but he couldn't pin down the why of it. When he couldn't remember, he grinned at Riordan. "I'm not sure either of us will be able to wait that long, Riordan."

"So I noticed," Riordan shot back. "However, there are more pressing needs demanding attention. We should be moving out soon, Ciaran," he continued. "Conchobhar's men have routed the O'Brien, and the king has released us. The men are ready to get on the road, afraid that he will change his mind if we're still here when he comes back."

"Aye, and probably right they are," Ciaran agreed. Besides, he'd seen the look the king gave Becca. Though he'd blessed her betrothal to Ciaran, under the false pretense that she was kin to Niall, he could just as easily change his mind. "We ride," he announced.

Chapter Ten

The journey back to Caisel Ailfenn was a nightmare for Becca. The wounded required constant tending, and Ciaran was the worst of the lot. Each morning he insisted on riding, but by the end of the day, he was ashen and wracked with pain. Becca felt every ache and spasm all the way to her bones. Niall, Riordan, and Taidhg did their best to shield her from the worst of it, but with little effect. Becca called them her Three Musketeers.

On the third day, she decided to get the whole bloody lot rip-roaring drunk and keep them that way until they reached home. At breakfast, she liberally dosed Ciaran and the most severely wounded with whiskey. By noon, Ciaran couldn't sit his horse, so Riordan and Niall rigged a litter between two horses to carry him. He regaled them with bawdy songs until they stopped for the night, at which time, he promptly passed out for which Becca was eternally grateful.

By the fifth day, the troop settled into a routine, and Becca fervently prayed that the liquor supply, which was running woefully short, would hold out. Niall and Taidhg reassured her there were any number of places to resupply should the need arise. Riordan wore a constant grin, fully enjoying his *Taoiseac's* indisposition. He did realize, though, that Becca had hit on a brilliant plan where all the wounded were concerned, as the troop traveled much faster than anyone anticipated. He and Niall originally estimated the journey would take near a fortnight, when in reality, they were only two, maybe three days at most, away from Ailfenn.

When Ciaran finally sobered up, his hangover was going to be vicious. Riordan had every intention of being as far from the keep as his horse could take him before the effects of the whiskey wore off.

Niall sent riders ahead with news of the wounded, and as the company drew closer, small groups arrived claiming husbands and sons and fathers, taking them home to nurse them. Each departure lessened Becca's responsibility, and the tired lines around her mouth and eyes eased somewhat, though Ciaran's wounds and fever still plagued her.

On the road, Becca enjoyed a certain amount of autonomy. She'd proven herself to these battle-hardened men, and there wasn't a one who wouldn't follow her. She was lucky this pocket of Ireland had clung to the old ways longer than most, as women had been on a more equal footing in Celtic society. Becca was reluctant to return to the castle. She didn't want to give up the freedom of her trews and boots. She didn't want to lay down her sword to take up needle and yarn. She was a twenty-first century woman. Granted, the last half of her life had been sheltered by necessity, but the first half had been a glorious exploration of her abilities. This was Becca's chance to live the second half over again, and she wanted to live it to the fullest.

She'd be riding along simply seething with rebellious thoughts, and then she'd look at Ciaran. Even drunk, he tied her stomach in knots. She remembered far too vividly how he'd made her feel back in his tent the morning after the battle. The memory brought a blush to her cheeks and liquid pooling low between her legs. A long, hot bath was the first thing on her agenda once they got back. Then she was going to sleep for a week. When she finally woke up, if Ciaran's stitches had healed properly... She squirmed in her saddle. Well, she wasn't going there just yet, but she had a great deal of unfinished business with a certain part of his anatomy. No thieving O'Briens, or anyone else for that matter, would stop her.

She circled Arien around so she could ride beside Ciaran's litter. He snored softly. Becca smiled, reining in Arien and stepping off him. She jogged a few steps to catch up to the litter and walked along side, leading Arien by his reins. Her hand stroked Ciaran's cheek, and the touch elicited a smile. Her hand found his and slipped into his big paw. She missed the looks her Three Musketeers exchanged as she walked for most of an hour by his side.

"If he doesn't tup her soon, the whole castle will be goin' up in flames," Riordan complained, shifting in his saddle to find a more comfortable position.

Niall chuckled. "Gonna' find a willing cailín when we get back, are yee?"

"Aye, or two or three. Niall, I'm tellin' yee, 'tis unnatural. Yee dinnit see him back in the tent. Him half dead yet as big as a horse, and her all hot and bothered."

"I did see it," Niall remarked dryly. "At least it's mutual."

"Oh, aye, 'tis mutual. Neither can keep their hands off t'other," Riordan groused.

When they stopped for the night, Becca recognized the place. They were only a hard day's ride from home.

"Day and a half at most, mistress," Taidhg confirmed.

Thank goodness for small favors. She'd only thought she was in riding shape, but after almost three continuous weeks in the saddle, she was ready to sit on something soft. She glanced at Ciaran. *Nothing soft about him, but I can't wait to sit there,* she silently amended. Niall and Riordan glanced at her, almost as if they'd read her thoughts. She blushed furiously, blood suffusing her cheeks. The two men had the good graces to look away before grins split their faces.

When it came time to settle down for sleep, just to prove them wrong, Becca chose to bed down away from Ciaran. She'd fed him and then dosed him with whiskey again before checking his bandage. Snoring, he rolled over as she gathered up her blankets and moved away. Even though Winken and Blinken snuggled her front and back, she was restless. She tossed and turned until well after midnight. Across the dwindling embers of the fire, Ciaran was having a bad night as well.

Becca gave up. She was too tired to fight the need any longer. Her body craved his, to be near him, to touch him. This was a need deeper even than the sexual desire he aroused in her. Her soul yearned for his. Her heart ached for his. Her longing was as elemental as life itself.

"Oh, bloody hell."

Gathering up her blanket and mantle, she trudged over to him. The dogs happily joined Bhruic as she checked Ciaran's forehead. He was running a fever again as he had intermittently during the trip. She was out of Siobhan's fever powder, and she hoped his symptoms didn't worsen before they got to Ailfenn. Ciaran stirred, his head tossing back and forth across the blanket stuffed behind his head. Becca spread her blanket next to him. Part of her still rebelled at her need for him so she laid down with her back to him. As she fell asleep, her hand brushed his arm. The simple contact was enough. As they slept, she turned to him, and his hand found hers. His strong fingers interlaced with hers. Becca sighed in her sleep, content and at peace. Ciaran's restlessness ceased, his soul finding solace in her nearness.

So close to home, Niall had posted only a light sentry. Unfortunately, the man was as worn out as the rest, and he fell asleep at his post. In the trees, two figures flitted between shadows.

"Told ya 'twas a woman," the larger of the two whispered.

"But she wears trews," the other denied.

"'Tis not a true man alive with curves the likes of that," the first insisted.

"The MacDermot lies injured," the second hissed, changing the subject. "And many of his men have fared the worse for their adventure. Mayhaps we need to visit his land soon and see what strays our way."

"Aye," the first agreed.

Bhruic stirred, lifting his head to sniff the air. Catching an unfamiliar scent, he got up to investigate, Blinken hard on his heels. As the dogs stalked around the camp, the two men beat a hasty retreat. The dogs prowled the perimeter for a few minutes. Satisfied the intruders had gone, they returned to nestle beside Ciaran and Becca.

Ciaran awoke with Becca beside him on his left. *Close to my heart,* he thought. He rolled over, ever mindful of his wound, and wrapped her in his arms. He pulled her back against him so they could spoon, his front to her back. Not surprisingly, he grew hard and his shaft burrowed into the soft curves of her *tóin.* Even in her sleep, Becca's body recognized his need for her, and she pushed back against him. Ciaran smiled and kissed her golden hair.

He had been extraordinarily blessed by the gods. This woman who appeared from nowhere, who haunted his dreams and hardened his body while softening his heart, was a gift. She was brave beyond all meaning of the word. His men now adored her and would follow her as they followed him. She was tender and knowing of the healing arts, yet she killed without hesitation to protect her own. Ciaran's right hand trailed over her waist and lay against the gentle swell of her belly. He couldn't wait to feel his child growing within her womb. Ah, what children they would make together. The lads would be strong and brave, and the cailíns? They'd be so fair every man would want them, but no man would be good enough. Ciaran chuckled. From what he was learning about Becca, the girls would likely be as strong and brave as the boys, and they themselves would decide if a man was good enough.

Ciaran was anxious to get home and in a hurry to heal. Though parts of his body were more than willing, other parts were not yet able. When the time came to claim Becca as his own, he wanted to be at full strength. Ciaran knew she'd been keeping him drunk, and Niall finally confessed why. Just as he'd felt every pain from her strange illness, she'd felt every pang of his wound and ache from his fevers. He marveled again at her strength.

As he drifted back to sleep, a thought nudged at the back of his subconscious. Words danced enticingly just beyond his memory. Important words; words he needed to say but didn't know why. *By the life that courses in your blood*, the wind whispered in his ear. *And the love that resides within your heart.*

Warmth spread out across her middle and Becca smiled. Ciaran's hand splayed across her stomach, warm and gentle. Her breath slowed to match the rhythm of his, and she'd almost swear that their heartbeats were synchronized. A breath of wind kissed her cheek, and words whispered in her ear. *Our love is a beginning with no end, until the end of time.* "I love you, too," she murmured.

Early the next morning, Niall and Riordan decided to push hard for Ailfenn. All the men were eager to return home. The wounded gritted their teeth and pressed on without break except when the horses needed rest. Ciaran rode in the litter without argument. The column traveled faster because of it. Becca rode close to his sling all morning, keeping a watchful eye on him. Taidhg rode nearby, keeping a vigilant eye on both.

Niall and Riordan rode up and down the line and made frequent detours into the surrounding area. The hair on the backs of both of their necks was prickling. The more seasoned among the soldiers remained alert. Someone watched, though no one spotted anyone spying on the column.

At noon, they stopped for a brief respite. They built no fire and paused only long enough to chew a quick bite and rest the horses. As the afternoon wore on, Riordan chose to ride next to Ciaran and Becca. The hair on his neck still bristled, and he would take no chances with the life of his cousin or Becca. The MacDermot was a man feared and resented by many of his neighbors. The land around Ailfenn was rich with fat sheep and cattle, it's harvests bountiful. The keep was large and well maintained, a most desirable prize for any raiders. Ciaran was a favorite of Conchobhar, and that, too, led to antipathy from lesser sept and clann chiefs.

Niall and Riordan were positive rumors of the MacDermot's injury had swept the countryside. They worried someone would try to finish the job the O'Briens had started or take advantage of Ciaran's incapacity in other ways. That Becca traveled with them made them doubly on edge.

They traveled along the edge of O'Flinn territory, and the O'Flinns had been notably absent from the defensive maneuvers in the south. Garbhan O'Flinn had two strapping sons, Darroch and Luthais, and a troop of both horse and foot soldiers. Ten years ago, the O'Flinn had offered his daughter to the MacDermot. Ciaran politely turned him down, stating the girl was barely fifteen, and when the time came for him to marry, he wanted to be a husband, not a father, to his bride. Since then, communication and trade remained strained between the two clanns.

Niall briefly wondered what had become of the daughter. He couldn't recall her name and only remembered she'd been a scrawny little thing, completely cowed by her father and brothers. Her mother died when the child was barely four, and Garbhan never remarried. The little cailín alone in the keep with that rough-and-tumble lot would not have had an easy life. Niall now hoped that O'Flinn had found another to marry the girl, and that her life had been tolerable thereafter.

Late in the afternoon, the column passed from O'Flinn country, and everyone sighed in relief. The oppressive sense of being watched waned, and the outriders relaxed a little. Just before sundown, they halted again. Like lunch, supper was cold. The men planned to stay only long enough to give the horses a breather. The road from here was well marked, and they'd be able to make Ailfenn before midnight.

Becca dutifully checked all of her patients. Despite the hard ride, most of them fared well. She avoided the two horses that brought up the end of the column. She couldn't look at their burdens without tears. Riordan sat down beside her and cocked his head.

"Why such a woeful face, cailín?" he teased. A glib retort about his cousin's constant state of arousal died as something in her expression stayed his tongue. He waited for her reply.

Becca inclined her head toward the two horses carrying their grisly cargo. "Did they have families?"

This was the last subject Riordan expected to be discussing with her. She never ceased to amaze him. What a lucky man Ciaran was. "Nay, Becca," he replied. "Manus was near sixty, and his wife died years ago. Padruig was not much more than a lad."

"Then he has a mother who weeps for him?" she asked, unwilling to let it go.

Riordan shook his head. "An orphan."

"Then I'll weep for him when the time comes."

Niall and Taidhg helped Ciaran to the fire. He sank to the grass beside Becca, concerned with the melancholy face she wore.

"What troubles you, dearest heart?" he asked before Riordan could warn him.

Becca turned tear-filled eyes to him. "Why do men have to be so stupid?" A little sob not much more than a hiccup escaped.

Riordan figured Ciaran's infamous temper was about to take away his good sense. He grimaced when Becca beat his cousin to the punch.

"Cows. This whole bloody war was over a couple of cows," she raged.

"Well, 'twas more than a couple, cailín." Ciaran spoke before Niall's warning cough cut him off.

"You don't get an old man and a boy killed over cows." Her blue eyes flashed angrily, and she balled up her fists. "The whole bloody countryside is covered with the fat buggers. You'd think there'd be enough to go around. But, no. Some idiot of a man decides he has to steal a handful. And some other idiot decides he has to retaliate. So all the idiot men go fight a war over nothing but leather and meat."

"Cailín, 'tisn't right to be calling the king an idiot." Ciaran's tone remained reasonable. "And there was more to it than the cows."

"Oh, yeah," Becca spat. "I can just imagine. I'm sure the king's honor was royally impugned because an O'Brien was presumptuous enough to steal O'Conor cows."

Ciaran's nose flared, and his lips clamped into a grim line. Honor was a very sensitive subject with him, because he valued it beyond all else. In fact, the clann's motto was *Honor and Virtue*. His father had been without honor. As a result, Ciaran vowed his honor would always come first.

Riordan and Niall surrendered and wisely backed away. Becca's tears dried. Red-faced, Ciaran clinched his fists so tight his knuckles turned white. Discretion being the better part of valor, the two men turned, but didn't quite run.

"To impugn the O'Conor's honor is to impugn mine." The words came out in a growl all the more menacing for being quiet. Ciaran's eyes glinted like winter ice.

"And to bury boys and old men over cows is a pointless exercise in male egotism." Becca's eyes narrowed, fire flashing in their blue depths.

Ciaran's stormy indigo eyes stared into Becca's fiery cerulean ones. Even though he was fuming, he noticed her eyes were the exact color of the stone in the center of the MacDermot Knot she wore on her mantle. A voice stirred to life in his head, a soft, whispery voice that sighed like a dying breeze. He didn't remember giving Becca the Knot, though it felt right that he had. She was still furious, and he suddenly saw the situation from her point of view. Despite the fact she'd killed more than her share of O'Briens, she'd done so to protect him and his, not for honor or glory. Women lived with the results of war—death, injury, hunger. Women buried the dead, nursed the wounded, and managed to feed their families when food was not to be found. Of course they would view war through different eyes. To men, it was all about honor. And glory. It was about victory, and in some cases, defeat.

Rather than retorting something that would further antagonize her, Ciaran reached over to caress her cheek. As his palm cupped her jaw, Becca tilted her head so that her cheek rested against his fingers. Her eyes closed, and when they opened, their color had gone soft with gentle golden swirls dancing in their azure depths. Ciaran bent his head to kiss her, and she leaned into him.

"Ah, love of my heart," he sighed. "May there always be such heat and passion between us."

His lips nibbled her full bottom lip, teasing and pulling. Then his mouth moved down to her chin, and his lips and tongue traced the curve of her jaw line until it met her ear. Ciaran smiled when he tasted the silky skin where her jaw met her throat. The spot was as soft and smooth as he'd thought it would be that long ago day when he'd looked up as she stood at the top of the stairs.

Ciaran's arms stole around her, and he felt her relax into his embrace. His heart was so full he thought it might explode. He'd never felt so protective of or so tender about any living thing. Just when he was at his mushiest, she took the upper hand. Ciaran burst out laughing when she muttered into his hair, "It was still stupid to fight over a bunch of bloody cows."

Ah, he feared his Becca would always demand the last word. And, as Ciaran thought about it, he wasn't sure he'd have it any other way.

Chapter Eleven

Becca guessed they were still a mile away from the castle when Ciaran called a halt and insisted he'd ride the rest of the way. She clucked over what she considered to be one more example of masculine pig-headedness, along with an unhealthy dose of superfluous male egotism. Her anger seethed at the unnecessary deaths and injuries to the men of the troop and bubbled just below the surface since they'd mounted up after the dinner break. She wasn't mad at Ciaran or the men of Ailfenn in particular, just men in general.

She rode quietly in the middle of the column, her back ramrod straight. Taidhg watched her for a long moment before nudging his horse closer to hers. He would brave her tongue. "He is *An Taoiseac.*" At his quiet reminder, she opened her mouth but he held up a hand to silence her retort. "He does what he must, mistress, not what he wants. He must put the needs and wants of his people above his own." They rode knee to knee for a short space before Taidhg continued. "He is a good man, mistress, and one who will love and protect you above all others, but he is *An Taoiseac,* and with that title come many duties a lesser man would find burdensome."

"It's not fair, Taidhg," Becca hissed. She kept her voice low.

Before Taidhg could reprimand her, the moon came out from behind a cloud. Tears glistened in her eyes, and a look of such compassion suffused her face. He thought his own heart might break. He'd misjudged the cailín, and not for the first time. Nor for the last, he suspected. She was turning out to be more than a fair match for the MacDermot.

As they neared the first crofters' huts, a river of torches flowed out to meet them. Becca rode in the middle of the column with some of the wounded. Ciaran was at the head, flanked on his right by Niall and on his left by Riordan. All three men rode tall and straight in their saddles. Becca knew how grueling this journey had been, and the sight of their proud bearing gave her pause. She'd picked the fight with Ciaran earlier because she was tired, frustrated, and just plain out of sorts. Her abdomen cramped and ached with each step Arien took, and she blamed it on Ciaran's wound. The men looked regal as they led the troop home to Ailfenn.

The column pushed its way through the growing crowd and entered the gate to the keep itself. Men came to lead the wounded soldiers' horses to the barracks where the injured were taken inside. Stableboys collected the horses and took them to the stables for a rubdown, water, and grain. People crowded around the rest, cheering and treating them like returning heroes.

Becca turned Arien toward the stable and wasn't too surprised when Eachan himself appeared. The big horse master lifted her to the ground. "I'll take care of the beastie, m'self," he told her. "Git along with yee, cailín. Yer fair worn out and all but asleep as yee stand here. Off to bed with yee."

Too tired to protest, Eachan's order made perfect sense. Becca skirted the main part of the crowd and stumbled inside to the great hall. Now that she was home, a great weariness settled on her. She no longer cared even about a hot bath. She wanted only to find a soft bed, throw herself onto it, and sleep for that week she'd promised herself. All but asleep on her feet, she wearily navigated the stairs and hallway to the chamber she shared with

Ciaran. She'd inhabited the room alone for so long, and she was so tired, she'd even forgotten it was his.

Alone in the chamber, Becca kicked off her boots and stripped out of her trews. The insides of her thighs felt raw from days in the saddle. Then she got a whiff of her shirt and peeled it off. Stumbling to the wardrobe, she pulled out one of Ciaran's shirts and slipped it over her head. The soft garment covered all the pertinent parts and, as she knew from previous experience, fit quite nicely to sleep in. She didn't even bother blowing out the candle. She just crawled beneath the covers and was sound asleep as her head touched the pillow.

****

After greeting Niall, Siobhan stopped by the barracks to check on the wounded. Becca had nursed them well. Knowing there'd be a celebration, she settled the injured solders as quickly as possible. She'd just finished checking the last man when Niall reappeared and asked her to look at Ciaran's wound.

"Where's Becca?" Siobhan asked her mate. "I thought she'd be looking after him."

Niall shrugged. "We rode in the lead, and she stayed back with the wounded. I thought to find her here, but found you instead. She's not with Ciaran."

Siobhan's brow furrowed even as her eyes widened in alarm. "Where is Taidhg? Or Riordan? Mayhaps they know where she is."

They hurried back to the castle where they found both Taidhg and Riordan, but when asked, neither had any idea of Becca's location. Ciaran sat at the head of the table as mugs of ale were passed around, but his gaze restlessly combed the room as if he looked for her, too. When Eachan came in from the stables, Siobhan questioned him, and he mentioned he'd sent Becca to bed.

Just to make sure, Siobhan slipped up the stairs to check. She found Becca sleeping peacefully in

Ciaran's bed, right where she belonged. Smiling, the older woman pulled the door shut. It was after midnight, and the whole castle needed to be abed.

Skipping down the stairs, she found Niall and told him Becca was upstairs asleep, and that's where they should be as well. She tossed a saucy grin over her shoulder as she sashayed away from him, the invitation unmistakable in the sway of her hips.

Niall yawned loudly, announcing to Ciaran he was done in and going to bed.

Grateful to his second-in-command for breaking up the celebration, Ciaran stood slowly. He'd never felt so tired in all his life. He glanced around, unable to find Riordan. He suspected his cousin had already slipped off with a willing cailín. As the other men drifted out with their wives and sweethearts, Niall waited for him at the base of the stone steps. Before he could ask, the man smiled at him.

"She's upstairs asleep, Ciaran." Niall explained as they climbed the stairs together. "Eachan took Arien from her and sent her on to bed."

Ciaran nodded, almost too tired to speak. Niall left him at his room. Ciaran pushed through the door, sighing at the vision greeting him. Becca's hair was strewn across the pillows like a golden web. Silver lights danced in its strands as the candles flared in the draft from the open door. He grew hard and heavy with wanting her, but he was too tired, and his body too sore to do anything about it. Quietly, he stripped out of his clothes. Pulling back the bedcovers, he stared at her, charmed that she'd donned one of his shirts to sleep in. Then he saw the pool of bright red blood beneath her hips.

"Siobhan!" Ciaran's panicked voice rang through the castle. "Siobhan, come now!"

Niall and Siobhan leaped out of bed. She quickly pulled a shift over her head and grabbed a mantle to toss around her shoulders. Niall pulled on a pair of trews and nothing else. They charged toward Ciaran's room.

Ciaran sat on the edge of the bed cradling Becca on his lap, crooning nonsense words to her as he rocked back and forth. The poor girl looked completely done in, but vainly tried to wake up enough to comfort Ciaran.

Siobhan noticed the bloodstain on the sheets and on the hem of the shirt Becca wore. "'Tis your time of the moon." Her voice was calm and matter-of-fact.

Becca blinked owlishly for a minute before figuring out what Siobhan meant. Her eyes widened. "My period? I haven't had one in over ten years, Siobhan." Too late, she noticed Siobhan's cocked eyebrow and realized what she'd said. "Oh, my god, I am so embarrassed." Becca groaned. This was worse than the nightmare every teenage girl had. The one where she wore white pants on a first date with the hottest boy in school, only to have her period arrive and ruin the whole evening.

Ciaran had the good graces to look slightly embarrassed as well. "'Tis so much blood," he muttered. "I dinnit know a cailín could lose so much."

Becca groaned again, partly in mortification, partly in pain. No wonder she'd had cramps for the last two days. Well, tampons were definitely out of the question, which led her to the next one, and it was one she didn't want to ask in front of the men.

"Niall, off to bed with yee," Siobhan ordered. "I'll be along shortly to warm yer feet. *Taoiseac*, the cailín isn't dyin' so let her be and go find something to do with yerself for a few minutes while we tidy up in here."

Reluctantly, Ciaran set Becca on her feet and stood. "Are you sure you're all right?"

Becca's cheeks burned. "Ciaran, puh-lease." The

look she gave him pleaded for privacy.

Ciaran shuffled out of the room, dragging his feet the entire way. Siobhan shut the door behind him, and Becca turned to her, panicked.

"What do I do, Siobhan?" She gulped. "Let me rephrase that. I know what to do, at least in my time. I just don't know what women *here* do when their time of the month comes. And while we're on the subject, what about underwear?"

"Underwear?" Siobhan tried out the unfamiliar word.

"Yeah, you know. Panties. Pantaloons. Knickers. Things you wear here..." She gestured at her midsection. "...that cover your front and rear and keep a cold breeze from blowing up your skirt?"

"Ah, I think I understand. The first problem I can take care of. The second thing you describe... I'll have one of the seamstresses come up tomorrow, and you can describe such a thing to her. If it is important to you, she will make you some... What did you call them?"

"Oh never mind. Let's just deal with the problem at hand."

Siobhan slipped out of the room and came back a few minutes later with a bundle she opened up on the bed. Inside was a piece of material that looked suspiciously like a thong and a stack of things that looked a lot like feminine napkins, made from rolled-up rags. Becca figured they weren't disposable, but at the moment, she didn't care. The older woman helped her into the thong contraption and then into a clean shift. Together they stripped the bed. A sleepy maid appeared with fresh coverings and retrieved the soiled ones, along with the dirty clothes strewn about the room. They'd just finished with the bed when someone softly tapped on the door.

"Can I come in, cailín?" Ciaran's voice beseeched.

Becca was still mortified by the situation, but Siobhan didn't give her time to dwell on it.

"Aye, *Taoiseac*, yee can come in," the older woman called. "I'll send up a warm stone if your tummy still hurts," she told Becca.

Becca shook her head, staring at her toes. The door creaked, and the latch dropped into place. She and Ciaran were alone.

He put his finger under her chin and tilted her head up so she would have to look at him. "'Tis all right, cailín. I've not been around womanly things much, and it took me by surprise."

Becca started to giggle. She hadn't been around womanly things much, either, and it had more than taken her by surprise. There were *some* advantages to being old, she decided. Her giggles threatened to become hysterical, and Ciaran's temper flared. How could she explain that she wasn't laughing *at* him but *with* him, especially since he wasn't laughing? The combination of being punch-drunk tired, and the shock of the last two months, finally caught up to her. A huge yawn choked off her giggles. She gazed up at him through drooping lids as her arms crept around his neck. She snuggled her check into the hollow where his chest met his shoulder. "I just want to sleep for a week, Ciaran," she murmured. "Is that okay?"

Without waiting for his reply, she turned away from him to climb into bed. Before she could, Ciaran scooped her into his arms and carried her. He laid her down gently and then crawled in beside her.

"If I can have you in my arms for the whole time, I, too, would like to sleep a week," he murmured into her hair. "Though I must say, I much prefer you in one of my shirts if you have to wear anything at all." He kissed her gently, almost reverently, and spooned up to her back. Her head rested on one of his thick biceps, and his other arm encircled her waist. "Good night, love of my heart."

Becca sighed as his comforting warmth surrounded her. *Love of my heart.* Twice he'd called her that. She could get used to hearing him say those words every night. She thought she'd answered him with "I love you, too," but she was so tired, she wasn't sure the words came out.

The sun climbed to midday before she stirred. Ciaran still slept heavily, so she carefully disentangled herself and made her way to the garderobe. She was tempted to throw everything down one of the holes but found a covered bucket in one corner filled with cold water. *Convenient,* Becca decided.

Becca returned to Ciaran's chamber, but no guard curled on a pallet beside the door. With the lord of the manor sleeping in her room she supposed a bodyguard was no longer necessary. As much as she had chafed under his stewardship, she would miss Taidhg.

Ciaran still slept as she slipped back into the room. Had he been awake she could summon Siobhan for a bath. Becca really wanted a bath. She also really wanted food—real food, served on a trencher at a table, not a bite of journey cake and dried meat eaten in the saddle or huddled around a small fire. Jerky was fine as a snack but not to live on for any length of time, and she'd been living on it for way too long.

The castle hummed with life. Even through the thick walls, she was attuned to its rhythm. Food was being served in the great hall, folks went about their daily chores, and life returned to normal now the troops were home. *Home.* Becca's thoughts lingered on that word. She felt like she'd come home. This *when* still felt strange, like wearing someone else's clothes. There were times when she reacted as if she were fifty, but her heart and her soul found the peace and happiness she'd never had before. She shied away from the bad memories of this *when*—of Ciaran lying mortally wounded, of fighting back-to-back with Taidhg, of the long ride home. Instead, she gazed at the man sleeping in the bed that still showed the outline of her own body.

What a magnificent man he is. Tall, broad-shouldered, strong. Becca could run her finger over the hills and valleys of his chest and abdomen and count every muscle group. Indigo highlights danced in his jet-black hair when the sun got caught in its ebony web. His stormy blue eyes, often turbulent like the North Sea, turned soft and gentle like the high mountain lake at her grandfather's ranch in Colorado when he looked at her. He did have a temper, but Becca decided there was a bit of fun to be had in provoking it. The only reason to fight was to have an excuse to make up. Making up with him would be delicious.

Ciaran was lying on his back, and Becca decided to take the opportunity to check his wound. Someone, most likely Siobhan, had cleaned and bandaged it when the troop arrived last night. Becca had been too worn out, and then with the arrival of that *womanly thing...* She blushed from head to toe just thinking about the scene last night. Now, she wanted to see for herself how Ciaran fared.

Carefully, she pulled back the covers, no longer surprised to find him naked beneath them. The poultice Siobhan had applied the night before was now askew so Becca peeled it off, carefully avoiding all contact with or looking at his manhood. Ciaran stirred, and Becca held her breath. He settled down and started snoring, a soft buzz saw of a sound. Becca suspected all the alcohol she'd poured into his system over the last week had finally caught up to him.

The wound was healing from the inside out, as it

should. It was no longer draining, and the angry, puckered skin around it looked pink and healthy. Siobhan had left an array of tins and boxes on the table by the hearth along with some bandages. Becca dug around for what she needed and applied a new poultice and bandage to Ciaran's side.

Finished, she just stood there staring at him. He was undoubtedly the most beautiful male specimen she had ever encountered in her entire lifetime. *Times,* she amended. *Lifetimes.* Her stomach knotted up, and she cursed the fact it was her time of the month. Even though she could stand there gaping at his magnificent maleness, she was still incredibly shy about her own femaleness.

"Dinnit anyone ever tell yee, cailín, 'tis rude to stare?" he growled at her, his eyes still closed.

"You're supposed to be asleep," she scolded.

"You're the one who said she wanted to sleep for a week," he reminded, quirking one brow and the corner of his mouth. "I only agreed if yee would stay in my arms for that length of time." He shrugged and made of cradle of his arms. "Since yer no longer in my arms..." His voice trailed off, and he grinned up at her impudently.

"Female prerogative," Becca replied. She lifted her chin as her mouth formed a moue like she'd bitten into a tart berry. "I changed my mind, and I've decided I want a bath."

Ciaran's suggestive gaze swept her from head to toe, and Becca felt her blush to the very roots of her hair.

"Aye, I could do with a bath myself," he suggested with a wicked grin.

"I am not going to bathe with you," Becca asserted. *At least not until my period is gone.*

"Yee need to get over this inordinate shyness yee have, cailín. I've seen yer body," he drawled. "All of it. And 'tis something to be proud of." He grinned lasciviously and added, "Especially since I'm the only man who will ever be seeing it."

Becca's face grew hot again. "It's not that," she stammered. "It's that *womanly* thing." *Ha, so there!* She gloated when his cheeks turned red. She had him there.

Ciaran shuddered, remembering the shock of finding her lying in so much blood last night. From the age of six, he'd been raised in the barracks with Niall and the soldiers. He knew absolutely nothing about female things and decided he didn't really want to learn. He'd grown hard under her scrutiny and though she now studiously avoided looking at his midsection, he suspected that part of his anatomy fascinated her. He remembered all too well the feel of her lips on him back at the encampment.

His body raged at him, demanding he take her right then, but his brain wondered if there was some sort of taboo or ban about making love when a woman...well, had her womanly thing. He watched her face looking for a hint of her feelings. She wanted him, he was certain, but her shyness about her body kept her from fully realizing her need for him. He could live with that, at least until this *thing* went away. He wanted to love Becca, love her truly and fully, wanted to bring her every pleasure he'd learned, and some he might even invent. Her bashfulness prevented her from fully participating with both mind and body. His own healing body would keep him from being a full participant. Aye, he could wait. He'd waited thirty years for her. What would another week mean?

Chapter Twelve

Ciaran waited for the tub and hot water to arrive. He balked as the women shooed him out. He exhaled, an exaggerated sigh so deep, his chest rose and fell. He plastered a look akin to a kicked puppy on his face in an attempt to look pitiful. Even though she wouldn't allow him in the tub with her, she could have at least let him stay and watch. Becca had the audacity to laugh at the suggestion, so he went in search of Niall and Riordan, hoping they would commiserate with him.

Both men were at the table in the great hall and in fine fettle. Niall politely inquired after Becca, with no mention of the night's escapade. Riordan was smart enough to follow the older man's lead. He, too, had heard his cousin bellowing in the night, but wisely made discreet inquiry before putting his boot squarely in his mouth. Riordan had enjoyed the company of a comely cailín last night, so he felt a great deal of sympathy for Ciaran.

A trencher of food appeared in front of Ciaran, and he took several bites before broaching a subject that had nagged at him the whole way back from southern Connaught.

"Your brother died without issue," he told Niall without preamble.

Niall ducked his head. Ciaran had overheard the entire confrontation with King Conchobhar. "'Twas the first thing that came into my head," he dissembled. Like Ciaran, he'd been concerned when no one looked for the cailín. If she were truly without clann or sept, Niall would happily adopt her.

"What happens if someone claims her?" Ciaran kept his voice low so no one but Niall and Riordan could hear him.

"We'll deal with it if it happens," Riordan interjected, supremely confident the MacDermots could handle whatever arose.

Ciaran glared at Niall. "Yee put yourself in danger with that claim." The words came out as a low growl.

Niall shrugged. He wasn't worried. "She belongs to Clann MacDermot. All of us. There isn't a man here who won't fight to keep her."

"I will not lose yee," Ciaran promised.

"And yee shall not lose her," Niall swore.

Outside, thunder boomed and the skies opened up. Riordan shivered, hoping the gods weren't sending a message. He'd just about come to the same conclusion as Ciaran—that Becca had been a gift from the faerie, and she could be snatched back just as quickly as she'd come.

The week dragged, raining every day, and keeping all close to the castle. Each night, Becca slept in Ciaran's arms, and each morning he kissed her awake. Each day, she prayed the "curse" would be gone, and she could come to Ciaran to discover all the passion he promised her with his gentle hands and lips. She grew accustomed to seeing his hard body, and familiarity did not breed contempt, only a healthy dose of lust. She chafed at the inactivity forced on her by the weather.

The sun finally broke through the brooding clouds a week later. Ciaran and Riordan left early that morning headed to one of the outlying crofts. A dispute had arisen between the crofter and the tanner, and as clann chief, it was up the Ciaran to sort it out.

Becca put on a plain dress and tugged on a pair of trews underneath. She was not going to waste a moment of the sunshine. She'd been stain-free that morning and couldn't wait for Ciaran's return. Rather than fret all day, she decided to give Arien some exercise. For some reason, Winken and Blinken had chosen to accompany Ciaran, and Bhruic was the dog waiting for her in the great hall. Patting the big animal's head, she skipped out into the sunshine.

Eachan was nowhere to be found, so she saddled Arien herself and led him out into the courtyard. Bhruic barked, his tongue lolling from the side of his mouth in a happy pant. She stepped into the stirrup, swung her leg over, and settled into the saddle. A stable boy appeared, and Becca called to him. "Tell your master I'm giving Arien a run. I'll be back before the nooning."

The boy ducked his chin in acknowledgement and hurried on about his assigned chores. Becca turned Arien's head toward the gate and nudged him with her heels. The guard at the entry saluted her but didn't ask where she was going. Arien trotted down the road with Bhruic happily loping along beside him.

****

Two brawny men hunkered down, trying to look small as they watched a herd of fat cattle grazing in the meadow.

"Aye, ripe they are for the taking," the younger said. Short but broad, they bore more than a passing resemblance to each other.

"And the MacDermot laid up with a wound from fighting the O'Conor's battles," the older one chuckled, his laughter an evil cackle. He licked his lips in anticipation. "Them cows out here all alone and in need of protection from thieves." He snickered. "Why, we'd be doing him a favor to nick them back to Ballinfaire where we can look after 'em right proper." He stood, thinking to round up the cows.

One of the cows lifted its head and looked off into the distance. Following the cow's gaze, the man swore and dropped back to his belly. "A rider comes," he hissed, "with a hound."

"We're goners for sure," the younger spat. "Can yee tell who it is?"

The older shook his head and crawled toward the scant protection the nearby woods might afford. Once they were under some semblance of cover, they watched the rider. They'd stayed downwind of the herd, and hoped the dog would also stay upwind of them where it couldn't catch their scent.

"Bloody hell," the oldest swore. "'Tis a woman." He scanned the area and then grinned lasciviously. "And a woman alone to boot."

"Wait," the younger cautioned, taking a good look at the rider. "By the gods, Darroch, 'tis Becca."

"Can't be," the older one growled at his brother. "She's dead, Luthais."

"Well, 'tis her for certain, and ridin' one of the MacDermot's best horses as bold as brass," Luthais asserted. The two exchanged worried looks. This was a wrinkle they didn't need and definitely didn't want.

Becca's excellent sense of direction led directly to the long meadow where she'd met near disaster before. Today, she wouldn't veer off onto that woodland path. She grinned. *At least not at a gallop.* She knew full well she would explore the path eventually. The lush meadow spread in front of her, and fat cows grazed chewing their cud, the quiet occasionally interrupted by their lowing moos. Becca urged Arien into a slow canter, meaning to circle around the cows without alarming them.

Today was a day to be savored, to stretch it out and enjoy. She didn't want to rush through it, even though tonight would be glorious. She guided Arien toward the path. She wanted to explore, albeit at a sedate pace, where it led.

Bhruic's ears pricked. Sensing prey, he took off. Becca reined up just before the trees, watching the wolfhound run with his nose to the ground. The dog flushed a rabbit, and for a moment, it looked like the rabbit might escape. Becca laughed, hoping the hare made it to safety.

The next thing she knew, rough hands grabbed her and yanked her off her horse. A dirty, calloused hand clamped over her mouth.

"Doncha' be screamin' now, Becca," the brute breathed into her ear.

Becca's first instinct was to struggle, but she was so shocked when the man called her by name, she lost her chance to fight. The man tightened his grip, turning her to face a second man. Becca didn't recognize him and doubted either of them belonged to Ailfenn. If they owed fealty to Ciaran, they would not have put their hands on her.

"Well, aren't yee glad to see us?" the man in front of her sneered. He held Arien's reins.

"Who are you?" Becca demanded, her voice muffled by the first man's hand. She hoped her voice still managed to sound as cold and haughty as she'd meant it to. "The MacDermot will hang you if any harm comes to me," she spat around the huge paw, wrinkling her nose at the smell emanating from it.

The two men snickered. "And risk a blood feud over a bit o' fluff like yee? I think not, Becca."

"Who are you?" she demanded again, her brain working in overdrive. Could these be O'Brien men come to exact revenge?

The man in front of her exchanged a dismayed glance with the man holding her. "Why, we're yer own dear brothers, sister." The man holding her snorted, the gruff bark of sound erupting through his nose. "Don't you recognize us?"

"But I don't have any bro..." Becca choked off her retort. *She* didn't have any brothers, but the Becca in this lifetime might have. She mentally kicked herself. Everyone had warned her about taking off by herself. Oh, but there would be hell to pay now. She forced air into her lungs, taking a deep breath to calm down. Though she couldn't see the one who held her, the one facing her looked like a toad. If he was as dumb as he looked, she might have a chance.

"If you take me back to Ailfenn, there will be a reward," she promised sweetly.

The one holding her tightened his grip around her waist. "Bah, we take yee back, yee'll have us hung. We aren't stupid, sister."

The man holding her flung Becca to the ground as a tornado of teeth and fur attacked him. Bhruic! She'd completely forgotten the wolfhound. His lightning-quick attack was vicious. Arien did his part by rearing and jerking against the reins. The second man could hang on to the horse or help his brother. He hung on to the reins for dear life. Bhruic yelped as blood spurted from his side.

"No!" she screamed. "Go, Bhruic. Go home. Get Ciaran," she ordered. The big man who'd been holding her rounded on her, and his fist connected with her face. Pain exploded in her head as everything went gray and foggy. Stars danced behind her eyelids. Becca sank into darkness.

"Catch the damn dog," Darroch ordered, trying to staunch the flow of blood from a nasty bite on his forearm. The dog had ripped away the whole sleeve of his shirt.

"I can't and hold the horse," Luthais complained.

Bhruic took off like a shot, running hard through the middle of the herd, scattering cows as he went. Blood dripped from the wound in his side but the valiant dog kept running. He carried a scrap of cloth in his mouth.

Treating the unconscious Becca as no more than a bundle of rags, Darroch flung her across the horse and loosely tied her wrists to her ankles beneath Arien's belly. Luthais gathered their own horses and brought them back. The two men mounted and put heels to their horses, riding hard for Ballinfaire. Becca, draped face down, bounced like a limp rag doll as Luthais led Arien in their mad dash to get clear of MacDermot territory.

Bhruic finally made his way to the village, crawling the last league. The smithy found the dog lying outside his forge, panting and bleeding. Bellowing for the guard, the huge man gathered up the dog and sprinted for the castle. He'd seen the MacDermot's cailín ride out that morning, the dog trotting along beside her.

Niall met the man at the gate. His eyes betrayed the sorrow he felt as he stared at the injured dog. With a gentle tug, he took the rag Bhruic still carried in his mouth. Niall called for Siobhan and ordered the smithy to take the dog to the stables. Eachan found an empty stall with clean straw where he and Siobhan worked on the dog. Niall grabbed a soldier and dispatched him on one of their fastest horses to find Ciaran and Riordan. Then he questioned everyone. Finally, a stable boy admitted that Becca had ridden out just after breakfast and had told him to tell Eachan she was going. Intent on other duties, the boy had forgotten. Niall glanced at the sun. It was well after noon.

Calling for a company of horse, he'd start the search for Becca immediately. Ciaran and Riordan could catch up. Too much time had passed as it was, but with any luck at all, he'd find the cailín. He was determined to have her back safe and sound before nightfall.

Backtracking the trail of blood from Bhruic's wound required keen vision and was time-consuming. The trackers eventually arrived at the meadow where the cows still grazed complacently. Scouting the perimeter, one of the men found where the struggle between man and dog took place. Niall recognized Arien's hoof prints and grimaced when he saw blood near them. Knowing the cailín, she fought and fought hard. He prayed she was still alive.

Ciaran and Riordan arrived at the gallop, and Ciaran threw himself off his horse even as it slid to a stop. Anguish radiated from his face and Niall winced.

"She lives," Ciaran proclaimed as he reached Niall. "She's hurt, but she lives. Who did this?" he demanded.

Niall held out the bloodied sleeve Bhruic had dragged home. There was nothing to distinguish it from a thousand other sleeves on hundreds of shirts worn by men throughout the country. The faint blood trail leading off into the woods disappeared a hundred feet away. One of their trackers managed to follow the dim trail of three horses to a stream where all traces disappeared. There was no way to guess which direction the raiders had gone.

"O'Brien?" Riordan asked the most obvious question, though he thought it unlikely. Any O'Brien raiding party would have to cross the majority of eastern Connaught to reach Ailfenn. He didn't dare voice his next thought. Riordan, along with every man at the encampment, had seen Conchobhar's lust for Becca. Surely, the king would not be foolish enough to test the MacDermot's mettle.

Niall shook his head. "I dinnit think 'twas planned. I think the cailín surprised some cattle thieves. They took her not knowing who she is." Both Ciaran and Riordan protested but Niall held up a hand to silence them. "She dinnit carry a weapon, else they would not have taken her. The brave beastie took a slash from a dirk to his side. 'Tis a wonder he made it home. At least one will be marked by Bhruic's teeth, and if they dinnit knock her out immediately, they'll bear hers as well."

Ciaran nodded his head, considering. Niall was right. He would dispatch riders to every corner to search for a man mauled by a dog, along with one scratched by a woman. He smiled grimly.

Ciaran and Niall discussed the situation. They reasoned the cowards could not travel very fast nor could they get far with an injured woman. Or one held against her will. The clann would find the miscreants and Becca within the fortnight, and when they did, Ciaran's retribution would be fast and furious. As soon as Becca was found, he would wed her, bed her, and that would be the end of it.

****

"How did this happen?" the female accused.

The male was silent. He had not anticipated the interference of these oafish fools.

"Ah." She interrupted his reverie, aptly reading his mind. "And you were the one who called them fools. Now, who is the fool?" She sneered.

"'Tis not over yet," he grumbled.

"Why do you delay the inevitable?" a second, deeply masculine voice interjected.

"You promised the time until Lughnasadh," *the first male insisted.*

"They must be bound and the Covenant consummated by the end of that day," the second intoned.

"Or what?"

Three breaths were drawn in sharply.

"How is this?" the second male barked.

"The veil is thin, Mac Lir," the woman complained.

"Who the bloody hell are you, and why do you keep mucking about in my life?" Becca demanded.

"She should go back," the second man decreed.

"No!" three voices cried in unison.

"'Til Lughnasadh, then!" the second pronounced.

Silence.

"Please?" Becca whispered.

"Hush, Child," the woman hissed. "Lest he hear you."

Silence came, followed by darkness.

She wanted to cry, or scream, or hit someone but there was no one to hit and she knew those others had gone so there would be no one to hear her cries. "Okay," she defied the dark. "You have really pissed me off now. I will not go back." She stamped a foot she couldn't feel. "I will stay here. Ciaran and I will be together. You can't make me go back."

"Empty threats, Child of the Mortals," the second male voice growled at her.

Becca shivered. Then she got really angry at her own fear and at these unseen voices that kept whispering nonsense to her. "Empty threats?" she snarled with more bravado than she felt. "We'll just see about that now, won't we?"

The woman smiled. The mortal had been right. The Child would always have the last word.

Chapter Thirteen

Every morning, men rode out from Caisel Ailfenn to search. Each day, they hoped one of them would find Becca or hear news of her whereabouts. Each night, they returned to the great hall with heavy hearts. As time passed with no sign of her, Ciaran grew more morose. Niall and Riordan often rode out together and shared their worry. Given Ciaran's temper, he would likely kill with his bare hands the man who'd taken Becca, especially since his wound kept him from joining the search.

Siobhan insisted that Ciaran take care of himself and she dutiful checked his healing wound and changed the bandages. She clucked about like a mother hen, until he ate something at each meal. His temper was a powder keg, and she was the only one who dared confront him.

Ciaran stalked through the keep, often standing on the walls. With a hand shading his eyes, he watched the distant hills. His feelings about Becca's disappearance waffled from hour to hour. One moment he'd swear she'd been taken from him, the next that she'd run away. He snarled at people, an angry wolf with his ruff up. Siobhan, finally reaching even her limit, ordered Niall and Riordan to get him roaring drunk. The castle would be able to relax for a few hours at least.

Taidhg, once her faithful guard, felt responsible for Becca's welfare. The night of her disappearance, he went to Ciaran and sank to one knee in front of his chief. Wincing at the pain radiating off Ciaran, Taidhg made his vow. "I will bring her home to you,

Taoiseac," he pledged. "On my life, I will see her safe again."

At dawn the next morning, he began his search at the stream where the trail had grown cold. Working his way upstream, in case one of the O'Neill had sneaked down from the north, he found no trace of the three horses and riders. At each croft and hut, he stopped to ask about two men and a woman. No one had seen or heard a thing.

Finally giving up, he turned his search to the south until he eventually found a shepherd boy who remembered seeing a campfire. The boy claimed he crept up on the camp to see who it was. He remembered two scrawny bays and a magnificent black tied to a picket line. Two men, broad and thick with reddish hair and beards, sat at the fire talking. The boy had been unable to hear what they'd said. He saw no woman, but he did remember seeing a bundle trussed up with rope not far from the fire.

Taidhg grimaced at the description, praying his mistress was still alive. The description fit any number of rogues running about the countryside, but Taidhg had a sudden hunch. Two thick-bodied men with red hair sounded all too familiar. Because they were headed in the right direction, he guessed they might be the O'Flinn brothers.

When the boy showed Taidhg where the men had camped, he pulled off the silver clasp holding his cloak and gave it to the boy in thanks. Thrilled with his prize, the youngster skipped off back to his herd.

The soldier scouted the campsite. Three horses had indeed been staked there. Taidhg also found sign of three different pairs of boots. That was the first hopeful sign he'd had. He would spend the night here and proceed to Ballinfaire the next day. At the O'Flinns' keep, he'd learn whatever he could about Becca's whereabouts, and then he would ride hard for Ailfenn to fetch Ciaran.

****

The first two days of her captivity were absolute torture for Becca. She came to once, only to find herself hanging upside down and bouncing along Arien's side. Blessedly, the darkness reclaimed her almost immediately. That night, she awoke, bound hand and foot with a nasty rag stuffed in her mouth as a gag. She fought down the vicious nausea and concentrated on stopping the ringing in her head. Becca spied on them by opening her eyes to bare slits so Tweedle Dee and Tweedle Dum would think she was still unconscious.

The oldest one was called Darroch, and the younger was Luthais. Luthais was slightly smaller than his brother, but since both probably weighed over 250 pounds, that didn't say much. They were dirty, stank, and thought nothing of standing to relieve themselves into the fire. If these two were indeed the *now* Becca's brothers, this Becca pitied her other self. She'd learned enough from their conversation to know they'd had something to do with the beating her body received just before Ciaran found her. She was, however, confused by the distance involved. The brothers spoke of leaving Becca's body near Balleymough, but Ciaran had found her not far from Ailfenn, nearly three days' ride away.

Exhausted and hungry, Becca finally let the darkness claim her again. She would find some way to escape and make her way back to Ciaran, or she'd think of a way to get a message to him so he'd come rescue her.

The next morning and every morning thereafter when she awoke, her first thought was of Ciaran. *I'm alive,* she'd whisper to the heavens. *I'm alive and I love you, Ciaran.*

She spent two more days hanging upside down over her saddle before the Tweedle brothers let her sit astride Arien. She figured they were close enough to their destination they no longer feared discovery by someone loyal to Ciaran. Late on the third day, Becca caught sight of what had been her alter ego's home. The place was dismal. Squalid huts huddled together beneath the grimy stone walls of the keep. Dirty faces stared at her as the three rode by. No guard in crisp uniform greeted their arrival. Skinny pigs and skinnier dogs milled about the courtyard.

Luthais pulled her off Arien and unceremoniously slung her over his shoulder as he slouched into the hall. The rancid air reeked with the smell of rotten food and human waste. The big lug carried her upstairs and dumped her into a dingy little room, pulling the heavy door shut behind him. A stout crossbar dropped into place with a grating thud. She wasn't going anywhere for a while.

Only the moonlight shining in through a high window lit the room. She noticed the bed was little more than a cot covered with a thin blanket and a small bench stood beside the empty hearth. In another corner of the room, there was a bucket. Becca guessed what it was for and at that moment, she didn't care if it was only one step above a bedpan, she needed to use it. She hoped someone would be around in the morning to empty it.

After taking care of business, she tried the door just to be sure. It didn't budge. Becca really needed more light to see what she was doing. That promising to be scarce until morning, she gave up and curled up on the cot with the meager blanket wrapped around her. The stones radiated a damp chill, and Becca was glad she still had her trews on beneath her skirt. The only familiarity they'd shown her were the clouts they periodically rained down on her head and shoulders to keep her in line. As she drifted off to sleep, she sought to touch Ciaran with her mind. "I love you," she told the darkness. "And I keep your heart within mine, now and forever." She could only hope she had reached him somehow.

****

Down in the great hall, the brothers asked about their father. The steward told them he was in the village, and they knew what that meant. He'd taken a woman to tup and would be back eventually. They called for mugs of ale and sat down in the great hall to await his arrival.

Just before midnight, the front doors banged open and Garbhan O'Flinn stomped into the great hall. He was an older, meaner version of the brothers. The two younger O'Flinns had gotten drunk waiting for their father. They'd nodded off, heads pillowed on the grimy table while their snores echoed off the rafters.

The steward crept forward, and in a dry, croaking whisper, told the O'Flinn about the bundle his sons had dragged home. He watched his master's face turn a mottled shade of burgundy, and scurried off before feeling O'Flinn's fist.

"An' what do you mean dragging that bit o' fluff back here?" O'Flinn roared.

Startled, both men fell off their respective benches onto the floor. "Yee don' understand, Da," Darroch pleaded. "'Tis where we found her and how."

His father struck him across the mouth before he could finish. "She's nothin' but bad luck, that one. I want her outta my keep."

Darroch crabbed away far enough so his father's long arm couldn't reach him again. "But, Da, she was ridin' one of the MacDermot's finest horses. On MacDermot land. She even told us the MacDermot would give us a reward if we returned her."

That stopped Garbhan dead in his tracks. "The MacDermot?" he roared. "I offered her to him ten years ago, and he turned her down without so much as a by your leave. Him turnin' her down caused all the rest to look down their noses at us. Now, he thinks to have her without any arrangement?" The man stormed around the hall kicking dogs and sleeping men out of his way.

The brothers cringed, waiting for his fit of temper to simmer down.

"How dare she not die?" he raged. "How dare she crawl to the MacDermot and bring shame upon this house?" The madder he got, the more outrageous his accusations against Becca. Before the old man was done, he'd conjured up an elaborate plot whereby the MacDermot had secretly seduced her and lured her away, all to bring shame upon the O'Flinn sept.

Grabhan stormed up the stairs and tossed aside the crossbar on the door to Becca's prison. He threw open the door, rushing inside. Becca rolled off the bed and cowered beneath it, hoping the dark would hide her from the raving lunatic standing just inside the doorway.

"Where are you, you *bitseach?*" the man roared, vainly trying to see in the dark.

Becca held her breath. It didn't matter what language the man spoke, Becca knew what the word meant. She choked back a cry as a leather strap sang through the air and battered the cot above her.

****

Ciaran sat bolt upright in bed. Wherever she was, Becca feared for her life. He was as certain of that fact as he was of his name. A cold, dark anger squeezed an iron fist around his heart. If anything happened to her, he would spend the rest of his days hunting down the man who had hurt her.

****

"Da? Da!" Luthais cried. "Yee'll kill her, and then where will we be? Da, I'm tellin' yee. The MacDermot will pay to get her back. Cattle. Horses. Gold, even."

The old man stopped swinging his arm and

rubbed his chin thoughtfully. "Aye, Luthais. Methinks you might have the right of it. Ridin' a good horse, was she? And dressed fine?" he mused.

The younger man led him out of the room. He hadn't stopped his father out of any pity for his sister. Pure and simple greed made him intervene. Something in Becca's tone of voice when they'd taken her convinced him a great reward could be had for returning her to the MacDermot.

The door closed, and she heard the crossbar being shoved back into place. Becca reached up and pulled the blanket off the bed, wrapped it around her, and rocked back and forth fighting tears. She had never been so scared in her life. Not lying in the cold and dark on the side of that Colorado mountain, not standing back-to-back with Taidhg and fighting two O'Briens at once—not even when she first saw Ciaran lying on that pallet looking like death itself. These men held her fate in their hands, and there wasn't a blasted thing she could do about it. If they killed her, no one would ever know. What would become of Ciaran then?

****

Taidhg rode into Ballinfaire just after sundown, but he saw nothing fair about this forsaken place. A poor excuse for a public house squatted on the outskirts of the village. Taidhg hadn't bathed or shaved since beginning his quest for Becca, so he fit right in with the rest of the denizens.

It took a couple of days to get the information he sought. Two men-at-arms, beard-deep in their ale, spoke of the cailín locked away in the keep. Taidhg bought them a round and expressed his interest. One man looked around to see who might be listening, then leaned forward. In a conspiratorial whisper, he told Taidhg all about the poor cailín.

"'Twas just before *Albun Eiler*," the man said. "The O'Flinn was in a right ferocious rage. Seems the last in a long line had turned down his daughter's hand. He beat the cailín senseless, then bade his misbegotten sons to take her out and leave her. Told 'em to finish the job he'd started." He swallowed most of his cup in one swig, wiped a grimy hand across his mouth, and continued. "When the brothers came back, they bragged 'twasn't an inch of her body 'twasn't bloody and bruised. They'd stripped her to make sure." He took another sip, swilling the ale around in his mouth before swallowing. "Then about a sennight ago, the brothers come riding hard leading a fine black horse with the cailín on it. Luthais spirits her into the castle and locks her in a room on the second floor."

The man finished his brew and looked at Taidhg expectantly. Taidhg obliged him by ordering another round for both men. After the scrawny serving maid deposited the drinks and scurried off, the man continued. "There was a fair uproar when the O'Flinn returned that night. Swore she was bad luck, and the sons shoulda' made sure she stayed dead."

Taidhg's hands formed tight fists under the table while he steeled himself, fighting to keep his anger in check. How could a man want to see his own child dead, especially one as fair and brave as Becca? When the man spoke of the O'Flinn charging into the room and beating his daughter, it was all Taidhg could do to stay calm with a blank face. He took a long steadying breath. It would not do to give himself away now.

The man finished his story by saying the girl was kept locked up in her room, and only the brothers were allowed in to feed her once a day. None of the men-at-arms had laid eyes on her since that first night. Some doubted she still lived.

"But as parsimonious as the O'Flinn is," the man continued, "he 'twouldn't be wastin' food on a dead body." The man winked at Taidhg. "Rumor has it the brothers stole her back from another clann, and even now, the O'Flinn is on his way to Tuam to press suit against the *Taoiseac* who'd been harboring his daughter."

Taidhg was torn. He could stay and try to rescue Becca. Or he could ride for Ailfenn to report to Ciaran and return to free the cailín. If she was still alive, Taidhg was fairly certain she'd manage to stay that way a while longer. If the O'Flinn had gone to the king, he had some plan in mind and a live Becca was surely a part of it. Ballinfaire was, even riding hard, two days closer to Tuam and the king than Ailfenn. It was a hard two days' ride back to Ailfenn, two back here, and then the ride to Tuam. Or four days ride to Tuam from Ailfeen. Taidhg had no choice. He had to ride for Ailfenn. Becca would have to fend for herself a bit longer.

****

Ciaran slumped in the chair drawn up before the fire. The flickering flames etched his face with shadows, emphasizing the melancholy radiating from him. Riordan, his feet stretched toward the fire, occupied a second chair in Ciaran's den. He watched his cousin over the rim of his mug. A fortnight ago, he'd had been envious. Becca was a comely cailín and the bond she and Ciaran shared was one he'd, thought he'd wanted. Now, he wasn't so sure. Every morning, Ciaran declared Becca was still alive, that he could somehow sense she was still in this world. Each night, he swore he would find her. Despair and hope raged a terrible battle in his heart and mind every hour of the day.

As Riordan peered at Ciaran's haggard face, his heart went out to the other man, remembering all too well the way Becca suffered after Ciaran had been wounded. Their bond was remarkable. If it was this bad for his cousin when his true mate was just missing and in danger, what would come of the one left behind when the other went to the ever after? He wondered if the grand passion attached with true mating was worth the desolation, the anguished loneliness, forming the flip side of that coin.

The guard on the walls called out a challenge, and every man in the great hall came to their feet, hands to swords. Tense, they waited, ready for anything. A few minutes passed before the front door finally opened, and the guards ushered in a man wearing the colors of the O'Conor. By the time he strode into the center of the great hall and looked around for the MacDermot, Ciaran awaited him. Immediately flanked by Niall and Riordan, a full company of men-at-arms also stood ready.

"Ciaran MacDermot," the messenger called out.

"Aye," Ciaran acknowledged.

"*An Rí* Conchobhar O'Conor, King of Connaught commands your presence at the seat of his Court in Tuam. You are to attend him there before *Lughnasadh.*"

"And why does the O'Conor command the MacDermot in such a way?" Riordan snapped, reminding the messenger that O'Conor got his power from the clanns.

"To answer the charges made by Garbhan O'Flinn, *an Taoiseac* of sept O'Flinn regarding the taking of his daughter," the man answered.

"His daughter?" Ciaran snarled. "I dinnit take her. I refused the child over ten years ago."

The messenger shrugged. "*Taoiseac* MacDermot, the king commands your presence to answer the O'Flinn's charges. Do you come of free will?"

"Oh, aye, I come of free will to get to the bottom of O'Flinn's deceit."

At that moment, Taidhg flung open the keep doors and marched in. Travel-worn, dirty, and weary, he'd all but killed his horse getting there.

Seeing the king's messenger, he knew he was too late. At least he could pass on his information. Ciaran would not be going to Tuam blind. He nodded his head in his clann chief's direction. "A word, *Taoiseac*, when you have finished," he said quietly as he passed the messenger.

Ciaran tossed his head, pointing with his chin toward the room under the base of the stairs. Taidhg retired to it without a backward glance. With a wave of Niall's hand, a serving girl scurried to heap food on a trencher, grab a full mug and follow the soldier.

"I give you host *this* night," Ciaran said, his voice coldly formal, "so your horse may rest. On the morn, you will return to Tuam." With that, he dismissed both the king and his messenger by turning on his heel and striding across the hall to his den. Niall and Riordan followed closely, neither of them completely turning their backs on the messenger nor removing their fists from their sword hilts. The messenger got their unspoken message loud and clear.

****

Becca knew the confines of her cell intimately and could now pace the room even in total darkness. The room held the rickety cot, a small wooden chest with a few threadbare gowns of the plainest material, the small bench by the hearth, and the bucket in the corner. Since the first night, her father had not reappeared. One or the other of her brothers came once a day with a bowl of thin gruel and a cup of water. She choked it down while whichever brother waited impatiently.

Ciaran remained topmost in her thoughts. He'd be worried sick about her. *She* knew she was relatively safe, as long as the other Becca's father didn't reappear, but Ciaran had no clue to her whereabouts or condition.

On the third day of her imprisonment at

Ballinfaire, Darroch appeared early in the morning with a knife in his hand. If he meant to kill her, she wouldn't go down without a fight. Becca wondered if the long-ago self-defense class would do any good now. The big lout grabbed her in a headlock. She fought, kicking, biting, and scratching, but the oaf just laughed at her feeble attempts. He cut a jagged hunk out of her hair, tossed her across the room like a sack of rags, and slammed the door shut behind him.

"Now what the hell was that all about?" Becca rubbed the sort spot on her head.

Ransom, a shadowy voice whispered in her head.

"That would make sense." She'd reverted to talking aloud to herself. "These slimeballs will try to get Ciaran to buy me back. Problem is, with that male ego of his, he'll be just as likely to storm the castle walls and take me back by force."

That thought warmed her all over. That a man cared enough to wage a war over her was a heady sensation. Then her twenty-first century sensibilities kicked in. Men would die—maybe even Taidhg, or Riordan, or Niall, or God forbid, Ciaran himself.

"If yee'd but let me love yee, cailín," Ciaran's voice whispered in her memory.

Becca realized she'd loved him from the first time she'd opened her eyes in this strange time, and her heart had recognized his, just as his had sought hers.

"Someday," she promised them both. "We will be together to love each other."

****

Ciaran, Niall, and Riordan all stared at Taidhg, aghast at what he'd just related to them.

"How could a man want to kill his own child?" Niall asked, stunned by the revelation.

"But how did she get from Ballinfaire to Ailfenn?" Riordan added, ever the logistician. "And why Ailfenn?"

"I refused O'Flinn ten years ago," Ciaran said with a heavy heart. "The child was just that—a child. Scrawny, frightened. Blue eyes too big for her face, with all that scraggly hair she hid behind. She was completely cowed by her father and brothers." He shook his head sadly. "If I'd only known," he whispered. "I could have fostered the cailín until she grew up to be my Becca."

Niall cleared his throat. "'Twouldn't have happened, Ciaran," he interrupted. Ciaran's eyes were almost black with suppressed rage, but Niall stayed his retort with a gesture. "Your Becca and his Becca are not the same."

Mistaking Niall's meaning, Riordan spat out, "What game does O'Flinn play? Thinks he to substitute one for the other?"

Niall shook his head. "He plays his own most likely, but he dances with a devil far more vengeful than even the MacDermots." A shudder ran through him as the other three men stared. "Your Becca once 'twas his," Niall began to explain. "Many lives ago."

"What mean you by this?" Ciaran demanded in a quiet voice sheathed in steel.

"You yourself once thought she might be fae," Niall reminded him. "And have told me so on more than one occasion. Siobhan and the Druid claim the fae returned her to this life."

Ciaran's eyes narrowed. "Explain!" He growled, anger swirling like bright sparks in the sapphire depths of his eyes.

Niall shrugged, remaining silent for a long time as he searched for the right words. He finally took a deep breath and said, "She is not from this *when*, Ciaran. She's from a time far distant in the future. She is your true mate, as promised by Finvarra to the first MacDermot, and the faerie returned her to you."

Ciaran was speechless, caught between thinking his captain of the guard had gone insane and wondering if he had the right of it after all. He glanced at Taidhg, who nodded at him. Riordan remained unconvinced and shook his head in disagreement.

"The words she spoke, Ciaran," Niall prompted the younger man. "And the ones that still roll off her tongue upon occasion. The way she rides, the way she fights." Niall grinned, remembering the sight of her. "Even the way she wears her trews. 'Tis all strange, Ciaran. What cailín would behave as she has? Even her pain, Ciaran," he reminded them all. "Odhran said it was from the two parts of her soul joining together."

"How did this come to be?" Ciaran whispered so softly the others had to lean forward to hear him.

"Because the O'Flinn killed his own daughter, *Taoiseac*," Siobhan replied from the shadows near the door, her voice just as sure as it was soft. "Becca's soul was too young when you first met, so she didn't recognize you, nor did you recognize her. When her life ended without the binding from you, all was lost. Both your souls were doomed to wander. In all your lives to come, you would not be findin' each other ever again.

"The Faerie made a covenant with the first MacDermot back in the dawning of time. Once each generation, a warrior 'twould be born. A man to follow in the ways of the legendary Fenian Warriors themselves. 'Twasn't necessarily father to son, but within Clann MacDermot, a Fenian would come. And then Queen Onagh made her own pact with the MacDermot Knot.

"The warrior was promised a bride, to have and to hold for his lifetime and the next and each thereafter, until the end of time. With the Knot and the binding oath their hearts would be made one. A love beginning, a love without an end, until the end of time."

Chapter Fourteen

Three days. Three days before someone besides one of her brothers came to the door. Three days before Becca got her chance to escape. Three days closer to *Lughnasadh*. That word, that date, burned in her mind. But for her life, Becca didn't know why it was important. She just knew she had to reach Ciaran before midnight on the first day of August, and the worst part was she wasn't sure what today's date was.

Becca tensed as the crossbar grated across the door. She had the bucket ready. When a burly guard stuck his head in, she flung the contents on him. He gasped in shock, and she bashed him over the head with the empty bucket with all the energy she had. Short rations had left her weak. Even so, the man sank to his knees as if he'd been pole-axed.

"Sorry. Nothing personal." Becca checked his pulse to make sure she hadn't killed him. She snatched his dirk from his belt.

She slipped out of the room and peered down the hallway. Midday, but no one stirred. Even the great hall was silent. Becca ran on tiptoes toward the stairway. Just before she reached it, a door suddenly opened on her right, and she came face-to-face with a little maid.

"Oh," the girl squealed softly.

Becca held a warning finger up to lips. "Shhh," she whispered. The girl nodded. "Will you help me?" The girl nodded again. "Go back in that room and shut the door. You've seen nothing, heard nothing. They won't hurt you that way." The girl gulped, but did what Becca asked.

On silent feet, Becca fled down the stairs. The gods, it seemed, were with her. No one was about the great hall, almost as if a spell had been cast keeping humans out of her way. It took all of her waning strength to open one of the massive doors at the end of the hall. No guards waited outside. Spying what she thought would be the stables, Becca took off at a stop-and-go scurry, keeping close to the wall and whatever cover she could find. At the door to the stables, she heard Arien squeal in pain. Her eyes narrowed to slits, and her mouth twisted into a grim line.

Luthais clinched a rope tightly in his ham-hock sized hands. Arien, on the other end of the rope, fought the big man. Without thought or plan, Becca slipped up behind her so-called brother.

"If you touch him again, I will kill you," she snarled.

Luthais whirled, dropping the rope in surprise. "How? Where? How did yee get free?" he stammered. He raised a fist to strike her. The next thing he knew, a very sharp dirk poked him in the groin.

"Hit me again, dear brother, and you'll be eating a different kind of sausage for dinner." She sneered at him, her smile belying the cold promise in her eyes.

Luthais shook his head, bewildered. "What happened to you, Becca? You used to be such a biddable little thing."

"I used to be such a victim, you mean," she spat at him. "I've lived a hundred lifetimes since you last saw me, brother. A hundred lifetimes filled with pain the likes you couldn't imagine. I am biddable no more, brother mine. You will return me to the MacDermot, and you will do it now."

Luthais shook his head. "Da would kill me," he whispered.

"Maybe," Becca replied, "but know this, the MacDermot will kill you for sure if you don't." She pressed the dirk further into his fat belly, pleased when the big oaf groaned. "Where is our dear *Da*?" she asked, saccharine dripping from her voice.

"He and Darroch rode for Tuam," Luthais answered quickly as she prodded him with the dirk again. "He goes to King Conchobhar to deal with the MacDermot for you."

"I will not be bartered over like a horse," Becca spat at him. She backed away, the dirk still at the ready, and snagged the rope holding Arien with her free hand. "Where's my saddle?" she asked without taking her eyes off her brother.

"Da uses it now," he murmured.

Becca led Arien out of the shed by the rope around his neck. She'd ride bareback style if she had to. Becca took just long enough to fashion a halter out of the rope before grabbing a fistful of mane and swinging up on the powerful horse. "I ride for Tuam," she told him. "If you value your life, you will not follow."

Luthais swallowed around the lump of fear in his throat. "Nay, I'll not follow, Becca." He spat on the floor. "You and your MacDermot be damned."

"Been there, done that." Becca grinned at him coldly. "And got the T-shirt," she added under her breath.

She wheeled Arien and headed for the courtyard. As they came around the corner, she almost ran down the little maid she'd seen in the castle. Reining Arien, Becca looked surprised to see the girl. The little maid quickly handed her a cloth bundle and a waterskin.

"You'll be needin' food an' water."

Becca smiled her thanks. "If nothing keeps you here, child, run. Run hard and fast for Ailfenn. When you get there, ask for Siobhan at the castle.

Tell her I sent you. She will find a place for you." The little maid nodded. Becca reined Arien's head toward the gate. She hesitated, and then turned back to the maid. "The date," she called. "What day is it?"

The girl looked confused for a minute. "Why, 'tis almost *Lughnassdh*," the girl answered. "The festival starts in two days time."

Becca groaned. She had two days and two nights to get to Tuam. Becca put her heels to Arien and headed for the gate at a dead run. She didn't slow him until they were well beyond the village and headed south on the road to Tuam. With no sign of pursuit, she finally pulled him to a walk.

Throughout the night, Becca pushed Arien hard, alternating between a fast walk and a gallop. If she didn't get to Ciaran before midnight on the first of August, something really bad was going to happen. She couldn't fathom what, but she knew she didn't want to find out. Just before dawn, she found a grove of trees back off the roadway. The sound of gurgling water bade welcome to both she and her weary horse. Becca slid off him and led him to the stream. As Arien drank his fill, Becca tried to ease sore muscles. Every inch of her body ached. She felt older than she ever had in this lifetime.

Becca turned Arien loose to graze, and she opened the bundle the maid gave her. She found a loaf of crusty bread and half a round of cheese inside. She ate sparingly and sipped from the water skin. After checking on Arien, she wrapped up in the thin blanket she'd brought from her cell at Ballinfaire and tried to sleep.

"I'm coming, Ciaran," she promised to the night.

****

"The change begins," the female said sadly.

"She'll get there in time," the male replied, supremely confident.

185

"Midnight tomorrow," the second male threatened darkly.

The first male and his mate stared at each other. They had done what they could, but their hands were tied now. The Child of the Mortals would have to find her own way to the Fenian Warrior.

****

Becca awoke stiff and sore. She glanced up to gauge the time by the sun's position. It was just past midmorning. Her body protested as she stood up, and a shooting star of pain danced from her hip to her ankle. "No," she whispered. Becca stumbled over to the stream and looked in. Her face was older, lines etching her forehead and around her mouth. "NO!" she screamed to the heavens.

She had to find a fallen log to climb up on so she could mount Arien. Back on the road, she urged him into a canter. Each step the horse took pounded her spine and head. "I will get there," she vowed.

****

Ciaran, flanked by Niall and Riordan, and followed by Taidhg and a company of horse, thundered through the streets of Tuam headed to Caisel Tuam. Their horses were covered in lather, and the face of every man showed grim determination. They would get Becca back or there would be hell to pay. In the courtyard before the doors to the great hall, the group reined in their horses. With swords already drawn, they took the unwary O'Conor guards by surprise. Ciaran, Niall, Riordan, and a handful of men, pushed their way through the doors and faced the Chair of Tuam, the throne of Conchobhar O'Conor.

"Where is she?" he spat at Garbhan O'Flinn, completely ignoring the king.

"What right have you to ask?" Garbhan sneered back. "You took her, and turned her against me."

"Nay," Ciaran denied. "I found her beaten and

186

left to die, by whose hand I can surmise," he growled back. "She is mine, and I will have her."

Conchobhar stared from one man to the other. That the fierce young woman he'd seen in the MacDermot camp a scarce month ago had come from the loins of Garbhan O'Flinn was highly unlikely. He remembered the O'Flinn's daughter as a browbeaten, shy little thing, not at all like the Celtic *banríon* who'd stared him down the day of the battle against the O'Briens. He'd had no doubt she was a MacDonagh, as Niall's line had produced many fine soldiers. The king glanced from O'Flinn to Ciaran. There was more here than first met the eye. He knew instinctively Ciaran's feeling for this woman ran so deep he would risk clann war for her.

"Where is the cailín?" Conchobhar asked O'Flinn.

"Safe within my keep," O'Flinn barked.

"Safe?" Ciaran growled. "How do I know you have her?"

O'Flinn gestured to his son. Darroch approached, pulling something from the pouch on his belt—a long, silken strand of gold hair laced with silver. Ciaran flinched.

"She'll not be safe from you until she is by my side once again," he snarled, his fingers curling into fists at his sides.

O'Flinn reached for his sword, but before his hand even touch the hilt, Ciaran had him by the front of his shirt, a dirk pressed to his throat.

"If there is a mark anywhere on her fair skin, if there be so much as another hair out of place on her precious head," Ciaran vowed in a voice as cold and as relentless as death, "you will die a long, slow death, Garbhan O'Flinn. I promise you this on the souls of all my ancestors and all my progeny to come."

No man dared draw a breath inside the hall.

Ciaran's blue eyes were as dark as a moonless midnight. His handsome face could have been carved from granite, and as the fire in the hearth flickered across his countenance, none there believed the devil himself could have bested the warrior.

"I ride for Ballinfaire," Taidhg said quietly to his liege. "I will bring her back or die in the attempt." Ciaran didn't move as the soldier slipped out of the castle, snagged his horse and rode north.

Conchobhar cleared his throat. He owed Ciaran MacDermot many things, including his life on more than one occasion. The MacDermot and his army had helped Conchobhar sit in the Chair of Tuam as King of Connaught. If Ciaran killed O'Flinn, the king would have to execute or banish him, neither outcome appealing.

"Loose him, Ciaran," Conchobhar ordered. He kept his voice low and calm. "We will settle this when your man returns with the cailín."

Ciaran stared deeply into O'Flinn's eyes for a long moment. When he finally released the older man, O'Flinn almost fell.

"Tomorrow is *Lughnasadh*," the king continued. "We will celebrate the Festival of Light, and when your man returns with her, we will deal with the situation," he promised Ciaran.

Ciaran nodded once, turned on his heel, and marched out the door, followed by his men. O'Flinn sank to a nearby seat, rubbing his neck.

"The cold hand of death has been wrapped around your throat as sure as the sun coming up in the morning." The king released a sigh, relieved. He wasn't sure that Ciaran wouldn't have killed O'Flinn on the spot.

The MacDermot men regrouped on the edge of the green outside the town. Many people had come to celebrate the bonfires and fair, but the troop managed to find a place away from the crowd to settle in. None let down their guard, and Niall set a tight perimeter. To a man, they would die for Ciaran and Becca if the need arose.

Ciaran wrapped his mantle around him and unconsciously fingered the MacDermot Knot at his throat. Becca had not worn the mantle the day she disappeared. Idly, Ciaran wondered if the Knot would have kept her safe. *Too late now*. The soft woolen folds of the mantle held her fragrance commingled with his own. Ciaran breathed deeply, drawing their combined scents into his lungs. He would not lose her. Not now. Not ever.

Chapter Fifteen

Taidhg rode as if a banshee was hot on his tail. He feared O'Flinn would dispatch a messenger to arrive before he could reach Ballenfaire to spirit Becca away. He would not fail Ciaran in this. He pushed his horse hard through the night, stopping only for brief watering rests. Worried any O'Flinn rider would know of a shortcut, he pushed hard.

****

The day wore on interminably. As each hour passed, her body aged a year. Each step Arien took was sheer torment, but Becca clung to his back determined to make it to Tuam. All would be right if she could but get there and fall into Ciaran's arms. Ciaran would keep her safe. Ciaran would keep her young.

Sensing his rider's discomfort, Arien picked his way gingerly. When he'd feel her knees lose their grip on his sleek sides, he'd stop, waiting for her to regain her strength. As the sun sank in the west, Arien wandered off the road seeking water and grass. He found a small spring and dipped his head to drink. Becca slid off his back, and sank onto the springy moss at the water's edge. Fiery pain branded every inch of her body. She squeezed her eyes shut trying to ignore the pounding in her temples. A tear rolled unheeded down her cheek.

"I love you, Ciaran," she whispered to the last soft ray of sunshine as it danced across the spring. "Now and forever."

****

Taidhg rode through the night, but at a more

careful pace, letting his horse choose the way along the rutted road. The sense of urgency still beat at him, but he knew any O'Flinn was also at a disadvantage in the dark. He finally stopped in the wee hours of the morning. His horse needed a good rest, and he needed a few hours of sleep before he could press on. Taidhg made cold camp, rolling up in his mantle and falling asleep as his head touched the wool.

The sun rode high in the sky when Arien raised his head from the spring. His nostrils flared as he got a whiff of a familiar scent. He whinnied.

His horse cocked his ears and turned his head toward a copse of trees well back from the road. "What is it, lad?" Taidhg listened. A whinny. His horse nickered back in greeting. On a hunch, the man reined him toward the trees.

He immediately recognized Arien. Then he caught sight of the huddled figure between the horse's feet. His heart leapt into his throat almost choking him. Jumping off his horse, he ran to the body wrapped in a thin blanket. Becca. It had to be Becca. He shooed Arien away and squatted beside the inert figure. "Mistress," he sighed softly. He rolled her over and gasped.

Becca opened her eyes, and squinted against the bright sun. "Taidhg?" she whispered between dry, cracked lips. She ran the tip of her tongue across them attempting to moisten them so she could speak. "I couldn't get to him. I tried, but I failed."

"Nay, mistress," Taidhg disagreed holding his shock at her appearance in check. "Time remains. I will get yee there."

Becca couldn't ride. His horse had been ridden hard from Ailfenn to Tuam, and then back toward Ballinfaire. Taidhg stripped the saddle from his horse and threw it on Arien. As he cinched the girth, he spoke softly to the spirited animal.

"Yer her only chance, Arien," he crooned. "She can't ride by herself. I must carry her, and yee are the fastest and the finest horse in all the land. Only you can save her."

Arien nickered softly, and brushed his soft lips against Taidhg's sleeve. The soldier smiled. "Aye, and yer a fine one," he told the animal.

Taidhg looped the rope that had been on Arien around his own horse and secured the end to the saddle. The man gently gathered Becca into his arms, feeling the shudder of pain race through her. He eased her up on Arien and then climbed up quickly behind her. Taidhg settled her as best he could in front of him and urged Arien back toward the road and Tuam.

Each step Arien took was absolute torment for Becca. She bit down on her lip until it bled to keep from moaning. Taidhg had come. There was a chance they would reach Ciaran in time. Several hours into the return trip, she managed to ask, "Why not Ciaran?"

"The king would not allow him to leave. O'Flinn claims yer his daughter, and that the MacDermot has no right to yee. The MacDermot would have slit his lying throat then and there, but for Conchobhar. Before Conchobhar could naysay all of us, I left for Ballinfaire to retrieve yee. None of us would leave yee in that place a moment longer than we had to," he assured her.

Becca shuddered. One hand twisted into his shirt, and she rested her head against him.

As the sun sank, Taidhg eventually gathered enough courage to comment on her appearance. When he'd rolled her over to see her face that morning, he would have started praying had he been a religious man. Her once young, beautiful face had aged to that of a crone. Her skin was dry like parchment, and lines of pain etched her countenance. "What happened, mistress?" he finally asked.

"I am turning back into the one who was," she murmured. "To stay the one who is, I must get to Ciaran before midnight, Taidhg, before the fires of Lughnasadh are extinguished."

"Aye, Siobhan and the Druid had the right of it then," His lip curled into a snarl. "'Tis the faerie who muck about in this."

Becca shuddered again as a vicious spasm raged through her body. "I will hang on," she promised. "No matter what, you must not fail us. Get me to Ciaran before the midnight turns." Her body trembled and then stilled.

She was unconscious. He tightened his arms around her. "Aye, mistress. I will not fail yee." He put his heels to Arien, and a screaming war cry erupted from his throat.

****

Twin bonfires lit up the green. Everyone for miles around gathered to celebrate the Festival of Light. More than a few couples took advantage of the old custom of handfasting. The *Lughnasadh* handfast was a trial marriage lasting for a year. At the end of the year, the couple could turn their backs and walk away—no harm, no foul—or they could remain together as husband and wife. Patrick's Church frowned upon the practice and was trying to usurp the old ways. The Church refused to acknowledge either the joining or the dissolution of such unions. Regardless, the Celtic way was slow to die out.

A solemn group of men watched the festivities. Garbhan O'Flinn was deep in his cups, the hulking Darroch not far behind his father. The two sat on the king's left. The O'Conor, flanked by two guards, sat on a small, raised platform. A full platoon stood nominally at attention at his back. Ciaran and his cadre sat a little apart on the king's right. To a man, they looked ready to fight.

Conchobhar rubbed his forehead. This was a bad business that left a bad taste in his mouth. If O'Flinn's charges were true, he'd have to take action against Ciaran and Niall. On the other hand, Ciaran had leveled serious charges against O'Flinn, claiming the man had tried to kill his own daughter. He just wanted the girl to appear so he could ask her what was going on, and put this whole unfortunate affair to rest.

Ciaran suddenly doubled over in pain. As one, Niall and Riordan stepped in front of him to shelter him from the view of the others gathered before the bonfire. After a long moment, Ciaran straightened, a grimace marring his perfect face. "'Tis hers," he groaned softly through clenched teeth. Sweat dotted his forehead, and he swiped at it with the back of his hand. "She draws near."

Taidhg cut his horse loose and spurred Arien. Becca hadn't uttered another sound, and her body grew light and insubstantial in his arms. They were close. He could see the glow from the bonfires up ahead. Glancing at the stars, he swore. They were almost out of time.

"Run, Arien," he urged the horse. "Run like you've never run before. Run for her life and his."

Arien faltered for a step then found his second wind. With pounding hooves, he charged through the darkness toward the promise of the glowing light ahead. As they got closer, people clogged the roadway.

"Get out of the way," Taidhg shouted. "Move afore I run yee down!"

The big horse swerved around a tent, scattering people in his wake. Horse and man had but one thought—get to the bonfire. Taidhg tightened his arms around Becca, fearful she'd slip through them.

As they reached the edge of the firelight, she shimmered in its reflected glow. Taidhg stared in fascination. For a moment, her face was that of the Becca he knew then it flickered, and her features changed to that of the Becca she'd once been.

She stared at him, sadness radiating from her eyes. "You did your best," she whispered. Then she was gone.

Ciaran watched the dark horse and rider approaching, and his gut knotted with fear as he rose to his feet. Taidhg had Becca, but it was too late. Ciaran knew it in his heart and his soul. Horse and rider slid to a stop on the other side of the fire. Everyone there saw her form shimmer and change, and then disappear from Taidhg's arms.

A huge man, glistening from head to toe as if clothed in drops of water, appeared beside Arien. He was so beautiful, the throng had to squint. He held Becca in his arms. With a wave of the giant's hand, Arien trotted off, taking a bewildered Taidhg with him. The *Tuatha dé Danaan* god set Becca on her feet, and as the flames of the bonfire flickered down to embers, her form wavered between youth and age.

"What witchcraft be this?" Conchobhar roared.

"Not witchcraft but fae," Ciaran exclaimed, drawing his sword, but knowing it would do no good.

"Do you know me?" the giant roared.

"Aye," Ciaran answered coldly. "You'd be Manannan Mac Lir, god of the sea and one of *An Tuatha dé Danaan.*"

The giant waved his hand. "The fires of *Lughnasadh* grow cold," he pronounced. He turned to Becca. "Your time here has ended. You are not bound, and so you return with me."

"NO!" Two anguished voices blended as one.

"But I choose," Becca's solitary voice cried out.

"'Tis too late." Manannan's pronouncement rumbled from his deep chest.

A log crashed in the fire and embers danced up into the midnight sky. All the mortals present blinked, and when they looked again, fae god and human woman had disappeared.

"*NO!*" Ciaran's cry was torn from the very darkest chasm of his soul. He sank to his knees knowing his heart had been torn out, and he would never be whole again. "No," he pleaded, tears streaming unheeded down his cheeks. His anguish was palpable to all standing near.

No one moved. No one spoke. Then another log fell and more embers waltzed skyward. When the smoke cleared, two figures stood beyond the flickering fire. Ciaran raised hopeful eyes to the pair.

"Fool!" Finvarra, King of the Connaught Faeries, spat at Ciaran. "She'd worn the Knot. Why did you not bind her fate to yours?"

"Fool!" Onagh, his queen, sneered at Finvarra. "Why did you bind his fate to ours?"

Every man there gaped in wonder at the woman. Tall and willowy, her gown shimmered with silver lights, and her long golden hair danced in the firelight. She was the most beautiful creature any of them had ever laid eyes upon. All but one. For Ciaran, no beauty would ever compare to Becca's.

Onagh turned to stare at Ciaran with cerulean eyes. His pain and anguish was more than she could bear. A single silvery tear formed in her eye and spilled down her cheek. It glittered and glistened, changing from silver to blue to a fiery opalescence combining all the colors of the rainbow. With one graceful finger, Onagh caught the tear. The iridescent drop quivered on the tip of her finger as she drew it to her mouth. With a gentle puff, Onagh lent wings to the drop. It flew across the fire and hovered for an instant in front of Ciaran's eyes. Then it mingled with his tears and fell to splash upon the

MacDermot Knot at his throat. There, it coalesced and solidified, turning into stone. Where one fiery tear had once graced the eternity knot, two now resided.

"'Tis all I can do," Onagh sighed, her voice as soft as the summer breeze. "Know that two hearts should have been one, now and for all time."

Finvarra had not moved since his first outburst, held speechless and enthralled by his mate's reaction. Now he turned sad eyes to his queen. "Come, my love," he whispered. "We must go. *Tir Nan Óg* awaits our return."

The woman turned her baleful glare on the O'Flinns. "Know you are not innocent in this, Garbhan O'Flinn. My wrath shall haunt you and yours for lives to come," she decreed in a voice so cold frost formed around her feet.

The fae king took his queen's hand, sadness still clouding his eyes. "Come, love," he whispered. The two figures wavered in the waning firelight, becoming insubstantial and ghostly before disappearing all together.

No human moved nor dared speak. Only the bravest among them even drew a breath. What magic had occurred this night? What terrible price had been exacted, they wondered, looking upon the ravaged face of Ciaran MacDermot and the cowed back of Garbhan O'Flinn.

Niall recovered his senses first. His strong, hard hands gripped Ciaran's shoulder. "Come, Ciaran," he commanded quietly.

"I can't live without her," Ciaran replied, his voice pitched so low only Niall heard it.

The older man knelt next to the man he'd have been proud to call his own. "You can, and you will. You must, Ciaran, for her sake and your own."

Ciaran turned anguished eyes to Niall. "I can't feel her," he cried. "She is now truly gone from this life."

Niall motioned for Riordan. Together, the two men hefted Ciaran to his feet and walked him back toward their camp. After a few steps, Ciaran straightened and pulled away from them. He whirled and marched back to Garbhan O'Flinn. He glared down at the old man.

"Know this, Garbhan O'Flinn," Ciaran vowed. "Upon her life, you and yours will suffer." Ciaran turned stiffly and returned to Niall and Riordan. "Saddle up the horses, men," he ordered in a voice straight from the cold halls of hell. "We ride for Ailfenn."

Riordan and Niall stared at Ciaran, both men deathly afraid for what was probably the first time in their lives. Ciaran's eyes held no emotion. They looked as dead and empty as his heart must surely feel. In the space of an instant, he became a ruthless, cold instrument of vengeance. The two men exchanged sorrowful looks. Ciaran had the look of death about him. They knew it was just a matter of time. This great warrior, this man they both knew and loved, would grow reckless on the battlefield. He would seek death and destruction, preferably his own.

King Conchobhar stood still, his feet frozen to the ground by what had just transpired. He was a more religious man than most, having embraced the Church of Patrick in his youth, yet deep within his Celtic heart, he knew he had just witnessed something beyond all human expectation. *Tuatha dé Danaan.* They existed. The *Sídhe* had returned to interfere once more in the lives of men. Conchobhar stared at the retreating backs of the MacDermots. *So the old tales were true. A Fenian Warrior did still exist.* He sighed, sorry now for his part in this affair. He turned around to stare at O'Flinn. The man had gone white, and the king could smell the fear emanating from his every pore. Looking once more at the broad back of Ciaran MacDermot, Conchobhar felt the fingers of fear skitter down his own spine. The MacDermot was not an enemy he would want. That went double for the fae.

Much later, as the disheartened troop rode silently for home, Riordan turned to Niall. "How do we keep him alive?" he whispered.

Niall shrugged, knowing in his heart the task was impossible. If Ciaran was truly determined to join Becca in the ever after, there was little they could do to prevent it. His arms suddenly ached for the feel of Siobhan's soft body. Every part of him longed to touch her, to get lost in her. With sudden insight, Niall realized a man wasn't complete without a woman. For some, any woman would do. For others, there was only one. He sent up a prayer of thanks that he'd been granted the boon of finding his.

For the whole long ride back to Ailfenn, Ciaran spoke not a word. He ate nothing and drank water only when Riordan or Niall insisted. He built a wall of isolation, retreated behind it and refused to join the world around him. Ciaran existed. Barely. But in his eyes, an ember began to burn, cold and bright. Death. In death he could join her, and by the gods, he would. He promised that to them both.

Chapter Sixteen

Becca walked listlessly among the standing stones. Shadowy tendrils of fog caressed her bare arms. She shivered.

"You cannot be cold," a deeply masculine voice, one vaguely familiar, rumbled at her elbow.

Becca turned to stare at the man who had appeared beside her. He was glorious. Tall, broad, every muscle defined in his sculpted torso. The gentle breeze combed his long hair with teasing fingers. Becca could not determine its color even as she stared in fascination. The strands first glowed dark chestnut, like her grandfather's favorite mare. She blinked. Now it was a golden palomino color. Another blink and it was deep copper with rays of the sun caught in its silken web. The robe he wore swirled about him with a life of its own. The garment caressed the thick columns of his thighs and molded his broad chest. Unconsciously, Becca ran her tongue over her lips, moistening them. The man watched hungrily.

"Who are you?" she finally asked.

"I am Manannan Mac Lir," he said, his tone intimating she should know who he was and that she might be daft for not recognizing him.

"And you would be...?" She let her voice trail off, leaving the question open.

"I am the King of *Tir Nan Óg*," he rumbled in a basso voice that would mesmerize an opera diva.

"And just what is *Tir Nan Óg*?" Becca shook her head to clear the cobwebs. She knew she didn't want to be here, even if she didn't know precisely where she was. There was something she needed desperately to do, but she couldn't for her life remember what it was.

The magnificent man at her side snorted. "*Tir Nan Óg*," he repeated. "Land of the Ever Young."

Becca pondered that for a long moment. "Why am I here?"

The man smiled and the whole landscape lit up, but Becca didn't care. She felt detached from all this somehow. By all rights, as gorgeous as this man was, she should have been trying to figure out how to get him to kiss her. Manannan touched her gently on the arm, then took her hand and urged her to walk with him. They left the standing stones and, below them, a wide valley spread welcoming green arms in the soft sunshine.

Her heart gave a little lurch. There once had been a man who held her hand like this. A man who... The fog rolled in again and Becca couldn't remember. She gazed up at the Adonis beside her.

"You *are* lovely, cailín." His deep voiced roughened, dropped. He murmured a husky sound meant to be intimate. His hand brushed a stray tendril of hair back from her face, and he leaned down as if to kiss her.

Becca averted her face. It was not his lips she hungered for. Who was that other? Where was he?

"Why am I here?" she reminded him.

He shrugged his massive shoulders. "You have lived many lives, Child of the Mortals, and your time is done. You have earned the right to eternal youth."

Becca stopped dead still. Shadowy voices whispered in her head. *Child of the Mortals, you have journeyed long through* Imrama Anam. *You have returned to* An Domhan *to fulfill your destiny. Your fate is tied to his, Child, and his to ours.*

She stared up at the man, hiding her sudden insight. She tilted her head, slanting her eyes toward him. She blinked slowly, hoping her long lashes kissed her cheeks in invitation, an irresistible temptation.

His eyes turned to warm amber, and there was a sudden stirring beneath his ethereal robe. One corner of her mouth curled, gratified by his reaction. He was so tall she had to stand on her toes to wind her arms around his neck. She pulled him down to her so she could nuzzle the soft skin just below his ear. He shuddered in anticipation.

"But, I don't want eternal youth," she whispered in his ear.

His eyes narrowed, and his mouth formed a bitter slit as he pushed her away. "You have no choice," he decreed in a thunderous voice.

Becca glared at him. "I want to grow old with Ciaran." She didn't ask, she demanded.

"You were not bound," Manannan roared

"But, we love," Becca argued.

"Love without the binding is simply lust," he declared, crowding her body with his own. He gathered her into his arms and forced her to accept his kiss. She clinched her teeth and jaw, refusing to open her mouth to his probing tongue. "I will show you what he would not." Manannan's breath whispered a seductive kiss against her unresponsive lips. "I will show you for an eternity." He held her pinned against the whole long, hard length of his magnificent body. "If yee'd but let me, cailín," he beseeched, his voice sounding so much like Ciaran's that Becca went weak in the knees. He ground his hips against hers to make sure she could feel his desire.

Rather than succumbing to his demands, Becca pushed against the hard wall of his chest, tears leaking from the corner of her eyes at his words. "I would choose one lifetime with Ciaran to an eternity without having known his love, without having known the magic of a true mating between mortal man and woman," she spat.

In a rainbow swirl that turned to dark thunderclouds and lightning, the fae abruptly disappeared. Becca looked around. She was completely alone. "Well, so much for that strategy." She glanced over at the standing stones. There had to be a way. She had to get back to Ciaran. He was her life, her very heart and soul. She would find a way. "We will be together," she promised to them both.

****

August passed into the first weeks of September. The O'Neill raided in the north, seeking cattle and crops. Like a pack of wolves, the MacDermot and his troops swept the northern border. Ever faithful, Niall and Riordan stayed by Ciaran's side, protecting him as much as possible. Ciaran's legend grew among their enemies. He was a Fenian Warrior come to life. He could not be wounded nor killed in battle. A head taller than any man, he could be seen in the thick of the fighting, his bloodied sword cutting down foe after foe.

When the O'Brien again reared their heads in the south, Ciaran led his pack in pursuit. They paused in Ailfenn long enough to re-provision and for the men to see their wives and sweethearts.

Alone in their room, Niall buried himself time and again in Siobhan's willing body. He tried his best to tup his brains out, and though his body finally succumbed to exhaustion, his heart still grieved for what might have been.

Riordan had sworn off women until he saw a comely maid he'd not noticed before. When he asked, she told him her name was Alys, though she was vague about how she'd come to Ailfenn. In the course of the night, when they paused in their lovemaking, Riordan finally pried her secrets from her. Alys revealed she'd been the one to help Becca at Ballinfaire, and that Becca had sent the girl to Ailfenn for her own safety.

The cailín cried against his shoulder.

"I should have helped her sooner," she sobbed. "'Tisna' fair, her lovin' him so fierce, and him her."

She gazed at Riordan through watery eyes. "She'll find her way back," she told him with a sniff. "I know she will. We just need patience and faith."

Riordan hugged her to his chest and kissed her hair. "We can only hope, sweet Alys."

"Bah," Ciaran snorted in the hallway outside Riordan's door. "Patience is for those with short lives, and faith is for those who cannot see beyond the next sunrise."

****

Finvarra looked sadly at Onagh. "Your words return to haunt, my heart," he sighed.

Onagh turned her luminous gaze on her consort. "Speak to Manannan," she urged.

Finvarra shook his head. "'Twill do no good, love. 'Twas hard enough to wring the first returning out of him."

"Bah," she spat. "You males are all the same."

She disappeared in a swirl of gold and silver, leaving Finvarra to stare sadly at the empty space she'd just occupied.

"We must be patient, my queen. Have faith in the Child of the Mortals."

****

Tir Nan Óg was an enchanted place. The temperature was always moderate, the grass always green, the flowers always nodding fragrant blooms in the gentle breeze which spread their perfumes for all to share. Becca seldom saw any of the other inhabitants, and the ones she did come across were all *Tuatha dé Danaan.*

She'd found a place prepared for her in the

woods near the standing stones—a silken tent with a soft bed. Each day when she arose, a fresh garment was laid out for her, along with food and drink of the richest assortment. Despite the beauty of the place and all the luxuries provided, she'd never been so lonely in all of her existence. When she closed her eyes at night, she dreamed of Ciaran. When she awoke, she prayed he'd be lying beside her on the bed.

Day after day, Becca was drawn to the circle of standing stones. Though it reminded her of the pictures she'd seen of Stonehenge, this place was smaller, more intimate, and sat on the crest of a high hill. At the far side of the circle, a massive stone, flat and worn smooth, lay across two smaller stones like a table or an altar. If one stood on the inside of the altar and looked out, misty, blue mountains stretched out to one side, the shining aquamarine sea to the other. Becca stayed there staring into the distance by the hour.

As she stood her lonely watch one day, haunting music drifted up to her. She left the circle and climbed down the hill to find its source. Another beautiful man, lithe, yet well muscled, sat on a boulder playing the pipes. His beauty was darkly masculine. Not as big as Mac Lir, he would still tower above all mortals but Ciaran. Becca watched his strong hands as they danced along the chanter of his pipes. When she approached, he stopped playing.

"Ah, the fair Rebecca. I wondered if I could lure you away from your solitary sentry," the man said in a voice as pure and sweet as spun sugar.

"Who are you?" She asked bluntly.

"I am Abhean," he said. "Harper of the *Tuatha dé Danaan*."

She glanced at the pipes. "I thought harpers played harps," she replied caustically.

A sardonic grin split the faerie's face. "A harper

plays many instruments." He took her hand and tugged her down to join him on the rock. He sighed, looking her over from top to bottom and back again. "Ah, cailín but I could play you like the finest instrument of all."

One strong finger traced her cheek as he stared deeply into her eyes and saw the hunger, the longing that lurked in her soul. "But 'tis not me 'twill have the pleasure," he added, the spun sugar in his voice no longer sweet but burnt.

"What is this place?" Becca didn't feel polite.

Abhean sighed again. "Land of the Ever Young." He tilted his head. "This should be a land of peace and joy for all mortals who find their way here. I fear 'twill never be so for you, cailín. Mac Lir thought to do you a favor when he brought you here. He did not want to return you to that other life, the one filled with pain and suffering. Without the binding, your heart would never be whole, so he sought to bring you what peace and solace he could."

"He tried to seduce me."

Abhean chuckled, but there was no mirth in the sound. "Nay, cailín. If he had truly meant to do the deed, he would have succeeded."

"Not bloody likely." Her lip curled into a silent snarl.

Abhean chortled, truly amused now. "Methinks Manannan Mac Lir underestimates you, Child of the Mortals." He stared at her again. "Rebecca." Her name dripped off his tongue like the finest melted chocolate. "Do you know what your name means, Child?" He took up his pipes and began another song, this one not quite so plaintive. He watched Becca out of the corner of his eye.

Becca stared off toward the misty blue mountains, listening to the music. When Abhean stopped to catch his breath, she quizzed him. "Do you?"

"Do I what?" he countered.

"Know what my name means."

"I never ask a question I dinnit know the answer to," he answered cryptically in his sweet, lilting voice.

"So what does it mean?"

"Bound. Or chosen, if you like." He put his full lips to the reed of the pipe and played again.

Becca gazed at the mountains, her chin propped in the palm of her hand. She glanced at the Harper out of the corner of her eye. A little smile tried not to twitch in the corner of her mouth. These faeries, or *Sídhe*, or *Tuatha dé Danaan*, or whatever they were called were an egotistical lot.

"If you are the Harper," she prodded, "then you must know all the old tales?" She cocked her eyebrow at him, daring him to answer.

The Harper's eyes glinted with mischievous lights, and he grinned down at the beautiful woman sitting at his feet. The puckish breeze teased her hair, wrapping a silken strand of it around his leg. He sighed. He understood now why the mortal wanted her so much, and why Mac Lir was so determined to keep her. Well, he had his own score to settle with Mac Lir. "Oh, aye, I know them all and wrote most of them," he hinted.

"Then tell me a tale," she challenged.

****

Bits and saddles, swords and pikes jangled in the early dawn light. Horses stamped, blowing steam into the chilly air. Men spoke to their loved ones in hushed tones, not wanting their words of love to reach the ears of the MacDermot. Already mounted, he looked fierce and proud on his prancing chestnut stallion.

Niall pulled Siobhan into his arms for one last kiss. "I'm glad yee never turned yer back on me, woman, to walk away," he whispered into her hair.

"Yee know I'd marry yee in the Church if that was yer choice," he added.

Siobhan clasped his face in her hands and laughed. "I do love yee, Niall MacDonagh, and I always will. It never occurred to me to walk away, husband." She kissed him soundly, then pushed him toward his horse. When he had mounted, she leaned against his leg, her hand caressing his thigh. "Watch him well, Niall, yee and Riordan. Don't let anything happen to him. She'll find her way back, and he must be here when she does."

Riordan stared down at the little maid who'd come to see him off. "Thank you, Alys," he told her sincerely. Her cheeks dimpled when she smiled up at him, and he longed to kiss each one. Instead, he leaned down to give her a quick buss. "Patience and faith," he whispered. "I pray for an abundance of both."

Without a word, Ciaran turned his horse and nudged him with his heels. As he rode through the gates, the troops lined out behind him. There were no cheers, no fanfare as the men rode out. Sorrow draped over Ailfenn like a shroud.

****

This time, Becca knelt on the outside of the standing stones and placed her palms flat against the smooth stone. Taking a deep breath, she opened her eyes and stared into the center of the circle. She gulped as the scene unfolded before her.

Men swirled in a macabre dance of life and death. Swords flashed. Arrows sang through the air to find their marks. Men cried out in pain. In the midst of it all, Ciaran stood like one of the standing stones himself. Tall, hard as granite, immovable. His sword dripped blood, and the pile of bodies around him grew deep. As he faced two opponents at once, a third crept up behind him. Becca watched in horror as the third assailant's sword found its mark, slashing across Ciaran's back and sinking deep between his ribs.

Ciaran dispatched the two before turning to the third. His sword flashed in the bright sun, then struck the man, severing his head. He stood tall for a moment, and then Ciaran collapsed, sinking to his knees in slow motion. Riordan and Niall were beside him in an instant. They dragged him from the field of battle and found a safe place. Men surrounded the area, prepared to die to protect their *Taoiseac*. An older man appeared with bandages and a wineskin.

Becca blinked. Ciaran now lay on a pallet in a rough tent, much as she'd seen him after the battle with the O'Briens. His face was drawn and pale, and sweat glistened on his forehead. Becca stared at his chest, watched it scarcely rise and fall. She heard the slow labored beat of his heart. She leapt over the altar to the center of the stones.

"Onagh," she called. Nothing. Becca stamped her foot in frustration. "Onagh," she demanded. "You will attend me."

In a swirl of iridescent light, Onagh appeared before her. "Who are you, Child of the Mortals, to command me?" the faerie queen responded imperiously.

"You once said he could not die without issue," Becca accused. She waved her hand and the scene she'd been watching appeared. "Well, he dies."

Onagh watched for a long moment. "His wound need not be mortal," she replied hesitantly. She refused to meet Becca's gaze, preferring to watch the scene unfolding before them.

"He dies, Onagh," Becca insisted. "Look in his heart. It is empty. A man cannot live with an empty heart."

Onagh sighed. "What would you have me do?"

"You could have told me. Instead of whispering in my mind, making me think I was crazy, you could have bloody well told me what to do. Since you didn't, you have to fix this. Return me," Becca demanded.

"I can't."

"Who can?"

Onagh's eyes filled with opalescent tears. "No one, Child," she finally admitted. "Mac Lir will have his way in this. He is *An Rí* of *Tir Nan Óg,* but I suspect that even his hands are tied."

"There must be a way," Becca vowed.

The next day, and the next, Becca searched for the Harper. Abhean had disappeared. She tried summoning him as she had Onagh, but he would not appear. He'd been the one to teach her how to use the stones to see into *An Domhan*. He had to know of a way for her to return. If he didn't, she'd seduce Manannan Mac Lir himself to find her way back.

Chapter Seventeen

Becca awoke to gray skies that threatened rain. The sun always shone in *Tir Nan Óg,* unless Manannan Mac Lir or one of the faerie was sad. In the distance, she heard the plaintive trill of the pipes.

"Abhean." Her breath sighed from her lungs and her heart wanted to break from the mournful music.

She found him once again on the boulder below the standing stones. "Tell me," she said without preamble. "Tell me how I can return."

"There is no going back," the Harper snarled.

Becca rocked back on her heels. Abhean's angry tears had darkened the sky. "Abhean, what has happened?" She choked back tears. Fear's icy fingers wrapped around her throat, and she could barely breathe. Something terrible had happened. She could tell by the look on Abhean's face. She prayed it wasn't Ciaran.

Only then did she realize that the Harper was dressed like a Highland Piper, replete with Scottish plaid kilt and the full kit. "Abhean?" she repeated softly.

"I know what is in your heart," Abhean growled, stalking toward her. "As I cannot leave this place, then neither will you."

He grabbed her hand and pulled her into a rough embrace. He tried to kiss her.

Turning her head away from his advance, Becca pleaded with the angry fae. "What have I done, Abhean? Why do you treat me like this? I don't understand."

"No, you wouldn't. *You* are the Child of the Mortals. A *chosen* one," he snarled.

Before she could react, the fae's arms tightened painfully around her. Her feet left the ground, and then the air filled with glittering stars. Becca's stomach sank to her toes, a feeling similar to riding an express elevator at top speed. The stars blinded her, and her stomach turned over. She squeezed her eyes shut, willing the dizziness away. In a few moments, she once again felt solid ground beneath her feet. Hesitant to see where they were, she opened her eyes one at a time. Her stomach still churned from the wild ride. She and Abhean stood on a rocky crag. Below them, the dark blue sea lapped against a beach of pristine white sand.

"What do you see?" Abhean barked.

Becca stared around her. She'd never gone beyond the standing stones or her bower in the forest. The ocean, a deep cobalt that reminded her painfully of Ciaran's eyes, swelled restless and prancing like a spirited stallion as it rushed toward the shore below her. The sky was a blue, so brilliant she squinted against its brightness. No cloud shadowed its expanse. She shrugged, not sure what she was supposed to be looking for.

His hand grabbed the back of her neck and forced her to stare out to sea. "Look again, Child," he ordered. Gone was the spun sugar and chocolate. His voice grated like the storm-tossed gravel beneath their feet.

Becca blinked away tears and saw a wavering outline, like a mirage far out in the ocean. She blinked again and saw another and another. Abhean's hand squeezed her neck causing more tears.

"Ah, you see them now, the Islands in Time," he whispered, his voice low and seductive like melted caramel. "Each island is a lifetime—yours or someone else's. Mac Lir thinks he is the only one with the secret to their manipulation. He believes he is the only one with the farsight."

Becca shuddered. Abhean's deadly cold voice froze her very soul.

Abhean continued. "He is not the only Timekeeper. There are others who can tinker with the lives of the mortals."

"Can you?" Becca whispered, almost daring to hope. "Can you send me back? Or at least show me the way?"

Abhean turned shrewd eyes on her. "First you must grant me a boon," he said in that spun sugar voice of his as he turned her in his arms.

Becca eyed him through narrowed eyes, not trusting the sudden change in his demeanor. "What do you ask of me?" She swallowed, her throat working to clear the fear lodged there.

Abhean smiled, but it didn't quite reach his eyes. "Lay with me, Child of the Mortals. Let my spear fill you up as no mortal man's ever could."

Becca stepped back, her anger and distaste plain for the faerie to read.

"Am I not fair to look upon?" he beseeched. He parted his robe to reveal his cock. "Am I not ready and willing to give you such pleasure as you have never known, nor will ever again?"

Becca stared at him with the same fascination as a mouse cornered by a snake. He was gorgeous in a dark, cold way, but he held no allure for her. "You wish to take my maidenhead?" she countered quietly.

Abhean's smile broadened. "'Tis better for me to do so than that mortal you claim to love."

He snatched her hand and guided it to his cock, forcing her to stroke and cup him. He purred at her touch. "I will give you much more than that mortal you pine for. And I will have what Mac Lir wants."

"Mac Lir?" Becca remained suspicious.

"Aye, Mac Lir would have you for his own, Child. He would bind you to him and this place, and then he would leave you with no memory of what went before."

Becca shuddered again, fear clutching at her belly. Abhean was playing some wretched game with Mac Lir, and she wanted no part it. She didn't doubt Mac Lir wanted her. She often caught him watching her from a distance, and then she realized the faerie stroked himself as he observed her. She felt dirty each time it happened. From what she'd gathered, fae men were not used to rejection by mortal women. Sooner or later, Mac Lir or Abhean would take her, and there would be little she could do to prevent it.

Becca got angry. She was not some prize in a sick game between immortal rivals. She squared her shoulders. "If this is the boon you ask, then I will find my way without you."

"But you declared you would seduce Mac Lir himself to gain the secret," he purred, sure he had the trump card. "I have the secret, and I am infinitely more inclined to make love to you. You would enjoy the experience with me, Child. Mac Lir would take you only to make you forget. You would derive no pleasure from his touch."

"I desire the touch of no man but Ciaran." Becca turned away from the faerie.

He snagged her hand, jerked her back, and forced her to look at him. Her eyes glistened with silvery tears. The hard-hearted Harper of the *Tuatha dé Danaan* felt his heart melt at their sight.

"Do you love him that much, cailín?" he whispered in an awed voice.

"He is my heart and my soul, Abhean," she cried. "I would give up a hundred lifetimes, nay a thousand, to live just one life and grow old with him."

The faerie harper stared at her for a long moment, digesting what she'd just said. *Ah, to love that deeply.* His heart felt like it was surrounded by a block of ice. There was one he had once loved nearly that much—one Manannan Mac Lir had refused to help.

He bent his head and captured Becca's lips gently with his mouth and murmured against hers,

"At *Albun Eiler* and *Alban Elued*, the spring and autumnal equinoxes, when light and dark, love and hate, good and evil are equal, the veil between this world and the next thins."

Becca grew still with hope growing in her heart.

"An unwavering soul, one with unfinished business and a burning desire, might find its way back to *An Domhan,*" Abhean told her softly. "You must find your own way, cailín, for none here can help."

Becca wiped the tears from her eyes with a determined hand. She was not surprised to discover Abhean gone when she could see again. "All I have to do is figure out how to get through the veil."

"Seek within your heart, Child. Seek with your heart to find what is missing," a mystical voice as sweet as spun sugar sang in her head.

****

Conchobhar once again stood in the war camp of Clann MacDermot to inquire about the Black Wolf of the MacDermots' health. His heart sank as Niall and Riordan exchanged worried looks. The king admired Ciaran for his prowess on the field of battle, but the MacDermot meant much more than that to Conchobhar. Ciaran was an honorable man, and there weren't many of those in the world. He glanced at the tent where Ciaran lay injured. Then he surveyed the faces of the men as they sat in small groups around their fires. The smell of death hung like a pall over the camp. Ciaran's men knew, just as the king knew, but he still had to ask, hoping someone would give him the answer he wanted to hear, not the one he knew to be true.

"The fight has gone out of him," Niall replied to the king's question. "I don't think he will survive this time."

The king turned to Riordan. "You are closest kin," he told the younger man. "The MacDermot men look to you as they did Ciaran. Will you take his place as *An Taoiseac*?"

"Nay," Riordan spat. "Not while he draws breath into his body."

Conchobhar shrugged. This fierce loyalty was what set the MacDermots apart from all others. "*Onóir bheith suáilce,*" the king muttered, *honor with virtue*. "Take him home," Conchobhar added aloud. "Let him die in his own place, then."

The journey home was slow and filled with grief. No man believed Ciaran would survive the trip. Not one man in the troop thought the *Taoiseac* would ever see Ailfenn again. Ciaran's body, however, proved stouter than his heart. He survived the journey.

Riordan and Niall laid him in the bed he'd once shared with Becca. Siobhan fussed over him even as he slept, unmoving, unfeeling, uncaring, willing his heart to quit beating so he could join his true love in the ever after.

A sennight passed, and *Albun Elued,* the autumnal equinox, came, yet Ciaran lay still as death. Siobhan attended to his wounds, and Riordan attended to his clann. Niall just paced the hallway outside, willing his *Taoiseac* to live.

Six months ago, Becca had appeared on the night of Albun Eiler. Niall thought back to his feelings that night, his fear that something terrible would come to pass. His premonition had come true, and he wished he could change things, make them right somehow. Niall loved the fallen warrior with his entire heart and soul. Loved him maybe even more than he loved Siobhan. Certainly loved him enough to die for him.

Siobhan softly closed the door to Ciaran's room and watched her husband's broad back pace away from her. There was nothing she could do to change the outcome. She knew of no spell, no prayer, no sacrifice that could be made. Even Odhran had all but blinded himself studying the old manuscripts, looking for some way to bring Becca back into this world.

Niall turned to find his wife watching him. The look on her face broke his heart. "Come, love," he whispered. She fell into his arms, and he kissed her deeply, blessing again the gods for bringing her into his life.

****

Becca stared into the stones, the tears on her cheeks streamed unheeded. Ciaran's once glorious hair lay in a ratted nest around his head. Lines etched his face, ones that hadn't been there before. His lips were drawn, and his skin pale. He wore the mark of death. Becca longed to lay her palm on his beloved cheek and kiss him awake. "You must live, Ciaran," she whispered, reaching through the stones. "You must live for me and ours. You must love me enough so I can find my way back to you."

Ciaran opened his eyes. Becca's beloved face swam in front of him. He reached out to touch her, and his finger captured a silvery tear as it caressed her cheek.

"How is this possible?" His voice, rough from little usage, cracked. *To be so close and yet so far from her,* his heart cried.

"Love, Ciaran," her sweet voice whispered again to his heart as butterfly wings fluttered against his cheek. "Love lives forever, and through it, all things are possible. Hear my words, and know your heart resides in mine for all time. Keep my heart in yours. As long as it is there, our love cannot die. Your love for me will light my way back to you. I *will* come back to you," she promised.

"Becca." Her name tore from his soul, a prayer and an oath.

Love me, Ciaran.

"I do," he promised the darkness.

Dawn wasn't far off when Siobhan slipped out of Niall's embrace. She'd heard a noise. She cocked her head to listen, but the entire castle was shrouded in silence. She shivered. The castle was never completely silent. Suddenly fearful, she slid out of bed, wrapping Niall's mantle around her naked body. She had to check on Ciaran, afraid he'd finally gotten his wish—afraid death had come to claim him. When she got to his room, she found his face wet with tears, and his heart beating stronger than it had in days.

"He lives," she told Niall joyously as her mate entered the room behind her. Niall wrapped his big arms around her and held her close. "What magic have you wrought, my love?" he asked, awed at his wife's power.

"No magic of mine," she declared. She sniffed the air and caught the faint scent of roses and something clean, like sea air or snow on the mountains. She stared down at Ciaran. "Love," she whispered. "'Tis the magic of love."

Chapter Eighteen

The greens and browns of September rolled into the frosty nights and boisterous colors of October. Autumn came to Ailfenn, painting the countryside with glorious oranges, riotous reds, and rich yellows. Though still slowed somewhat by his wound, Ciaran was up and about, overseeing his clann once again. His face was lined now, and he looked older than his thirty-one years, but he regained strength daily.

As the days grew shorter, the people of Ailfenn prepared for *Samhain*. Inventory was taken in the larder and the buttery. Crofters finished harvesting their crops and shepherds brought their herds back from the far grazing lands. The weakest animals in the herds were killed and dressed, the meat preserved for eating during the cold months to come.

Women cleaned their houses, airing their linens and clothing in the soft light of the last warm days of the year. At night, families gathered around their hearths and told the old tales and some new ones. All the girls longed to hear the tale of the taking of *An Taoiseac's* true love by the faerie. The boys scoffed at the story, wanting to hear about the glorious battles in which their fathers had fought.

Each night after the evening meal, Ciaran, dark wolf that he was, retired to his den. Sitting on a chair made soft with sheepskins and woolens, he stared into the flames, imagining he saw Becca's face reflected back at him. As midnight approached and the flames died, he vowed to love her until the day he died. "And I plan to be a bloody old fool before that happens," he spat into the fire. When the last ember burned to black, he heaved out of the chair. With plodding steps, he climbed the stairs to his chamber. He went the oaken chest at the foot of the bed and took out one of Becca's gowns. Pressing his face into its folds, he drew hungry breaths deep into his lungs, savoring the faint scent of her still lingering there.

Reverently, he replaced the gown and climbed into bed. Drawing his mantle into his arms, his fingers traced the MacDermot Knot over and over, occasionally caressing the two fiery stones in its center. "You will come back to me," he whispered repeatedly into the darkness. "Love of my heart, light of my life," he murmured as he drifted off to sleep.

****

"Light of my life, love of my heart," Becca whispered. "Oh, Ciaran how I miss you!" Her fingers stroked the altar at the standing stones like a lover's caress. She laid her head down, and her tears gently fell upon the stone.

Manannan, King of *Tir Nan Óg*, stared at the beautiful woman, his body hard and aching for her. He knew she came to the stones each day, and he knew why. He'd chastised the Harper for telling her their secret. Now his heart was heavy. He watched this Child of the Mortals survive each of her lifetimes, growing stronger and wiser with each, yet her heart remained empty, and her soul filled with sorrow. He above all the other faerie kings and queens took any covenant with the mortals to' heart. It was he who watched over the chosen ones to ensure that they were bound together each lifetime.

He'd thought to spare the Child of the Mortals any more suffering in mind or body by bringing her to *Tir Nan Óg* rather than returning her to her former life. Manannan realized he'd been wrong. As he watched her melancholy grow each day, he thought his own heart would break. He considered taking her himself, for laying with her would erase her memories of those other lives, but each time he sought to do so, something stopped him. He wanted her as he'd never wanted another mortal woman. He ached to feel her long fingers wrap around his cock, to taste the sweet essence of her. But whenever he looked deep into her eyes, he knew that neither he nor any other in *Tir Nan Óg* would ever be able to sate the hunger of her soul. There was only one who could. He could not force her. Unlike some others of his kind who took what they desired regardless, to Manannan, even a seduction against the woman's will was still rape. He turned away from Becca, steeling his heart against her pain. He could not return her. He would not. Not without the binding.

****

The week before *Samhain*, Ciaran himself oversaw the laying of the bonfires on the hilltop above Ailfenn. Odhran chanted over each piece of wood added to the two piles, sending up special supplications to all the gods, old and new. All around Ailfenn, people bustled about, preparing. The last of the harvest had been laid by, meat cured for the cold, dark times of winter, and the people were ready to celebrate. While their joy was tinged with sadness, the folk of Clann MacDermot had much to rejoice this *Samhain*. Ciaran had returned to them, though his soul ached for the loss of his true love.

Tinkers, minstrels, and harpers arrived daily, their chanting spiels and music filled the air. The tanner and weaver offered their finest goods for the women to haggle over. Breads, sweet treats, and rounds of cheese spilled across overloaded tables. The blacksmith laid out his wares, as did the silver and gold smiths. Life was finally returning to Ailfenn.

Men raced their horses in the meadow below the

hill, wagering good-naturedly on the outcomes. Lads and cailíns cast loving eyes at each other, sneaking away from the adults to hold hands and kiss behind the assorted tents. Children danced with delight from one stall to the next table, oohing and aahing over each newly discovered treasure. The clann gathered from the four corners of the territory to celebrate before the dark days of winter arrived to shut them in.

Ciaran walked among them, greeting each by name, stopping to share a moment of conversation, to learn about a marriage or a birth or, sadly, a death. At his throat, the two stones in the MacDermot Knot glimmered softly in the muted sunlight. The men exchanged cheerless glances behind his back, while the women breathed poignant sighs after he passed. Many of them had sought to woo the *Taoiseac*, and now they knew he would woo none back. The story of Ciaran and his true love had spread far and wide among the people who owed allegiance to Ailfeen.

Samhain arrived at last. All the fires in Ailfenn were extinguished, and the people gathered on the hill. Ciaran struck flint with iron. A small spark jumped from the flint into a small wad of wool. The wad flamed, and Odhran the Druid fed the sacred fire with rowan and oak. The flames grew stronger, lapping at the kindling laid around it. Soon, it had ignited the entire pile, and flames danced merrily across the bonfire. Ciaran stuck a torch into the first bonfire. When it flamed brightly, he tossed it into the second. Harpers, pipers, and drummers struck up a lively tune as couples danced around and snaked past the fires. Shepherds drove their herds between the two piles. Soldiers carried their weapons and led their horses through, all to protect and purify everything that belonged to Clann MacDermot.

His heart heavy, Ciaran turned away from the fires and the dancing couples. Walking among the tents and tables laden with food and wares, the excited giggles of a group of children drew him. A harper settled in to tell tales. Ciaran cocked his head, trying to place the man. Handsome in a cold, dark way, the harper was a stranger to him.

"And would yee like to hear the tale of the first MacDermot," the harper began. The children squealed with delight.

"Tell us about his battles," one boy shouted.

"Yeah, tell us about the Fenian Warriors," another agreed.

"I shall tell yee the tale of how the MacDermot saved the life of King Finvarra and thus won his true love," the harper said in a voice as sweet and rich as spun sugar.

****

"I cannot listen anymore," Finvarra decreed.

"How do her tears not break your heart?" Onagh said to Manannan.

He shrugged, the gesture more nonchalant than he truly felt. "There is naught any of us can do, Onagh," he replied, his voice thick with some unnamed emotion, for in truth, her tears continued to break his heart.

****

The fires died down as midnight approached, and people lit their torches for their walk home. Ciaran stood between the fires, his legs spread wide, and his hands stretched to the heavens. He'd stripped down to nothing but his trews and boots. His muscles rippled as he beseeched the stars. Firelight danced across his bronzed skin, the flickering flames defining each well-developed muscle. All stopped to stare in awe for he appeared to be some faerie warrior of old.

"Becca," he shouted to the firmament above.

223

"Hear me. By the life that courses within my blood and the love that resides within my heart, take thee to my hand, my heart, and my spirit to be my chosen one."

The three stared at each other in wonder. Was it possible that the warrior had discovered how to bring his true love home? The mortal's voice echoed around them.

"The binding," Onagh whispered.

"At last," Finvarra sighed.

"She returns," Manannan decreed.

"To desire thee," Ciaran vowed, "and to be desired by thee. To possess thee and to be possessed by thee without sin or shame for naught can exist in the purity of my love for thee. I promise to love thee wholly in this life and beyond, where we shall meet, remember, and love again. There is no beginning, there is no end but in you. Our love is a beginning without an end, until the end of time. You are my chosen." Ciaran sank to his knees, his chin falling to rest on his chest. He was completely drained.

Becca blinked, blinded by the fires on either side of her. A man knelt at her feet, his chin sunk on his chest. His hair was so black the light cast by the fires burned blue in its silken depths.

Ciaran looked up, his dark indigo eyes met ones of cerulean. His heart turned over, and his gut clenched.

"You," the vision before him breathed. She sank to her knees and placed her hand above his heart. "Ciaran, by the life that courses within my blood," she repeated. "And the love that resides within my heart, take thee to my hand, my heart, and my spirit to be my chosen one. To desire thee and to be desired by thee. To possess thee and to be possessed by thee without sin or shame for naught can exist in the purity of my love for thee. I promise to love thee wholly in this life and beyond, where we shall meet, remember, and love again. There is no beginning, there is no end but in you. Our love is a beginning without an end, until the end of time. You are my chosen."

Ciaran buried his hands in her golden hair and claimed her lips with his own. Her mouth opened for him, and his tongue drove into her mouth, teasing her with what was to come from the rest of his body. Becca wrapped her arms around his neck, swearing never to let him out of her sight again.

"Love of my heart," he whispered against her mouth.

"Light of my life," she replied.

He kissed her again, so hard, so deeply that he pulled the breath from her lungs, sucking it into his own. His erection pressed against the sweet vee of her thighs. He gazed at her, wonder softening the hard sapphire color of his eyes to a rich cobalt. Then he realized she was wrapped in his mantle and wore nothing else. The MacDermot Knot shimmered above her breast. As he watched, the two fiery stones blurred, turning into opalescent liquid and joining, coalescing back into one large, heart-shaped stone.

"Two hearts forever joined as one," Ciaran whispered, fingering the brooch. "As she once promised."

Becca stared up at him, love and desire radiating from her eyes. "Take me home, Ciaran. Take me home and love me tonight and tomorrow and forever."

"Aye, cailín."

Ciaran stood and pulled Becca to her feet. He gathered her into his arms and held her against his bare chest. The silent crowd parted as the magical warrior strode toward his keep, his faerie bride in his arms.

Riordan was the first to come to his senses. He grabbed a torch and thrust it into the fire. Racing down the hill, he caught up to Ciaran and Becca, passing them at a full run. He burst into the great hall, strode to the hearth, and jabbed his torch into the waiting wood, lighting the fire already laid there. Jogging up the stairs, he dashed to Ciaran's chambers where he lit that fire and went about the room lighting candles—no small feat with only a torch. He raced back to the top of the stairs and touched the flame of his torch to the rush lights lining the stairs as he descended.

Gair, the steward, appeared with another torch. Together, the two men hurried to light every candle, every rush light, and every fire in every hearth in the entire castle.

Ciaran and Becca made it back to the great hall just as two men-at-arms entered. The men turned to stand at guard as the MacDermot, with Becca still in his arms, entered. The whole of Ailfenn followed hard on their heels.

Riordan smiled at the couple, his heart full to bursting. Becca's return was nothing short of a miracle. His cousin's bride was positively radiant, and he'd never seen Ciaran so happy.

Riordan jabbed Gair in the ribs. "Babies," he crowed. "Grand, glorious babies the like this clann has never seen, nor will likely ever see again. And we'll live to see it, Gair. Aye, we'll live to see it."

Niall and Siobhan, with Eachan and Taidhg close behind, joined Riordan and the steward. Siobhan's face was wet with happy tears, and the men grinned from ear to ear.

"Do you come willingly into my keep as my bride, to live and love, now and forever?" Ciaran asked formally.

Becca kissed him deeply before replying. "Aye," she sighed. "I do."

A shout erupted from every throat. "MacDermot!" the gathered clann roared.

Ciaran looked down at Becca, his gaze tender and sweet. Until he noticed one long, bare leg peeking from beneath his mantle. His gut clinched in anticipation, and his cock strained against the leather of his trews. He couldn't wait to wrap her legs around his middle as he thrust into the very heart of her. His mouth descended upon hers, utterly devouring it. He sucked her tongue into his mouth where it dueled with his own. Blindly, he climbed the stairs still kissing her.

As the couple disappeared at the top of the stairs, Niall grabbed Siobhan and kissed her. He guided her hand to his groin. His own *boidín* was straining against the laces of his trews. "If he doesn't tup her soon, the whole castle will go up in flames," he whispered against her willing mouth.

"I'm willing to douse your flames," Siobhan replied with a husky chuckle.

The two made their way through the crowd filling the great hall and drifted up the stairs, never taking their eyes off each other.

Riordan turned to Gair. "'Tis time to celebrate," he told the steward. "Food and drink for all!"

Little Alys appeared at Riordan's side, and he swept her into his arms, sealing his mouth to hers in a deep kiss. "Patience and faith," he told her breathlessly, gazing into her soft azure eyes.

She smiled at him, dimples appearing in her cheeks. Boldly, she let her hand trail across his stomach, then lower where his trews were hard. Riordan sucked in his breath. "I know a man who needs tupping," she told him, her lips pursed in sassy invitation.

"Aye," Riordan agreed. They, too, slipped up the stairs arm-in-arm.

"Thank the gods that's over," Eachan told Taidhg.

The old soldier nodded at the horse master, and

the two of them moved out of the way as trays of food and pitchers of drink appeared from the kitchens and from outside as well. The whole crowd milled about, either in the great hall or in the courtyard outside. By morning, the whole lot would be roundly drunk. Not wanting to waste a moment, the two men grabbed mugs from a tray and tossed back the ale.

"To the faerie," Taidhg said, spilling the last swallow of his mug on the floor.

"Aye," Eachan agreed, following suit. "To *An Tuatha dé Danaan.*"

Chapter Nineteen

The closed door to his chamber proved problematic with his arms full of Becca. Ciaran couldn't get it open. Becca squirmed against him, and the mantle she wore gaped open, revealing her lush, firm breasts. Ciaran sucked in air. If he didn't get out of his trews immediately, he was going to strangle. She wrapped her arms around his neck, kissing him fiercely, her teeth nipping and pulling at his lower lip as her tongue darted into his mouth. She wrapped her luscious legs around his waist, and Ciaran groaned. His *boidín* grew even harder, thicker, and longer. At least his hands were free, and he could get the door open.

Once inside the room, he kicked the door shut and stumbled to the bed. The two of them fell on top of it in a tangle of arms and legs. Through all the long lonely nights, Ciaran had dreamed of this moment, Becca had always been fully dressed and he'd taken his time to undress her one lace, one piece of clothing at a time, pausing to kiss and suckle to arouse her beyond distraction. Now, as she lay beneath him, her body was open to his adoration. Her hands fumbled at the laces on his trews and he moaned, but he grabbed her hands away and held them above her head.

"Let me look at you, Becca," he whispered. "For this moment in time, let me just look at you and worship you as you deserve."

She sighed. She didn't want to be worshipped, she wanted to be loved. She wanted her hands on his body, touching and inflaming him, as his hands did to hers. Slowly, Ciaran lowered his head and his mouth claimed the rosy tip of her breast. She arched against him. His tongue teased her nipple, flicking the now hardened tip, then swirling around the rosy areola. He loosened one of her hands so his hand could be free to explore.

His hard, strong fingers closed on her other breast, and Becca panted. "Yes," she sighed, as his thumb piqued her nipple, and his hand cupped her. "Oh, yes."

He let his tongue wander down and across the valley between her breasts, then lower still, trailing across her ribs and seeking her belly button. His hair spilled across her shoulders and chest, and the soft tickle almost drove her insane. Her hips bucked. He raised his head and smiled, wicked lights glinting in his eyes.

"All in due time, cailín," he promised. "All in due time."

Becca could feel the hard evidence of his arousal pressed against her thigh, and that wasn't where she wanted it. She wanted him squarely between her legs, and she wanted him there now. She had waited too many lifetimes for this moment. She squirmed, trying to maneuver beneath his heavy weight. He laughed, wrapping a massive arm around her hips.

"Lie still, Becca," he ordered, his voice roughened by desire. His tongue strayed across her hipbone and into the soft skin where her thigh met her abdomen. He nuzzled that area, then slipped his hand between her legs, smiling when he found liquid heat waiting for him. *Aye, she's ready for me.* His cheek nudged her leg, and Becca spread wider for him.

He knelt between her knees, his hands on her hips. He smiled, his full mouth curling at the corners, while his eyes glinted with a flash of diamonds in their sapphire depths. "I have much to teach you, Becca, and the first lesson is your pleasure."

She watched in fascination as his head dropped between her legs. She choked back a scream as his tongue found the nub at the entrance to her slick folds. His lips teased, and his tongue lapped her nether lips, kissing them before his tongue sought the very core of her. Ciaran's finger replaced his tongue, and he gently inserted it into her waiting sheath. She was hot and wet and ready for him, but he was not ready for her. He wanted her too much, and his *boidín* was large, much too large for the virgin he knew her to be. Ciaran had to slow down and take his time preparing her for his entrance. He would not hurt her this first time, nor at any time. He wanted only to bring her pleasure for the rest of their days.

When she relaxed against his one finger and the press of his hand, he pulled it out, and she whimpered. Ciaran smiled. He inserted two fingers, and Becca gasped. She pushed against his hand, rolling her hips from one side to the other, in exactly the response he sought.

"Please," she begged.

With two fingers and then three, Ciaran caressed and stretched her, marveling at her body's reaction to his invasion. Becca's whole body was flushed, and her nipples taut buds as she writhed against his hand. "Yes, love," he encouraged her.

Becca spiraled out of control. Waves of heat, generated by his hand, washed across her body. Her muscles clamped around his fingers, pulling and caressing. Wanting more. Wanting him. Her hands found his face, and she pulled his mouth down to meet hers. "Kiss me," she implored.

He did. Hard and demanding, his tongue mimicking in her mouth what his hand and fingers did between her thighs. He felt her sharply indrawn breath, which she held for a long moment, and then the shudders began.

Like a ticking bomb reaching critical mass, every part of her exploded, beginning in her center and spreading out to the ends of her fingers and toes. "Ahhh." Her breath hitched in her chest as another shudder consumed her, turning her sigh into a whimper.

Ciaran groaned as she quivered against him. Even though his *boidín* was still hidden in his trews, he almost spilled his seed. "'Tis but the first of many," he promised.

She'd never felt so alive, so aware of her body. Rather than sating her, his foreplay just whetted her appetite. She wanted him, all of him, buried deep within her. She wanted *him* to bring her back to that dazzling place she'd just been. She pushed at his hard chest and rolled away from him.

"Turnabout is fair play," she purred at him, one eyebrow cocked as she favored him with a smile.

She pushed him back on the bed and straddled his midsection.

He groaned. She leaned over to kiss him, her hair trailing across his chest. Her lips nipped his bottom lip, and then her mouth sucked his tongue into it.

He wrapped his arms around her, savoring the feel of her taut nipples pressed against his chest.

Becca kissed him long and hard, and as much as she loved his mouth, she wanted to explore his body, tasting and savoring. Her tongue found a path along his strong jaw. She traced the line of it to his ear. Nipping and suckling, she pulled on his earlobe with gentle teeth, blowing softly, pleased when she felt his whole body shuddered beneath her.

She nuzzled the soft skin at his pulse point and rubbed her smooth cheek against the shadow-bearded roughness of his. She rained kisses down his neck and across his chest, bestowing attention on each of his nipples. Her head dipped, her tongue following the fine feathering of hair down the center of his abdomen.

Strong hands gripped her biceps, but she put him off, her voice both tender and determined. "Fair is fair, Ciaran. I have waited just as long as you have, and now it is your turn." She looked as smug as a cat licking cream off her lips.

He smiled, knowing how headstrong she was. Her silken hair trailed lower down his abdomen setting his skin on fire. Her fingers found and defined each muscle along his ribs and abdomen. She kissed the scar just above his hipbone before her tongue and lips went back to find the downy dusting of hair sprinkled across his chest. Once again, her tongue tracked to the trail arrowing to his belly button—and lower. Her hands kneaded his hips as her tongue followed the dark trace until it disappeared into his trews.

With sure fingers, Becca unlaced his trews, and his erection eagerly spilled out. Ciaran managed to kick off his boots as Becca curled her fingers into the waistband and peeled the tight garment from him.

With his trews finally off, she sat between his feet staring at him in awe. "Oh, my God," she whispered. "You are magnificent." She licked her lips in anticipation.

Ciaran's gut clenched, his gaze following the pink tip of her tongue. He gulped.

She skimmed her fingers up his muscled legs, her touch as light as a feather. Curious, her hand shaking a tiny bit, she cupped the sac beneath his erection. When her touch elicited a sharply indrawn breath, she smirked. Using only one finger, she skimmed her nail up the ridged underside of his cock. *Silken steel*, Becca thought as her hand wrapped around the thick evidence of his virility.

She wondered how anything so hard could feel so soft and smooth beneath her touch. Becca trembled, a tiny aftershock going off in her middle. Soon, what she held in her hand was going to be right where she wanted it, and she could barely contain herself.

She bent her head to taste him. Her tongue swirled around the tip as if she was tasting an ice-cream cone. Except this cone was formed with fire and heat, not ice and cold. Ciaran groaned and went rigid beneath her. She felt him grow even more beneath her hand—longer, stiffer, thicker. Her lips replaced her tongue, and she drew him into the moist satin of her mouth.

Ciaran thought his cock would burst if it got any harder. He had to bury himself in Becca, and he had to do it now. They would have lifetimes to explore and tease one another. Now, his need was as elemental as life itself. His hands fisted in her silken hair and he dragged her head up. Kissing her hard enough to bruise her lips and steal the breath from her body, he rolled them over.

"Now," he growled. "I will have you."

Becca sighed. "Finally," she agreed, the word escaping from her mouth to his.

She spread her legs and Ciaran fitted himself between them. As he'd once suspected, her hips were made to cradle a man. *Not just any man,* Ciaran amended silently. *Me!* He would be her first and her last. His smooth tip hovered at her sweet entrance and she squirmed, trying to fit them together. "'Twill prick but just a bit," he whispered into her mouth.

Ciaran used his hand to ensure she was hot and wet, and still ready for him. She pushed against his hand, panting into his mouth as he kissed her. He guided his *boidín* into her core, where it was surrounded immediately by slick, pulsing silk. Ciaran pushed into her, wanting to be gentle, and stopping so her muscles could relax to accommodate him.

"Bugger this," Becca cried. She grabbed his buttocks with both hands and arched into him, driving him deep into her center. There was momentary pain and tears glistened at the corner of her eyes, but for the first time in her life, in all of her lives, Becca felt complete.

Ciaran lay still, buried deep within her. Afraid to move. Afraid of spilling his seed too soon. He kissed the tears from her eyes, most of his weight propped up on his elbows so his mass wouldn't crush her. He brushed a tendril of golden hair back from her forehead. "I dinnit want to hurt yee, cailín," he murmured.

Becca kissed the hollow of his shoulder. "Nay," she argued, her eyes glinting with mischievous lights as her mouth formed a teasing pout. "You'd have taken all bloody night to do the deed."

He grinned at her impudence, once more in control. He pulled back, his shaft retreating from her. She groaned and tried to hold him in her. He drove into her, and she cried out, this time in relief. Slowly, he withdrew again and the muscles in her sheath tightened, trying to hold him inside her. He pushed back, keeping his thrusts slow and sure as he rocked inside her. With each withdrawal and answering plunge, her hips rose to meet him. Then her tempo changed. No longer slow and easy, Becca pushed against him, urging him deeper and deeper, wanting him harder and faster.

Their breaths escaped from their lungs in gasps. Her sheath was hot and wet, and the sweet honey of her liquid passion trickled down Ciaran's thigh. Her legs wrapped around his waist, and he put his hands under her hips, tilting her pelvis up so he could drive deeper and harder still.

Shooting stars gathered in Becca's middle, and skyrockets went off behind her eyelids. She moaned in delight, her body gathering in on itself, the relentless waves of pleasure building to a crescendo she could no longer endure. "Please," she beseeched.

His *boidín* throbbed and felt like it was going to explode. The silken sides of her sheath stroked and caressed him, driving him mad with the sensation of liquid fire. When her plea reached his brain, the stars themselves exploded. He buried himself deep as he gathered her into his arms. His very life pumped out of him into her. She opened wide to receive him, then gathered him close to keep him.

Feeling his seed pumping into her, finally sent Becca over the edge, the pain and the pleasure all mixed together. She lay whimpering in his arms, knowing joy beyond all bounds, and completely awed by the experience.

Ciaran brushed soft tendrils of hair back from her face and kissed her cheeks, her forehead, and her eyes—trying to comfort her. "Did I hurt you, cailín?" His voice was taut with fear. He'd not wanted to hurt her, had only wanted to bring her pleasure this first time, but he knew he'd been too rough, too demanding.

She smiled into the hollow of his chest, and he felt her lips as they curled into that smile.

"How long before we can do that again?" Her voice was muffled against his warm skin.

He pushed up onto his elbows, arching his back so he could see her face. His expression registered his shock. "What did you just say?"

Her fingers trailed down his sides to find the hard muscles of his buttocks. She caressed and petted him while she flexed her inner muscles and squirmed. "You heard me," she replied, grinning so wide her dimple added a period to her words. "When can you do that again?" Her hands traced the wicked scar slicing across his back. Becca winced. She'd come so close to losing him to that wound. She kissed him, a furious barrage of kisses meant to erase that sight from her memory forever. She would forbid him from ever going to war again. In fact, she was never going to let him out of her bed.

Ciaran's shaft grew hard within her. He blinked, amazed he could. Moments ago, he'd felt so sated, so completely satisfied that he'd wanted nothing more than to gather her into his arms and sleep. She arched her hips against him.

"Well?" she demanded.

Stunned, he wasn't ready for her next move. Before he could react, she rolled them over so he was on his back, and she was astride him. *By the gods, but she is beautiful.* Her golden hair danced with silver highlights, and her cerulean eyes twinkled in the candlelight. Broad shoulders many a lad would envy tapered to her glorious breasts—full, firm, with rosy nipples beckoning for his mouth to taste. Her long waist nipped in below her ribs then flared to those wonderful hips made to hold him. Then came her long, lithe legs now curled beneath her so she could rock on her knees. She drove him wild with delight.

As Becca swayed above him, he watched in rapt fascination as their bodies joined together. The nest of her golden curls teased the jet-black fur surrounding his *boidín*. He reached up to cup her breasts in his rough hands. Becca moaned and leaned into them, her taut nipples rubbing against his palms.

Ciaran let her set her own pace. The first time had been for them both. This time was for her. She rode him, setting the pace of a gentle canter—slow, rolling, her eyes closed, her face set with a tender expression. She took one of his hands and guided it between her legs. Ciaran smiled. Virgin she might have been, but his Becca definitely knew what she wanted. His hand splayed across her golden down as his thumb found her secret nub. He touched her, and every muscle in her body tensed. He cried out his own pleasure as her sheath tightened around him. Now she rode him hard, almost desperate as she rocked against his thumb while her muscles flexed and squeezed his shaft. They both panted, so close to the edge that a gentle breeze could have blown them over the cliff.

"I love you, Becca."

That was all it took. Becca collapsed on his chest, her body shuddering and trembling as a major earthquake and myriad aftershocks rocked her body. Ciaran pumped his seed into her once again, his shaft throbbing and pulsing with life.

"I love you more than life," Becca whispered against his throat, exhaustion starting to claim her.

When he finally slipped from her body, she gave a little moan of protest. Her body nudged against his, seeking to draw him back inside her. He smiled and settled her against his side. With his free hand, he found the bedcovers and pulled them up. She was really and truly his now.

Becca's eyelashes fluttered over her cheeks. "And forever." She was asleep before the last syllable passed her lips.

Chapter Twenty

Ciaran nuzzled the back of Becca's neck where soft skin met silken hair. She snuggled back against him and sighed in her sleep. His *boidín* nestled between the cheeks of her *tóin* and grew hard as his hand splayed across her rounded abdomen possessively. When the tiny being growing inside retaliated with a kick, Ciaran grinned.

"Aye, a fine, strong son," he murmured into Becca's hair.

"Don't count on it," she mumbled. The caustic tone of her voice was not lost on him. "Could just as well be a girl."

He laughed out loud. "Oh, aye, it could. Any daughter of yours 'twould be more than likely to kick the hand that feeds her."

She wriggled her bottom. His immediate reaction brought a smile to her face. "Well, you aren't feeding her...or my hunger either, for that matter. I should kick you, too."

His hand caressed her swollen stomach, then trailed up to cup a full, round breast. "Do you hunger for me, cailín?" he growled in her ear.

A delicious shiver danced down her spine to settle in her toes. She flexed her buttocks and was rewarded by his sharp intake of breath.

"Nay," she protested. "I don't hunger for you." She dismissed him airily, then squeezed again for effect. "I hunger for *him*." She batted her lashes and purred.

He laughed and shifted her in his arms so that she was propped on her elbows, and her knees were drawn up beneath her. He grabbed a pillow, one of the innovations she'd added to their life, and stuffed it in under the top of her thighs. He positioned himself behind her, his *boidín* playfully rubbing against the crease between her cheeks. A little moan escaped her throat as she pushed back against him.

His long fingers teased the soft folds between her thighs. He tested her readiness and found her hot and wet. With a growl, the dark wolf of the MacDermot claimed his mate, driving into her very core. She pushed back against him, frantic to drive him deeper.

"Easy, cailín," he soothed. "The babe."

"Making love with you will not hurt the baby," Becca promised him as she pushed and squirmed.

He wrapped one massive arm around her middle and held her, his other hand caressing her hip. She made little mewling noises in her throat. He pushed into her again and again as she bucked back against him. Her inner muscles contracted, and then a shudder ran through her. He drove into her one more time, and shooting stars exploded in his brain as his seed pumped into her. She convulsively contracted around his pulsing cock, as shudder after shudder rocked her body.

At last, she drew a long, shaky breath and collapsed onto the bed. He followed her down and gathered her into his arms. Her head rested in the hollow of his shoulder, her one leg thrown possessively across his middle. His fingers idly combed the tangles in her hair. After a few minutes, their hearts regained a normal rhythm, and their breathing slowed.

"Love of my heart," he murmured.

"Light of my life," she replied. The baby kicked again, and she gasped.

"Son," Ciaran asserted.

"Daughter," Becca avowed.

****

The months flew swiftly, and life at Ailfenn was good. Both the O'Neills and the O'Briens stayed within their own lands. Snow fell on the winter solstice as the Yule log burned merrily in the hearth, the white flakes softening the bleak winter landscape. In time, the dark days of winter grew longer and spring began to awaken the land.

Albun Eiler, the spring solstice, dawned warm and bright, and Ciaran smiled at his wife, as she lay snuggled in his arms. "One year," he whispered into her silken hair. "You came to me one year ago."

"Yeah, and if I remember correctly, you wanted to kill me," Becca reminded him, an arched brow and sarcastic tone making her point.

"Nay, cailín," he insisted. "'Twould have been like cutting out my own heart. I loved you. Loved you the first moment you opened your eyes and looked into mine."

She kissed his chest. "You're just saying that to keep your pregnant wife happy."

With a gentle finger, he tipped her chin so she had to look up at his face. His indigo eyes, normally as dark and stormy as the sea, softened to cobalt. His mouth sought hers and he kissed her, his lips gently nibbling hers. "I will do whatever it takes to make you happy, Becca. You are a gift. One I almost lost, and one I cherish the more for it. I will not lose you again." His voice was thick with emotion.

Becca sighed happily and snuggled closer to the warmth of his body. It might be March twenty-first, but the air was chilly, and the fire had burned down to gray embers. "It's my birthday," she announced. "I'm fifty-one."

Ciaran snorted.

"Well, technically, I am," she retorted.

A soft tap at the door postponed his teasing. "Yes?" he called instead.

"'Tis Alys," a timid voice called from the other side of the door. "Come to stir up the fire."

"Come in."

The little maid scurried about laying wood kindling before poking up the dying embers. She added some logs, and soon the fire crackled, spreading warmth throughout the room. She bobbed a little curtsy and hurried out the door. Ciaran was too busy kissing Becca to notice the look on Alys's face. The little maid's dimples made deep divots in her cheeks.

"All is well," she whispered to the shadows in the hallway.

Spring arrived in all her glory. Flowers nodding in the gentle breezes dotted the meadows, and lambs cavorted around their fat, wooly mothers. Cattle chewed their cud contentedly, and grain crops stretched green stalks to the warm, blue sky. Spring soon bowed out to welcome the warm days of summer.

Becca grew larger and more cantankerous with each passing day. Although Ciaran was fascinated by the changes to her body, she felt fat and unattractive no matter how he tried to soothe her.

Siobhan talked to him about the moods a woman endured. She even had Niall talk to him, but he still fretted. He loved her dearly, and it distressed him that she thought he might not.

The last sennight of July grew busy as tinkers and traders arrived to set up their tents and offer their wares. Most of the clann arrived to celebrate the Festival of Light, anticipating the birth of *An Taoiseac's* first child. Had Becca discovered the number of wagers being made on the gender of the child and the date of its birth, she would have been mortified...or laying bets herself. People arrived from far and wide to honor Ciaran and his lady on this *Lughnasadh*.

On the first day of August, he insisted she accompany him to the green. She protested, saying it was too far to walk. He offered to get a cart or carry her himself. She demurred, saying she had nothing to wear. Siobhan appeared with a new linen gown in shimmering shades of blue and green. Becca balked just because.

"I am as big as a house, Ciaran. I don't want anyone to see me like this," she grumbled.

He pulled her into his arms and kissed her, his lips and tongue teasing her mouth. When she finally relented a little, his tongue darted into her mouth. He kissed her long and hard, leaving them both breathless.

She leaned against him, needing him and wanting him in much more than just a physical sense, though she couldn't wait to renew that aspect of their relationship, too. This man was her strength and her stability. Even when she was the biggest shrew in the country, he kissed her, held her, and told her how beautiful she was.

"I wish yee could see yerself through my eyes, cailín," he whispered into her hair. "Yee could be as big as the castle itself, and I wouldn't care." He ran his hands across her body. He'd memorized every curve, every secret place, and he loved all of her. "'Tisn't your face or your body that makes you beautiful, Becca." He placed his hand on her head. "This," he said. Then he touched her heart. "And this." Both of his hands cradled her rotund abdomen. "And the miracle growing here. These are the things I love about you. These are the things that make you beautiful."

Tears stained her cheeks silver, and she brushed them away with the back of her hand. "I'm sorry I've been such a beast," she sniffed. "Hormones." He looked completely perplexed at the word. "Oh, I forgot. Hormones are nasty little buggers that run amok in pregnant women's bodies making them weepy and bitchy, and bloody well useless."

Ciaran smiled down at her. "So, cailín, will yee come to the fair of *Lughnasadh* with me?"

She smiled back. "Aye. I'll come."

She changed into the linen dress, and the little maid, Alys, brushed out her hair. With deft fingers, the girl wove the plaits and then wound the intricate braids around her head. Becca felt infinitely better by the time she joined Ciaran in the great hall, and they strolled out to the courtyard. True to his word, he'd had a cart brought around so she wouldn't have to walk. Eachan himself drove the cart, while Ciaran mounted his stallion.

All was in readiness up on the hill. The bonfire stood ready to be lit, and both the priest and the Druid did a brisk business. Lughnasadh traditionally was the time of handfasting. A couple could have a trial marriage lasting a year and a day. They could return to the fair the following year to make their troth a permanent one, or they could turn their backs on each other and walk away in opposite directions, effectively divorcing.

Ciaran did have an ulterior motive for bringing Becca to the fair. Though he had bound her to him at *Samhain*, he also wanted the blessing of the Church. He'd directed Eachan to take Becca directly to the priest. The cart rolled to a stop near the man in his faded brown cassock, and Ciaran dismounted. One of his guard led the stallion away.

When she realized what was going on, she started laughing. "Talk about a shotgun wedding," she chortled, and then realized not a soul had a clue as to what she meant. That just made her laugh harder. She wasn't prepared when the first contraction hit. It stole her breath and doubled her over. Then her water broke, and she looked at Ciaran, her eyes wide and worried.

He knew what was happening before she did. A huge smile split his face, and he pulled her into his arms. "Tis time, cailín. The babe comes."

He asked Niall to call for his horse, but Taidhg had already reacted and led the stallion forward. Ciaran mounted and then Niall carefully picked up Becca. He handed her to his *Taoiseac*.

"I'll send Siobhan," Niall told them. "And the midwife." He turned on his heel and darted into the crowd to find his wife.

Cradling her across his hard thighs, Ciaran urged the big horse back to the castle. The whole crowd stopped to watch the couple, and Becca was so embarrassed she hid her face in his shirt. Riordan was in the courtyard as they cantered in. He helped Becca down, and then took the horse from Ciaran as the big man scooped Becca into his arms and strode into keep. Up in their chamber, Ciaran set her on the bed, wondering what to do next.

"Get out," she ordered as if reading his mind. His face fell. Hurt radiated in his eyes. Taking his face in her hands, she kissed him tenderly. "No offense, Ciaran. I might be a twenty-first century woman, but men in the delivery room never seemed like a good idea to me. Please, when Siobhan and the midwife get here, go find Niall and Riordan, and get rip-roaring drunk. Okay?"

"I'll not leave you to face this alone, Becca," he vowed, his fierce expression emphasizing his words.

Siobhan and the midwife sailed in before Becca could reply. One got her undressed and into a simple linen shift, while the other laid fresh coverlets across the bed. Ciaran paced the room like a caged wolf.

"Relax," Siobhan chided him, keeping her voice calm. "The babe will come in its own good time. If yee have to stay, then do some good." Ciaran looked hopeful. "Get into bed with her and let her lie back against yee."

Ciaran did as he was told, leaning up against the wall on a couple of pillows. He pulled Becca back against him and wrapped his arms around her. She finally found a comfortable position by bending her knees up. Siobhan draped a coverlet over her legs to preserve some modicum of her modesty.

By noon, Ciaran was cursing his *boidín*, his selfishness, and men in general. By mid-afternoon, Becca was cursing one man in particular, but didn't dare voice her opinion. As shadows fell across the room, Alys came in to light candles and rush lights along the walls. Her cheeks dimpled as she watched the couple on the bed. A really strong contraction hit, and Alys's brow knitted in consternation. She slipped out of the room. A few minutes later, she returned with several new candles and some sprigs of herbs. She lit them all, and soon a soothing mixture of scents wafted about the room. Becca closed her eyes, drew deep breaths of the perfumed air into her lungs, and relaxed.

"I can do this," she murmured. "This is a piece of cake compared to what I've been through."

Hard dark came and with it, contractions so close they might as well be one continuous spasm.

"Where is Riordan?" Becca panted between one set of contractions. "Get him in here now," she ordered through clinched teeth.

A few minutes later, Riordan appeared hesitantly at the door. He peeked in, curious as to why Ciaran laid on the bed cradling Becca against his chest and between his legs. Siobhan and the midwife waited at the foot of the bed. Becca's face shone with sweat, and she made little huffing noises. Riordan looked closer at his cousin. Ciaran's face was white, and sweat beaded on his forehead.

A contraction built in Becca's middle, and she gathered all of her strength to push, waiting for the pain to build and recede.

"Now," Siobhan agreed.

Ciaran's hands knotted into fists where they crossed beneath her breasts, and his knuckles turned white. He bit down so hard on his bottom lip that blood actually spurted. Fascinated, Riordan watched as the contraction passed, and Becca relaxed, as did Ciaran—but only barely.

Becca looked up at Riordan, her eyes blazing. "Well, it took you bloody well long enough to get here," she snarled. Riordan held his hands up in front of him to ward off her bark. "Will you get this bloody bugger out of my room and as far away from here as you can?" She glared at her cousin-in-law when he didn't reply immediately. "I mean it, Riordan. Take him far away. And while you're at it, get him drunk and keep him that way until this bloody birth is done."

Ciaran mopped her brow and kissed her hair. "I won't leave yee, Becca," he whispered in an attempt to soothe her, all the while trying not to let his panic show. Her labor had gone on far longer than any he'd ever heard tell of, though Siobhan and the midwife seemed unworried.

"If you stay for the rest of this, Ciaran, you won't let me be having any more babies," she snapped. "And I plan to have at least a dozen."

Ciaran blanched, and Riordan had the audacity to laugh. "Aye, cailín," he finally grinned at Becca. "I'll get the bloody bugger drunk for you. I want the two of you to have babies enough to start a whole new clann."

Niall appeared at Riordan's elbow, prepared to help the younger man carry out Becca's wishes. "She's a woman, Ciaran," Niall reminded him. "She'll have her way by hook or by crook."

Becca's azure eyes gazed into Ciaran's stormy ones. "Please," she whispered. "I can't be taking care of you and me, and the babe when she comes."

"He," Ciaran corrected, but he disentangled from her. He plumped up the pillows he'd been laying against and helped her settle back against the cushions. He bent and kissed her forehead. "I'd be takin' the pain from yee if I could," he whispered.

"I know." She kissed his cheek. "But you can't, Ciaran. Please. Just go. This is hard enough as it is."

"I'll be right outside," he promised.

"No, you won't," Becca ordered. "At least as far as the stables, Riordan. And drink. Strong drink. Whiskey. Lots of it." She started panting again as another contraction built. She was damned tired of this.

Ciaran ran his hand through his hair, wanting to go to her and hold her again. Riordan stepped to his side, his hand on Ciaran's arm to draw him away.

"Get him out of here. NOW!" She barked the words out from between clinched teeth.

Niall and Riordan each grabbed an arm and forcibly dragged Ciaran from the room. The midwife followed them and shut the door with a resolute bang behind them. She dropped the crossbar into place for good measure.

Dumbfounded, Ciaran stood in the hallway. His own wife had chased him from the birthing chamber and locked the door behind him. "Of all the..." he muttered. Then the contraction hit. He doubled over as Becca cried out from the other side of the door.

"Whiskey," Riordan said.

"Aye," Niall agreed. "And lots of it."

As his two friends escorted him down to the great hall, Ciaran understood the wisdom in Becca's actions. Gair filled mugs for them, and the three men slunk into Ciaran's den to await the outcome.

****

Just after midnight, Alys burst from Becca's room, ran down the hall, and called excitedly from the top of the stairs, "'Tis here, *Taoiseac*. The babe is here. Come quick."

The door to the den crashed open. Ciaran took the stairs three at a time, Niall and Riordan close on his heels. The three slid to a stop at the door as they listened to the baby crying inside. All three wiped moisture from the corners of their eyes.

"'Tis a son, *Taoiseac*," Siobhan called. "A fine, strong son."

Ciaran stumbled into the room. He peeked at the tiny bundle in Siobhan's arms, marveling at the tiny fingers and the perfectly shaped head. His hand carefully cupped the baby's head, covered with dark peach fuzz. He turned to Becca, his eyes shining with a love so intense, it rivaled the bonfires burning on the hill above the castle. "Son," he told her smugly as he took her hand and kissed it. "Aye, but you're a fair cailín, and I love you more than words could ever convey."

Becca's hand gripped his, squeezing hard enough his fingers went numb. She grunted and bore down, and as Ciaran stood there dumbstruck, his daughter entered the world only a few minutes after her brother.

"Girl." Becca smirked without even looking at the baby.

Ciaran gathered her into his arms, raining kisses upon her face and neck and shoulders. As she held his face in her hands, she kissed his tears away. "I thought you wanted one of each," she teased him.

"Oh, aye, cailín," he whispered in awe, brushing her hair back off her forehead. "Aye."

****

"Aye, indeed." Abhean stared into the center of the standing stones. The bland expression on his face camouflaged the emotions churning in his heart. He flinched as the air shimmered beside him, and Onagh appeared. Ignoring her, he continued to watch the tender scene unfolding before him in the center of the standing stones.

"I know what you did," she murmured.

He shrugged, still holding his emotions in check. "So now they will have all their lives as was written." His flat tone didn't fool her as he'd hoped.

"Play not the fool with me, Abhean," Onagh chastised.

"You have what your heart desired. Let me be." He felt her stir beside him as if she meant to touch him. She didn't.

"You have seen." Her voice held no question. "Their lives stretch out before them, each one full of both happiness and heartache, as the lives of mortals should be." She remained silent for several heartbeats. "You got your way." Her voice betrayed nothing.

"No." His voice betrayed more than he wanted.

"He will have his chance." Her voice was softer than a whispered summer breeze but he heard her.

"Aye. He will. Despite Mac Lir." His nostrils flared, the only sign of his anger.

"'Tis a dangerous game you started."

A tendril of her golden hair tickled his forearm and he recoiled from its touch. "'Tis not for sport, Onagh." He dismissed her with a gesture. Even as the scene in the center of the stones shifted to show a horse and rider, Abhean disappeared.

Chapter Twenty-One

The hair stood up on the back of Becca's neck, and cold fingers skittered down her spine. Someone watched her. She glanced around surreptitiously, but noticed nothing out of the ordinary. Still, she had the distinct feeling that someone was staring at her. The big black horse she rode tossed his head.

"Easy, Ari," she soothed as he danced between her legs. "They're all depending on us. This has to be the ride of our lives," she whispered to the spirited animal.

Becca leaned over his neck, took a deep breath to steady her nerves, and tried to shake off her unease. She touched Arien lightly with her heels. Horse and rider became one, a molded partnership of gentle hands and legs with muscle and strength. She sat the large horse like she'd been born to him, and he carried her like she were a Valkyrie maiden of yore.

His eyes narrowed as he watched horse and rider. He'd come to see the horse, but it was the rider who captured his attention. She was glorious—broad shoulders, slim waist, and legs that went from here to there and back again. He briefly fantasized about those legs wrapping around his middle. He squirmed uncomfortably as his *boidín* stretched the front of his riding breeches.

"Bloody hell, Neal," he muttered, wondering if he'd be able to sit his horse during the competition.

The big sandy-haired man on his left chuckled appreciatively. "Ayo, Irish hotblood, Keiran," he commented in a rich brogue.

"Yes, she is," Keiran murmured.

A third man, this one with rich, auburn hair and a rakish grin, joined the first two. He watched the horse and rider then glanced at the dark man in the middle. He guffawed, clapping the big man on the back. "I think Kieran has met his match, Neal."

Misunderstanding the younger man, Neal replied, "Aye, Rory, 'tis a fine horse for certain. If he jumps as good as he looks, I think we should add him to the stable."

Rory hid his smile. Neal could be so dense at times. "*She* sits a horse as well as Kieran, does she not?" he pointed out.

"She?" Neal blinked in confusion. "Oh, yee mean the cailín ridin' him." He studied horse and rider for a long moment. "Aye, she does have a good seat."

"And her *tóin* ain't so bad either." Rory chuckled under his breath. He chortled when that comment drew an exasperated growl from the dark man at his shoulder.

Neal turned to stare at both men. Kieran was obviously uncomfortable in his abruptly tight riding breeches, and his cousin, Rory, enjoyed that fact immensely. The older man tried to hide his smile. In all the years he'd known Kieran, this was the first time he'd ever noticed him react to a woman like this. Neal glanced at the other man. Unlike Rory, who'd tupped every cailín who was willing. Neal decided he was going to enjoy watching the outcome of this contest, too.

"And yee notice, Rory," Neal added with a devilish grin, "she's got good hands as well."

Kieran groaned, imagining those hands touching him. *What in the bloody hell has gotten into me?* He squirmed again. He'd grown even harder during the course of this conversation. Much more, and he wouldn't be able to walk, much less ride in the next round.

"Clean round," Rory commented as the girl and horse finished. "And she's under the time." He glanced at Kieran's mid-section. "Going to be a bloody hard jump off," he sniggered.

Kieran punched him in the arm. "Then we'd best get ready," he growled.

Becca circled Arien at the end of their ride. They'd jumped clean, and she glanced at the clock. They were well under the time limit, too. Exhilarated, she patted Arien's neck and guided him out of the arena. As they neared the gate, she finally heard the applause. Becca glanced up into the crowd by the gate trying to locate her family. Her grandfather waved at her and flashed a thumb's up sign. She smiled and dipped her head at him.

She scanned the crowd and locked gazes with the most intriguing pair of blue eyes she'd ever seen—so dark they were almost black. Then she glimpsed the face and body those eyes belonged to. With the face of a Greek hero, he was tall—at least six and a half feet—with broad shoulders, short hair so black and thick it almost looked blue in the sunshine, and long, muscular legs. Oh, those legs almost made her swoon when she thought about them touching hers skin-to-skin. Her gaze lingered on his mid-section and she grinned, thinking of the old Mae West line about guns and pockets. He was certainly glad to see someone. Becca blushed to the roots of her hair and resisted the urge to fan herself. The man absolutely took her breath away.

She urged Arien down the runway leading from the arena to the holding area and the practice ring beyond. Her parents and grandfather waited in the holding area. She slid off Arien and hugged everyone. They all babbled, so excited their words tumbled over each other, but Becca couldn't concentrate on the conversation. A flurry of feminine sighs pulled her gaze to the practice ring.

The man she'd seen in the stands had just entered the ring on his horse. A crush of female bodies jockeyed for fence-side position. *God, but he's magnificent.* Becca blushed as a hot pool of desire settled between her legs.

Her grandfather took Ari's reins from her unresisting fingers and led the big horse away for a quick rubdown. Becca's parents still jabbered, their voices floating around her. All of her attention centered on the man cantering in the ring. She was lured to the rail like a moth drawn inexorably to flame. Without a word to her stunned parents, she glided over to the fence as if in a trance. Two men parted to give her room and exchanged grins over her head. With her attention focused on the ring, she ignored them.

Becca stared, bemused by the dark man watching her from the dark chestnut horse. Without thinking, she swirled her tongue across her lower lip. He made her mouth dry, and she felt a nervous flutter low in her belly. Then her top teeth tugged at her bottom lip, and the men on either side of her shook their heads when the rider wheeled his horse away from her and rode across the ring.

The auburn-haired man on her right chuckled, and she glanced at him. He was good-looking in his own way, but her attention was drawn back to the rider again. The man beside her was sunset to the other's midnight. That they knew each other was obvious by the fierce looks the rider flashed toward the man beside her.

The loudspeaker announced something, but Becca didn't have a clue what it was. There was a loud buzzing in her ears accompanied by a thumping bass drum. Blood sang in her veins and her heart pumped to keep up with the fire burning within her.

"Yee'd best get a move on, cailín," the older man on her left urged. "Yee need to be mounting up for the jump off."

"Oh. Yes. Of course." She nodded, distracted, never taking her eyes off the rider as he left the ring.

The younger man grabbed her by her upper arms, physically picked her up, and turned her to face the opposite direction. "Cailín, yee need to be goin' now if yer competin' in this round." His thick brogue didn't hide his amusement.

"Uh. Yeah. Thanks." She stumbled away. Her brain finally processed that the man had called her *colleen.* She smiled. Her grandfather always called her that. Maybe it was a sign.

Her grandfather had Ari ready for her to mount. Her dad gave her a leg up, and then patted her thigh. "Ride like you know how, Becca," he encouraged.

She flashed her family a smile and shook her head to clear it. She needed to focus. Still in a daze, Becca let Ari find his own way to the staging area at the gate. Nine other horses and their riders waited in the runway. One by one, each pair entered the arena. The first four all garnered either time faults or jumping faults during their rides. The dark man on the chestnut horse was the fifth rider. As he entered the arena, Becca urged Ari up to the gate so she could watch, and when he looked up, their eyes locked on each other.

She took his breath away. Her smile was radiant as her cerulean eyes stared into his. Though her hair was tightly bound in a bun at the nape of her neck, Kieran imagined its golden strands trailing across his chest and... He jerked his thoughts back from that dangerous trap.

Kieran broke eye contact first, and circled at a controlled canter. "Easy, Fen." He kept his voice low. He was damned uncomfortable, but he had no choice. He rode for Ireland, the Army, and his Clann. He let out a slow breath, pointed Fen's nose at the first jump, and released the big animal.

Becca watched man meld with horse to become one. The horse was an awesome example of Irish breeding and any other time, she would have paid close attention to the animal. Today though, it was the rider who held her enthralled. His wore a dark green military jacket over pale fawn breeches. The patch on his left shoulder flashed gold and red against the somber color of his uniform. His riding helmet now covered his close-cropped black hair. The uniform in no way diminished the man's astounding musculature. In fact, it only enhanced it.

Becca sighed, feeling inordinately foolish. This was 1978 for goodness sake. This was a time for women's lib, burning bras, and "I Am Woman" rhetoric. It wasn't politically correct to act like the swooning heroine in some bodice ripper. But there was a nasty little voice in her head that kept whispering, *"Aye, but wouldn't yee like him to rip yer bodice? Yee'd be lovin' ever bit of it, yeah?"*

Horse and rider finished the course to thunderous applause. Clean round. Four seconds under the time limit. He'd be hard to beat. If she'd been mounted on any horse but Arien, he would have been impossible to beat.

"Riding a clean round, ladies and gentlemen, is Captain Kieran MacDermot of the Irish Defense Forces on Fenian Warrior."

Well, that certainly explained the uniform. Army man. Irish. Dark. Brooding. Yummy. Becca forced her thoughts back to reality. As the captain rode through the gate, he looked straight at her and Becca thought she would melt right there. No man had the right to be that gorgeous. No man had the right to have that much sex appeal. She grinned. That man could seduce the most ardent, man-hating libber and make her ask for seconds. Ask? Hell, he could make her beg.

Well pleased with himself, Kieran passed by the cailín on the black horse. He'd managed to stay aboard without too much affront to his masculinity. And, the look on the cailín's face as he'd ridden past was most gratifying. He couldn't wait until this blasted event was over. He had six weeks of leave coming, and he knew exactly where he was going to spend it. He grinned. And precisely what he was going to do while spending it. Unlike Rory, he didn't have a cailín at every stop. Now he knew why. He was going to woo this one, win her, and make her his. Kieran's grin broadened into a smirk. He didn't even know her name. He was bloody well losing his mind!

Becca was the last rider. The only clean round belonged to the Irish Army captain. She took a deep breath. Her insides quivered as a tingly spasm ran from the pit of her stomach all the way to her toes at the thought of him. Her knees wanted to clamp together, but horse and saddle prevented them from doing so. She'd laughed when girlfriends had told her of getting off while riding. Now she was grateful there was something to rub against. *Oh, my God. I cannot believe he can turn me on by just looking at me. How juvenile am I?*

She reminded herself there was time enough for such thoughts later. Right now, she had a jump-off to win. She patted Ari's neck and urged him into the arena. She circled, made sure Ari had the correct lead, and then gave him his head. They soared over the first obstacle.

Kieran had ridden out to the holding area after leaving the arena. The cailín and her horse, the last pair to ride, were announced. *Rebecca Miller riding High Meadow Poseidon's Arien.* He dismounted, and led Fen back to the gate. The cailín really was an excellent rider. Her hands and legs were quiet. She stayed balanced. She stayed focused. She let the horse do his best. She rode a clean round.

"Ladies and gentleman," the announcer said, "Ms. Miller and Arien had a clean round and were four seconds under the time limit. We have a tie."

Becca couldn't believe it. She tied the big Irishman. As she rode toward the gate, she almost reined Ari to a halt. He was standing there, leaning insolently on the gate, watching her intently. She dragged another one of those quivering breaths into her lungs. This was so not fair. A win would give her enough points to qualify for the Grand Prix. If she could win this event, she was sure the U.S. Equestrian Team would move her up from alternate to team member. She'd dreamed of riding in the Olympics since she'd been a little girl—had trained her whole life for this one moment. This man was not going to jeopardize her chances. She'd just ignore him.

Kieran almost laughed out loud as he watched the emotions flit across the cailín's face. That she was as affected by him as he was by her was reassuring. He considered knocking down a rail just to get this thing over with so he could properly introduce himself, and then seduce her at his leisure. Unfortunately, his honor wouldn't allow it. He was an officer, and though he was Irish, he was gentleman to boot. He wouldn't throw the competition.

Becca rode through the gate, determined to ignore the big man. She reined Ari around so they were facing the arena. Glancing out of the corner of her eye, she was pleased he seemed to be ignoring her. Good. That meant he had no interest in her.

His instincts were more finely honed than most soldiers'. His active duty unit was the *Sciathán Fianógloch an Airm,* the Army Ranger Wing of the Irish Defense Forces. The unit drew its name from the legendary Fenian Warriors of ancient times.

Kieran knew she was checking him out and her perusal had stopped at his groin.

She hadn't meant to look at him, but since he wasn't paying attention to her... She took her time looking him up and down, and... *Ohmygosh, ohmygosh, ohmygosh*, she chanted in her head. Was he ever up!

Slowly, he turned his head and his indigo eyes stared into her cerulean ones. She blushed furiously, and Kieran confirmed her thoughts were as prurient as his own. He grinned unabashedly, cocked an eyebrow, and winked.

Becca ducked her head, and tried to stifle her mortified groan. Oh, God. He knew exactly what she was thinking. She was mortified at the decidedly sexual direction her thoughts had taken. Unlike most of her peers, Becca had not jumped into the sexual revolution. In fact, she was probably the only twenty-four-year-old virgin in the entire U.S. of A. However, one more look from him, and she might just jump into his arms and demand he take her virginity right here, right now, in front of God and everybody.

He watched her worry her bottom lip with her teeth again. The subconscious gesture was enough to send his *boidín* to full attention. Damnation, he was never going to get through this next round. He wanted only to drag her off her horse, find a stall full of new hay, and tup her until neither of them knew their names.

The course stewards made their adjustments to the obstacles, and the chief judge came over to discuss order with the two riders. Ever gallant, Kieran deferred. "Ladies first," he offered in a brogue as thick as honey and just as sweet.

"But I'm not a lady," Becca retorted before she could stop herself.

"Then, I'll go first," Kieran replied smoothly,

flashing a cocky grin.

He mounted effortlessly, and Becca's breath caught in her chest. *Ohmygosh, omygosh.* She chanted the mantra again. She was never going make it. She could actually feel wetness between her legs. She glanced down, hoping it wasn't visible. *Sweat. It's just sweat.*" She didn't believe a word of it.

She tried very hard not to watch, but couldn't help herself. As he rode, she let her imagination have full sway. She pictured him as some ancient warrior, his blue-black hair flying in the wind, a sword at his side. She couldn't breathe, and got dizzy from the vision she conjured. She almost fell off Ari again.

"Whoa, cailín," an amused voice said.

She glanced down. The good-looking man from the practice ring patted Ari's shoulder, and the horse whickered. He wore a uniform with riding breeches and boots as well. "You're with him." She took a deep lungful of air, then let it out slowly.

Rory grinned at her. "Aye, cailín, 'tis true. Lieutenant Rory MacDermot at your service."

Becca glanced to the rider still in the ring, then back at the man standing next to her stirrup. They certainly didn't look anything alike. Was MacDermot a common name like Jones or Smith or Miller?

As if reading her mind, Rory grinned easily at her. "Cousins. I got all the personality, and he got all the brooding good looks."

Becca giggled and relaxed. This was what she needed to get her focus back, this harmless flirting and banter. That other, he was too dark, too intense, too...well, just too much of everything.

Kieran and Fenian once again had a clean round, though they just barely beat the time limit. Becca rode out into the arena before he came through the gate. She couldn't be anywhere near him and maintain the focus she needed.

"Watch the turn on number six," he called to her as they passed several feet apart. "'Tis sharp."

Becca nodded. She'd been watching him on the course. His horse came off jump number five on a left lead and had about two strides to gather himself, change to a right lead, turn and take the double oxer that was number six. Any but a skillful horse and rider would turn too wide to come square at the fences on six. Becca briefly considered changing leads right before five. She questioned whether Ari would have enough time to gather himself for the tall jump. It was a risky move, especially since five was close to the arena wall and faced a sea of spectators. However, she was a fierce competitor. If it worked, it could shave off enough time she'd win. If it didn't, she would probably come in second anyway.

She leaned over Ari's neck and petted him. "In for a dime, in for a dollar," she told the big horse.

Kieran dismounted and stood beside Rory at the gate. They watched silently, knowing this was the make or break round. Becca cleared the first four obstacles, her time was neck and neck with Kieran's. As they watched her approach jump five, Kieran caught the subtle shift in her weight and watched the big black horse switch leads.

"Smart." Her audacious decision impressed him.

Horse and rider approached the high triple-barrier fence. Becca was in complete control, and Arien launched himself effortlessly. They would clear the fence with little problem. There was a blinding flash, and time clicked into slow motion. The big horse seemed to hang suspended in mid-air, and then he was falling, crashing through the top bar of the fence. That rail splintered, and the rest came crashing down around him. His left front foot hit the ground, and his leg buckled. His body followed, twisting as it plunged. Becca was flung from his back by the force of the fall, and she hit the ground several feet away.

Pandemonium erupted. Kieran and Rory were through the gate at a dead run. Kieran actually beat the nearest course steward to Becca's crumpled body. His hands skimmed over her body as he checked for broken bones. Her helmet had been knocked loose, and Kieran carefully removed it. As he'd suspected, she had golden hair shot with silver highlights, and its luxurious mass escaped its bun. Her eyes fluttered, but she remained unconscious.

****

"Not again," the male said, disgruntled.

"You worry too much," the female said.

"Well, he took so long to find her, 'twouldn't do to lose her now," the male groused.

"He'll bind her, give her the Knot, and all will be well in our world," the female declared.

"S'cuse me," Becca interrupted.

Silence.

"Hello?"

Still silence.

****

Becca moaned and slowly opened her eyes.

"Don't move, Becca," her hunk in green uniform commanded.

"Ari," she groaned. "Is Arien okay?"

Kieran glanced over his shoulder. Rory held the horse and checked him over as the event veterinarian, along with a couple of paramedics, ran up. "He's up and movin', cailín. I think he'll be fine. 'Tis you I'm concerned about. Just lie still 'til the medics check you over."

Becca smiled at his worried, blue eyes. "I'm fine," she asserted. "Guess this means you win."

"Doesn't matter." Kieran dismissed the idea out of hand. "What happened?"

Becca screwed her eyes shut, trying to remember around the headache pounding her temples. There was the ghost of a bright flash behind her eyelids. "Flash," she finally replied. "I think from a camera."

"What bloody idiot would use a flash camera at an event like this?" he growled.

"A bloody stupid one," Rory responded at his shoulder. "Yer beastie will be fine accordin' to the vet," he added.

"Thank goodness." Becca closed her eyes and bit back a groan. She peeked out from under her long, dark lashes. "Can I get up now?"

"Not 'til the medics give their consent," Kieran asserted.

He moved back to give them room, and found he had to bite back a huge dose of jealousy to keep it in check. He didn't like the idea of another man touching Becca one bit. In a few moments, the paramedics cleared her, and Kieran took their place at her side.

"Now?" she asked him, cocking an eyebrow.

He gave her a little room, but not much. His body wanted to crowd hers, to touch, to savor and taste. He tried to get a grip on his emotions. She could have been killed or severely injured, yet he could only think of one thing—getting her into a nice soft bed where they could spend the next six weeks tupping and getting to know one another.

He helped her to a sitting position, and then stood to pull her to her feet. She swayed against him for a brief moment, and white-hot heat burned a hole in his skin where they'd made contact. Her gaze jerked up and stared into his eyes, mesmerized. Kieran smiled at her. "Aye, yee feel it, too," he whispered.

Becca was unhurt. The crowd applauded, seemingly captivated by the fact that her staunchest competition had been the first one to reach her side. Kieran paid them no attention, and she suspected he'd be bemused by the dreamy looks many of the women cast his direction as he and Rory escorted her to the gate.

The vet and a steward had already led Arien out of the arena, and Becca was anxious to check on him. If her head didn't hurt so badly and it weren't so undignified, she'd have run to the holding area. As it was, she was awfully glad Kieran and Rory walked beside her.

The three of them moved through the tunnel from the arena. The chief judge and the chief steward were talking loudly to a man with a large assortment of camera equipment dangling around his neck.

"There's yer bloody idiot," Rory pointed out.

Kieran took off like a shot. He stalked up to the man, grabbed his arm, spun him around, and landed a haymaker squarely on the man's nose. The photographer went down like he'd been poleaxed. Kieran glared down at him, his eyes the color of the North Sea in December. The man on the ground muttered something about the police and wanting to sue.

"Yee bloody well deserved it, yee friggin' bugger. Yee want to come after me, yee go right ahead, but I guarantee there's more where that came from," Kieran snarled.

Becca stood there gaping. A very secret feminine center buried deep within her relished the thought that this man was willing to fight for her. One look at his face would tell even the most stupid of people that he was a warrior. Most smart men wouldn't be dumb enough to take him on.

"Close yer mouth, cailín," Rory chuckled. "Absolutely overwhelming, 'tisn't he?"

"That's the understatement of the year."

When Kieran rejoined them, they followed the vet and the steward as they led Arien toward the stables. Walking side-by-side, Becca's arm brushed Kieran's and the next thing she knew, he was holding her hand. It felt like the most natural thing in the world, as if holding his hand was something she'd done a hundred times before. Her body sought every excuse it could find to brush against his as they walked. His did the same.

The vet checked Arien again in his stall, pronounced him fit, but as a precaution, he wasn't to be moved or ridden for several days. "Use some liniment on his legs to help with the swelling and stiffness," the vet instructed before he left.

"Won't be a problem," Kieran told the vet. "Becca will be tied up for several days. She won't have the time to be ridin' *him.*"

She cut her eyes at him, her cheeks flushing bright red when she realized what he was implying.

"Well, yee will be," he whispered in her ear.

His warm breath against her neck sent a shiver all the way down to her toes.

Becca's parents and grandfather hovered at the stable door, along with Rory and Neal. Kieran chafed at the restraint the crowd put on his designs. He planned to spirit Becca away, and it would be several days before they'd return to the world.

He introduced himself to her family, told them the outrageous lie that he and Becca were old friends from the circuit with plans to get reacquainted after this meet. Becca didn't deny it. Kieran gave her no chance to get away. He snagged her hand, and pulled her toward the stable door. If they didn't get somewhere private soon, he swore he'd take her right there in an empty stall.

"Hey, cousin," Rory called after him, grinning from ear to ear. "You'll be needin' the keys." He tossed the keys to their rental car to Kieran, who caught them deftly with one hand. He watched as Kieran hurried Becca out, the two of them all but trotting to the parking lot. He turned to the older man who'd come up beside him. "He's absolutely gobsmacked by her," he chuckled.

"Aye," Neal agreed.

Rory sighed. "Makes yee want to weep for joy, doesn't it? What babies the two of them will make." Becca's parents stared at Rory, shocked by his statement. The cocky Irishman flashed them an impudent grin. "Trust me. Kieran's an honorable man. He'll be weddin' her before they make those babies."

"I should hope so," Becca's mother sputtered.

Once Kieran had Becca safely in the front seat, and he was behind the wheel, he let out a long breath.

"What's your hurry?"

Kieran grabbed her hand and placed it on his groin. "If I don't have yee soon, cailín, I'll burst for fair certain."

When Becca realized what she was touching, her eyes widened. He was hard and huge, and she very suddenly wanted to be flat on her back with him between her legs.

"How fast can you drive?"

"Fast enough."

Chapter Twenty-Two

They barely made it inside Kieran's hotel room, before his mouth descended on hers. As soon as they stepped off the crowded elevator and the doors whispered shut, he sucked her tongue into his mouth, his lips claiming hers. All the way down the hallway, her tongue dueled with his, until he kissed her so hard, he sucked the air right out of her lungs. Panting, Becca clung to him as they stumbled through the door. He kicked it shut with one foot while he stripped off her riding jacket. She fumbled with the buttons on his uniform jacket. He swatted her hands away.

"Let me," he growled. While he fought the buttons, Becca unfastened his belt. "'Twould be easier if we each worked our own," he suggested.

"Smart idea."

The tiny buttons on her formal shirt stymied her, though. She kicked off her boots and peeled out of her breeches. Socks soon followed, but she couldn't decide about the lacy scrap of underwear she wore. She went back to work on her shirt buttons.

Impatient, Kieran grabbed her shirt. "I'll buy you a new one," he growled against her lips as he ripped the buttons free. He pushed the material off her shoulders and gazed adoringly at her breasts as they peeked out of her bra. "Ah, cailín," he murmured before he buried his face in the valley between them.

They fell back on the bed, and Becca realized that Kieran was completely naked. The hard evidence of his desire pressed against her belly, but that wasn't where she wanted it. He kissed her hard, then released her lips to rain kisses down her throat and across her chest. His tongue worried the edge of her lacy bra. She squirmed even more. He discovered the clasp to her bra in the front and as soon as he undid it, her breasts slipped from the lace. He lowered his head, and his mouth claimed the rosy tip of one breast. She arched against him. His tongue teased her nipple while one of his hands paid homage to her other breast. His free hand traced across her ribs and down to caress her hip. It slipped inside her panties and found moist heat waiting.

He shuddered. She was as ready for him as he was for her. His hand dipped lower, between her legs, and his thumb found the nub at the entrance to her slick folds. He teased it, and her flesh grew slick as warm liquid pooled. Slipping a finger inside, he was amazed at how tight she was.

Becca gasped when his finger pushed inside her. When a second joined the first, she couldn't decide if she was feeling pleasure or pain. At that point, they were almost the same thing. She might be a virgin, but she wanted this man inside her with every ounce of her being.

Kieran could wait no longer. She was ready and willing, and he was more than able. He stripped the scrap of lace from between her legs and nudged her thighs apart with his knees. He settled between her long legs, teasing the tip of his *boidín* against the slick folds hiding the entrance to her very core. His hand guided the tip inside her, and he pushed in with a thrust of his hips.

Becca gasped as his hard thickness spread her. She took a deep breath, trying to force the muscles in that area of her body to relax. The anticipation had her so keyed up that not a single muscle in her body was relaxed. Her friends in college had spent hours in the dorm talking about sex. She knew this first time would hurt. She just wanted it over with so she could relax and enjoy the next time.

He pushed in farther, still amazed by how tight she was. Then the head of his *boidín* met resistance—the thin membrane of her maidenhead. He stared at her, confused. She had so much latent sexuality, and was just has hot and excited as he was. It hadn't occurred to him she might be a virgin—not in this day and age for sure. He grinned despite himself when he saw her face. Her eyes were screwed shut, and her brow was knitted into a ferocious frown. He kissed the corner of her mouth.

"Why dinnit yee tell me?" he whispered against her lips.

Becca cocked one eye open to look at him. "Does it make a difference?"

"Absolutely," he affirmed. "'Tis all the difference in the world." He kissed her, his lips softening against hers. He traced her jawline with his tongue, following it up to the soft skin beneath her ear. "I want only pleasure for you, Becca, not pain. Are yee sure yer wantin' to do this?"

"Absolutely," she sighed, opening both eyes. "You tie me up in knots, Kieran. Completely and absolutely. I've never felt like this." Her long lashes shuttered her eyes. "I'm just afraid that it won't be good for you," she admitted self-consciously.

"Ah, cailín, how could yee worry about such a trivial thing? Just let me love yee and 'twill be good for me." He slipped out of her while kissing her lips again, long and hard, his tongue diving deep and withdrawing, mimicking what he was going to do with the rest of his body eventually.

When he'd kissed her breathless, his mouth wandered down her neck and across her chest. He paid rapt attention to each breast, teasing the rosy tips into hard little peaks. Lips and tongue then skittered down her ribs to find the soft skin where thigh met belly. His hand splayed across her belly and he liked the little swell he found there. Someday, his child would grow there. He was as certain of that fact as he was of his name.

His finger once again found her sheath hot and wet, but still too tight to accept the size and length of him without pain. He nuzzled the inside of her thighs then slid off the bed. Kneeling beside the bed, he grabbed her by the hips and swiveled her around so he would have easy access. He put her legs over his shoulders and dipped his head to taste her.

At the first touch of his tongue, Becca almost jumped out of her skin. His tongue lapped at her silken folds, then flicked across the nub. His lips greedily sought that tiny little bud, his teeth nipping and gently pulling. A spring coiled tight inside her. His tongue pushed into her, tasting and testing. He raised his head to watch her as his long, strong finger replaced his mouth. That spring wound tighter. In and out his finger danced, until she was pushing against his hand. Two fingers went in and still she pressed for more.

Slowly, surely, his fingers stretched and soothed her deep inside, preparing the way. His thumb found the nub again and rubbed. He was rewarded by a soft mewling noise. The muscles in her sheath contracted, claiming his fingers. His free hand found one of her breasts, cupping its soft firmness while his finger and thumb teased the nipple. Becca panted now, frantically pushing against his fingers and hand. He felt the shudder that began in her central core.

The rolling tremble starting behind her belly button spread out all the way to her fingers and toes. "Ahh." She exhaled. Just before another spasm consumed her, she managed a quick breath around the hitch in her chest.

Kieran groaned as she shuddered against his

hand. He almost came, too, but forced himself to hang on. He put her legs down, and slowly slid up her body. He kissed her long and deep. "'Tis only the first of many," he promised.

He thought his cock would burst if it got any harder. He had to bury himself in Becca, and he had to do it now. "Now," he growled. "I will have you now."

Becca nodded, panting. "Finally," she agreed.

He'd already fitted himself between her legs, and his smooth tip hovered at her sweet entrance. She squirmed, trying to fit them together. "It will still hurt a bit, but 'twill be easier now," he reassured. Once again, he guided his *boidín* into her. It was immediately surrounded by wet, pulsing silk. He pushed into her gently, stopping to allow her muscles to relax and accommodate him.

"The hell with this," Becca cried. She grabbed his buttocks with both hands and arched into him, driving the full length of him to her very core. It hurt more than she'd anticipated, and tears glistened in the corners of her eyes, but for the first time, she felt truly complete and alive.

He lay still, afraid if he moved, or if she moved, he'd spill too soon. He kissed the tears from her eyes, propping most of his weight on his elbows, making it easier for her to breathe. He was a big man and didn't want to crush her. He brushed a tendril of golden hair back from her forehead. He kissed the spot on her forehead where his fingers had brushed her soft skin, and then he kissed the tip of her nose before his lips found hers, kissing them tenderly as well. "I dinnit want to hurt you, cailín," he murmured.

Becca kissed the hollow of his shoulder. "No," she argued, her eyes flashing with mischievous glints. "You'd have taken all damn night to get it done."

Kieran grinned at her cheekiness, but he was once more in control. He pulled back, his cock sliding out of her. Becca cried out, trying to hold him in. Kieran drove back into her and she cried out again, this time in relief. Slowly, he withdrew again, then pumped deeper. Each time, her muscles flexed, trying to hold him deep within her. Slow, sure, in control, he rocked inside her. Withdrawing, then plunging with more intensity. Her hips rose to meet his, and then she took control. She sped up the tempo, urging him deeper and deeper still. Harder. Faster. She clung to his shoulders, wrapped her long legs around his waist, and locked her ankles behind his back. He groaned.

They both spiraled out of control, reaching higher and higher. Becca's sheath was slick and hot, and the sweet moisture of her passion trickled down his thigh. He put his hands under her hips, tilting her so he could drive himself into the very center of her.

His *boidín* throbbed in time with the contractions running through her sheath. He was about to explode so he gathered her into his arms. She opened wide to receive him, and as he pumped his seed into her secret depths, she gathered him close to keep him. Becca shuddered as wave after wave of shooting stars imploded in her middle. She whimpered and Kieran immediately shifted his weight, afraid he was crushing her.

"Did I hurt you?" His voice was tight with fear. He'd planned to take it slow and easy, but when she'd arched into him, forcing his *boidín* so deep, he'd lost a little bit of control. He grinned, ruefully admitting to himself, he'd lost a lot of control. She smiled into the hollow of his chest, and he could feel her lips curling against him.

"How long before we can do that again?" she asked, her voice muffled by his warm skin.

Shocked, Kieran braced his hands on the bed and reared back. He stared down at her. "What did you just say?"

Becca trailed her fingers down his muscled sides and across his back, stopping when she got to the hard muscles of his buttocks. She squirmed, and then flexed the muscles in her vagina, caressing his entire shaft. "You heard me." She grinned. "When can you do that again?"

Kieran groaned. She'd completely drained him and now, not five minutes later, she wanted to do it again. "You are insatiable," he teased.

"Yes," she replied truthfully.

****

Two days later, Rory and Neal met Kieran in the bar of their hotel. When the big man was slow to sit and grimaced as he settled on the wooden stool, Rory guffawed and slapped him on the back. "And where are yee hidin' the fair Rebecca?" he teased his cousin.

"She's gone back to her hotel to pack. I'm picking her up in an hour. I called the colonel, and he's given me three weeks' leave. Not much time to plan and execute a wedding, but Becca says her mother can handle it with her eyes closed." Now it was Kieran's turn to smirk. Rory and Neal both had to force their gaping mouths closed.

"Yee've known the cailín only briefly, Kieran," Neal counseled the younger man. "Are yee sure you aren't thinkin' with the wrong part of your anatomy?"

Kieran smiled at his mentor. "How long did you know Chavonne before you married her?"

Neal choked and had to cough, clearing his throat before he could speak. "That's different."

Rory stared at the older man, a wicked gleam flickering in his eyes. "Bloody hell, man, you've never married her, have you?"

Neal coughed again. "I would have," he blurted. "In the Church even, but she'd have none of it. Your Uncle Finn fixed the papers for me so the Army would recognize her as my wife should something happen."

Kieran smiled at the big man. "Relax, Neal. Your secret is safe with us." He kicked Rory under the table just to make sure. "Be that as it may, yee still haven't answered my question. Yee knew the minute yee laid eyes on her she was the one."

Neal sighed in defeat. "Aye, lad, I did."

Satisfied, Kieran ordered a Guinness from the bartender. "Rory, like it or not, you've been granted leave to be my best man. Neal, you're to go with Evan and the horses back to Ireland." As the older man started to protest, Kieran held up his hand. "Becca and I are coming to Ireland for our honeymoon. We'll have a second ceremony at Boyle with the full clann in attendance so I can bestow the Knot. I'm fully aware of what Uncle Finn would do if we didn't follow custom, however archaic it might be."

Neal and Rory exchanged a long look.

"Kieran, we've all known forever you'd be Uncle Finn's heir." Rory shrugged. "Face it, you're going to be the MacDermot whether you like it or not. Since Uncle Finn isn't gettin' any younger, and especially now you've chosen Becca, you have to give her the Knot." Rory chuckled. "I swear there are times you'd think the clann would cease to exist if that bloody brooch wasn't handed out once a generation. I'm just glad you're the one who's cursed with the true mate thing." He leaned back in his chair and let out a satisfied sigh. "Me? I like the cailíns way too much to tie myself down to just one."

Kieran stared at the man who was not only his cousin but also his best friend. "Be careful what you say, Rory," he cautioned. "You never know when foolish words like those will come back to haunt you."

Rory snorted. "Aye, and next you'll be tellin' me to spill a drop of ale to pay tribute to the fae." The younger man stood up and stretched. "An' speakin' of the cailíns, I've got a hot date. Cousin, you know how to find me."

Without a backward look, Rory strode out of the bar. Kieran and Neal exchanged a long look, then glanced around the room to make sure no one watched. They both spilled the last drops of their beers on the bar.

"To the faerie," they toasted.

Epilogue

Becca floated in that delicious state halfway between falling asleep and dreaming. She snuggled into Kieran's side and sighed, the sound happy and relaxed to her ears. On this first night of her married life, she was completely and totally satisfied. Oh, how this man had made love to her. And, oh, the things she had done to him. Her cheeks grew hot just thinking about all they'd tried in bed. She felt complete, like a huge hole in her heart had been filled and for the first time in her life, she was truly at peace and content. She snuggled closer to her new husband. How could she not feel whole when he filled her so completely?

She rubbed her cheek against his shoulder, her thoughts returning to their wedding. It had been a simple ceremony with family and a few close friends. He'd added some vows of his own for them to repeat.

"By the life that courses in my blood and the love that resides in my heart, I take thee to my hand, my heart, and my spirit, to be my chosen one," Kieran had pledged to her that morning in front of their guests. "To desire thee and be desired by thee. To possess thee and to be possessed by thee, without sin or shame for naught can exist in the purity of my love for thee. I promise to love thee wholly in this life and beyond, where we shall meet, remember, and love again. There is no beginning, there is no end, but in you. You are my chosen."

They'd be married again in a church ceremony in a few weeks' time when they arrived at his home in Ireland.

Kieran stirred restlessly and tightened his arms around her. He made her feel cherished, as if she were the only woman in the world.

"You *are* the only woman in the world as far as I'm concerned," he murmured in her ear.

She kissed the hollow of his shoulder and laid her head on the spot. "Love of my heart," he told her looking deep into her cerulean eyes.

"Light of my life," she had replied as her eyes drifted shut and her breathing became deep and regular.

Becca smiled in her sleep and he kissed her forehead. His last waking thought was that her eyes were the exact color of the fire opal mounted in the MacDermot Knot. As soon as they got back to Ireland, he'd give it to her.

****

"He must still bestow upon her the Covenant," the male complained.

"'Twill be done. The binding is made. 'Tis all that matters," the female replied.

"Excuse me, but who are you?" Becca broke in.

Silence.

"I know you can hear me. Why won't you answer me?"

Still silence, and then a sharply indrawn breath.

"She still hears us. How is that so?" The male was distraught.

"How could she not?" the female replied smugly. "She is our daughter."

A word from the author...

At the age of four, I lined up my stuffed animals and told them stories I made up. At thirteen, I committed my first "novel" to paper—in a black-and-white-plaid spiral notebook. "The Talisman" had a decent plot along the lines of "Connecticut Yankee in King Arthur's Court" though processed through the brain of an adolescent girl. Needless to say, it was abysmal.

I've been married to my best friend, who also happens to be an attorney, for twenty-five years. Our wonderful daughter is in college, majoring in museum studies and history, a love she came by honestly from her dad and me both.

Over the course of my lifetime, I've been a military officer's wife, state appellate court marshal, airport rescue firefighter and forensic fire photographer, crime analyst, and technical crime scene investigator. I've since retired from the "real world" and live in Oklahoma. I spend my days at the computer with my two dogs, the "lolcat" who owns us all, and myriad characters all clamoring for attention. Eventually, I'll get around to telling each of their stories.

For more information about Silver and her books, visit www.silverjames.com

Thank you for purchasing
this Wild Rose Press publication.
For other wonderful stories of romance,
please visit our on-line bookstore at
www.thewildrosepress.com

For questions or more information
contact us at
info@thewildrosepress.com

The Wild Rose Press
www.TheWildRosePress.com